I0760765

CAPTIVE OF TWILIGHT AND TREACHERY

CAPTIVE OF TWILIGHT AND TREACHERY

THE ZHENINGHAI CHRONICLES

ANASTASIS BLYTHE

CAPTIVE OF TWILIGHT AND TREACHERY

www.AnastasisBlythe.com

Hardcover ISBN: 978-1-960606-04-4

Jacket Cover design by Moorbooks Design.
Laminate Cover and Interior Design by Dragonpen Designs.

FOR ELYSE, READING BUDDY AND DEAR SISTER.
HERE'S TO A LOT MORE LIBRARY TRIPS.

CHAPTER 1

THE GLIMPSE OF night sky visible through the small window of the bunkroom told Shang it was a couple of hours past midnight. Only the guards would be awake now. He eased off his bunk and slipped out of the room, silent as death, his clothes bundled to his chest. No one stirred behind him. *Good.*

The fortress hallway before him was bleak and dark. Nothing but a sconced torch in the main hallway beyond this one shone any light into this crevice of Liafugen. He dressed as fast as he could—in all black.

In the weeks since Meiling's capture, he and Fen had been kept at this fortress to rest and recover before returning to Suguan, but Shang hadn't been doing much resting.

It was quick and careful work to dodge patrol's prying eyes and sneak a few wings down to the infirmary. The only delay was when a feral-wielder with augmented hearing made his rotations close to where Shang was crouched in the shadows. He waited, not breathing, until the guard was long past before he moved again.

He slid the infirmary door open, ducking behind a changing screen before the medic on duty could see him. The infirmary was quiet, with Fen as the only overnight patient. She was finally sleeping soundly from dusk to dawn, instead of waking every few hours moaning with pain. The space between those moans had nearly shredded Shang's sanity when he'd been here. It was already too much that Meiling was captured, but to lie awake for hours hoping he wouldn't lose Fen too . . .

The medic probably spent most of the night dozing against his desk. Shang might check, but if he was wrong, he didn't want to risk getting discovered.

Any moment now.

Sure enough, a pair of running footsteps came straight for the infirmary. A groan sounded from the medic.

"If that is Yaozu and his delicate stomach again . . ."

Loud retching in the hallway dragged another groan from the medic. Paper shuffled and robes swished, and then his heavier footsteps thumped across the infirmary.

"All I want is one night in the span of a week where I'm not cleaning up vomit," he grumbled. Then he slid the door open. "Am I going to have to put you on a stricter diet, boy? This is the third time this week!"

Sorry, brother.

Shang leapt into motion, leaving the shelter of the screen. He skirted around empty bed mats, the medic's desk, the cabinets of herbs and medicines. Candlelight bobbed and winked against the darkness. His fast movements sent a sharp burst of pain down his spine. Cursing inwardly, he slowed just slightly, until the pain was only an ache.

The medic would have a fit that Shang wasn't following his instructions to rest and recover. If Shang listened, however, and waited until he was recovered, he'd find himself en route to Suguan for trial. Besides, there just *wasn't time*. It had killed him every waking minute to delay this long.

He reached the one bed concealed by a screen to block out the candlelight. Fen lay sprawled on her back, her mouth open. Her shoulder was freshly bandaged, the color returned to her cheeks. A small chest was at her feet, containing her clothes.

He dared not touch her for fear of waking her. The time he had was already slipping through his fingers. Still, he couldn't help mouthing a silent, *"Goodbye, friend. Heal quickly."*

Then he flipped open the lid of the chest, dug beneath Fen's robes, and pulled out the things he'd been slowly pilfering and hiding away over the last couple of weeks.

Extra knives. Rope. Flint and steel. Some food things. A mask and gloves. His father's signet ring. The broadsword he'd hidden in the tall potted plant by the bed.

The infirmary door slid back open, and the medic's voice carried through the small space. "Sit yourself down, boy. I'll brew you *another* ginger tea."

Shang buckled on his weapons silently, keeping his breathing steady to calm his heart rate. He slid the tight coil of rope and sack of food onto his belt. He hated that he didn't have a *jiaun*, but those were carefully cataloged in the armory. Even one's absence would have been noticed.

The earthy aroma of ginger was abruptly cut off when Shang tied on the mask, hiding his face except for his eyes. He drew the hood of his cloak low and pulled on the gloves.

He was just about to stand when he looked down—and found Fen's eyes wide open. Faster than a heartbeat, he clapped his gloved hand over her mouth. She lowered her brows, glaring at him. He held a finger to his masked lips, then let go of her.

She said nothing, just kept her eyes locked on his. Then she reached out and clasped his hand. Something inside him twinged with regret. He squeezed back. He hated leaving her like this. Hated it more than words. Fen was his comrade. Warriors didn't leave their comrades behind.

He forced himself to let go.

The moment Yaozu had his cup of ginger tea and the medic had left the infirmary to clean up the hallway mess, Shang slipped to the window. He eased it open, swung himself out onto the sill, and pulled it closed behind him.

If he didn't do this right, he'd be shot.

But if there was one thing his father had taught him from the moment he was born, it was that failure wasn't an option. Getting shot off Liafugen's walls was not an option. Even though he'd spent most of the last fortnight in the infirmary, he hadn't wasted a single moment. All those hours staring outside that infirmary window, he'd been planning. Watching the patrol rotation. Asking innocuous questions. Working out exactly how to pull this off.

He braced himself, then dropped onto the roof of the armory. Pain shot into his ribs as he rolled into a crouch. He allowed himself three seconds to press a hand to his side and wince. Then he was in motion again.

He slinked across the armory roof, to the edge nearest the parapets. When a patrol came near, Shang dropped to his stomach, laying flat on the roof, waiting for her to pass. The moment she was gone, he pulled the rope from his belt, worked a slip knot, and eased himself back into a crouch.

The loop he threw landed around a merlon. He counted to three, waiting for the window in patrols, and then tightened his grip on the rope and swung himself off the roof, landing with his feet flat against the side of the parapets.

Quickly, he pulled himself up to the parapet, fitting between the crenels.

And right in front of him, with his back to him, was an armed guard.

A comrade.

Sorry, Shang thought before slamming the side of his hand into the man's neck. He crumpled, and Shang caught him, easing him to the ground and hiding him in the shadows before unlooping his rope from the merlon and slinking to the opposite side of the parapet.

He ducked below a crenel, his hands working the rope into a different, more complex knot than the first. One that would support his weight but come undone with a sharp pull.

Voices drifted on the chill night wind. They came from below. Not a risk for him. Even so, sweat slicked down his brow, dampening his mask. Despite his carefully measured breaths, his heart raged in his chest.

He finished the knot, got to his feet, and slipped it around the merlon he hid behind.

Then, with a last check over his shoulder to be sure he hadn't been spotted, he swung himself out over the battlement. Hand over hand, his feet flat against the stone outer wall of Liafugen, he walked himself down the steep incline.

When he reached the bottom, his lungs were heaving. He yanked hard on the rope, and the knot came undone, falling around his feet. The aches plaguing his body grew more insistent, but he ignored them as he rewound the rope and hooked it on his belt.

One step down. Now he just needed to knock out the guards at the bridge over the chasm, and then the hardest part of the first half of his plan would be done.

After that, he had to get a horse. His father's signet ring would accomplish that.

The road before him was long, treacherous, even *traitorous*. Defying orders like this was enough to get him executed. The emperor would have his head—twice over. But Shang didn't care.

Not when Meiling was in the hands of a monster.

It had been hard enough to imagine leaving her alone in the hands of allies.

The few times he'd let himself imagine what Fang Zedong and his minions could be doing to her, he'd nearly lost his mind. Which he couldn't afford. He had to stay calm and rational. Recklessness wouldn't save anyone.

But when Shang snuck up behind the guards, all remorse that these men were his comrades was swept aside by the burning ice in his gut. As their unconscious bodies fell to the ground, he broke into a run and sprinted across the bridge. He only had seconds now before the fortress watch realized their gatekeepers were down.

So he ran, plunging into the darkness, ignoring the pain of his partially healed wounds.

Come hell, high water, *mó guǐ*, an entire empire—he was getting Meiling back. He swore it on the graves of his fathers, the grave of his mother. *Dragons*, he'd swear it on anything. If he had to tear apart both Butagin and Zheninghai to find her, he'd do it.

He was getting her back, or he'd die trying.

CHAPTER 2

MEILING HAD TO get out of here.

Darkness hung. Black, thick, heavy, *moist*. Each tremulous intake of breath tasted like damp midnight without the welcomed light of a silver moon or a starlit sky. No crisp, clear wind. No soft scuttling of bugs in the trees and underbrush.

Only a persistent, faraway *drip, drip, drip,* the occasional echoing jangle of iron-wrought keys, and the shuffling of ragged clothing on the cold stone of the dungeon.

And the healer's dry, insistent voice.

"I really cannot believe you came here without a knife," said Feiyan. "I can't *promise* I could pick the lock, but I definitely cannot do it without a knife. Though, now that I think of it, a knife probably wouldn't be the most helpful tool for breaking us out of here. Do you have a hairpin? But see, the advantage of a knife is that you can kill people with it. I'm going to guess any hairpins you have are not serrated."

Meiling licked her parched lips. Her voice snagged in her throat when she spoke. It always did here. "They threw my penknife away when I tried to kill myself. All I have is a hair ribbon and the clothes I'm wearing."

"Kill yourself? Seems counterproductive."

"Depends on what you're trying to accomplish," said Meiling.

Feiyan seemed to shrug in her cell. "Fair enough." There was silence for a long minute. A distant door clanged open, then shut, and loud footsteps stomped in another direction. When the noise had died back to the near silence of this place, Feiyan said, "So . . . why *were* you trying to kill yourself? You don't strike me as the thrilled-to-die sort of person. I admit I'm curious."

It almost *felt* like Feiyan scooted closer to the bars separating them, propped her elbows on her knees, and jutted her chin out in interest. But she might have been leaning back against the frigid stones for all Meiling knew, disengaged and half-asleep.

"Do you know many people who are thrilled to die?" Meiling asked cautiously.

Feiyan barked a half-laugh, which slowly died into a contemplative huff. Still, she didn't answer.

Meiling blinked in the blackness. "Um . . ."

"Killing yourself. Why?"

Through the thin fabric of Meiling's clothes, cold wetness seeped into her skin. Wetness from the dungeon floor. She grimaced despite herself. "I was trying to save my companions. They were going to be killed. I was not."

"Shangdi and Fen? I'm surprised they needed saving. Shangdi, in particular, is positively allergic to being saved. He prefers to be the savior."

"I noticed." Meiling's lips tilted in a tiny smile. Such a strange thing to smile within such despairing walls. "They were wounded.

We were nearly to the fortress Liafugan. Fen was incapacitated, and Shang was weakened by wounds. I knew if I didn't do something, the brigands would kill them. It was all I could think of."

"Interesting. What sort of mighty brigand or monster wounded them so severely? And how did *you* escape, mostly unscathed? Some secret magic of yours? Invisibility? You know, I'm being dragon-spawn for saying this, but having magic like invisibility would have been much preferred to healing. Perhaps healing would not be so bad if people weren't getting sick and dying so much! Why can't they stay healthy for five minutes? But nope . . . I apologize. I digress."

Meiling cocked her head, knitting her brows together. She hadn't thought much about what it must be like to be the only healer of all Zheninghai. Now that she considered it, it sounded exhausting. "We came upon a herd of qilins," she said, squeezing her eyes shut against the memory of those terrible, beautiful horned monsters. Those jewel-like scales running down their deer-like bodies. Heads like lions with beards and manes and those death-tipped horns . . .

"Fathers and stars and moons above! You must have been remote indeed to stumble upon such a horror. How did you even survive?"

"We were just outside a village."

Feiyan balked. "Just outside of a village? What sort of toothless, spineless, worthless village patrol had not discovered the herd and hunted them down? Phoenixes scorch those idiots! You know, Princess Meiling, I think our world is stupid. Do you agree? Here, let me convince you. The most powerful wielders in the empire go where? To the bureaucracy. To sit at a desk and run the empire. And where do the useless wielders go? To hunt down *mó guǐ* and brigands. It's an utterly nonsensical situation. Whose idea was it? Idiots." She let out a spew of frustrated air, which was the closest thing to wind in this dungeon.

She had a point.

Feiyan continued talking. "We must depart from the conversation of the qilins and incompetent wardens, otherwise I'll lose my mind and you will hear more than you ever wanted to know of my opinions on the subject. So . . . backing up here. Why in the world were you even with Shangdi and Fen in the wilderness? Afternoon picnic?"

Should Meiling tell her about her magic? She bit her tongue, tightening her arms around her knees. She leaned her head back against the stone and shuddered as harsh cold flowed into her scalp. "They were taking me to Liafugan."

There was silence. Feiyan was no fool.

She might sound like one, but Meiling remembered those eyes she'd seen in the forest, set in that pretty face. She remembered the glimpse of her in the illusionist's memories. However she may act, Feiyan was no fool.

Strange as it was, the desire to confide in Feiyan overcame Meiling. There was something about her, or perhaps something about being alone in a dungeon, that made her want to trust her.

Her spirit suddenly revolted at the thought, terrified. Shang's calculating eyes flashed before her, his menacing smile when he'd discovered what a powerful weapon he could hold sharp against her throat. After all, Meiling used magic outside of the emperor's sanction. It was secret, forbidden. And giving that knowledge to anyone was giving over power to destroy her and her family.

Bitterness rose hot and heady in her breast. It tasted sour on her tongue, making her swallow heavily. With each inhale, she breathed in the permeating darkness of the cell straight into her lungs.

"Well," said Feiyan brightly, "fortresses are my very favorite vacation destinations. I love the coziness of rock and iron. What made you pick Liafugen? The food?"

"I didn't pick it."

"You didn't, now? Don't tell me it was His Imperial Majesty, our own Glorious Emperor, who did?"

Hesitation locked her tongue. Then, softly, "How did you know?"

"An intriguing question, but one not nearly as interesting as my next one for you. Were you hiding from Fang Zedong?"

"I . . . well, yes."

"Then what kind of magic do you have?"

"Magic?" Meiling blurted, drawing back in alarm. "I didn't say . . . I didn't say I have magic!"

"You didn't have to. You know what this good-for-nothing Fang person is doing? Collecting magic-wielders. He's not collecting useless princesses—no offense to you, of course. So if he sent his brigands after you, then you have magic."

Once again, Meiling could not argue with her logic.

"What does your magic do? You've kept it a secret this long, which is impressive. And not only that, but you're one of the few wielders that Fang felt necessary to kidnap. Which means you must be powerful."

Meiling would never use the word *powerful* to describe herself. Shang, yes. Pa, yes. Never herself. Not a short, slender princess curled in the corner of a darker-than-night dungeon. "I . . ." She licked her lips. What did she have to lose by sharing? "I can leave my body. And enter minds."

It seemed the most concise way to describe whatever her magic was.

"Oh, now *that* is exciting. That was what you meant earlier when you said I was in the illusionist's memories. I was not quite sure at the time. I figured it was a good thing, though." It almost sounded like Feiyan was smiling. "Are you in my mind now? That would be embarrassing."

"I can only do it when I'm asleep," Meiling said. "So, no, I'm not in your mind."

There was an exaggerated sigh of relief. "Phew. The thought was only *slightly* unsettling, I assure you, but unsettling nonetheless. Now, where were we? Fen and Shangdi take you on a little escapade to find out which village patrols need replacing and keep you out of Fang Zedong's hands."

Meiling recounted everything she could recollect from their journey. It was a little halted, but she managed to explain most of it.

She told about how an evanescer had attempted to kidnap her from the palace, how her parents sent her away to Liafugan for safe keeping until they could resolve the threat. How Shang and Fen were assigned to escort her, how their journey proved much more hazardous than initially anticipated.

That, of course, was mostly due to the group of brigands who hounded their every step. And the qilins—they had not been prepared for such significant foes.

She told of their harrowing battle with the brigands outside the fortress. *So close* to their destination. But Meiling had bartered her life for her companions' and had been captured. The last she had seen of Fen, she was lying on her back in the middle of the bridge passing over the chasm cut into the valley below the hilltop fortress. She had been barely lucid, cursing Meiling for trying to save her life.

The last she had seen of Shang, he had been prostrated on the ground, burned and bleeding. He had been struggling to get to his feet, to fight with the last ounce of his strength. All he could do was watch as she practically flung herself into the arms of their enemies.

Feiyan interjected comments and questions here and there. Meiling answered as best as she could, though she was left confused more often than not about whether her remarks were serious or facetious.

The longer they talked, the more the tension eased out of her shoulders, and the unending fear faded. Was this what it was like to have a friend? To not be alone? Did it truly take her getting imprisoned in a dungeon to find a friend?

"The brigands," Meiling said quietly, "were dispatched to capture you as well as me. How did they find you?"

There was a long moment of silence. Serious silence. She waited, hardly daring to breathe.

When Feiyan spoke, it was her usual carefree chirp. "They just swooped in when I stepped away from the dying masses to relieve myself. Truly? Let a girl do her business in peace and *then* kidnap her. That's what I always say."

"That's what you always say?" Meiling repeated, almost cracking a smile.

There was a quiet chuckle, and then silence reigned for several long minutes. Minutes that made her conclude that silence in darkness always seemed to last longer.

"I have an idea," Feiyan said eventually.

"About how to escape?"

Feiyan seemed to wave her hand impatiently. "No, well, yes. But more importantly—how to handle the flocking crowds to be healed. There needs to be some serious categorizing happening. You only have a papercut? Go back to work. It'll heal. You've been dismembered? Burned half away? All right, come here and I'll heal you. Do you know how little sleep I've gotten these years at the Academy? They want me to be a proper Academy graduate. No token graduation. Nope. I've got to know all the things about people who died a long time ago. And if they've been dead for centuries, it's not like they mean anything to me. I can't heal them and honestly, I'm not sure I'd want to. Imagine all the problems that would cause." The soft swish of hair suggested she was shaking her head. "So I must be a *proper* Academy graduate, but it's not like people can wait years for me to graduate before dying. They've got me working all day, studying in the fringes, and then I'm still supposed to be *healthy*—they don't seem to realize that I can't heal myself. Ironic, don't you think?—and they make me do the arena fighting too."

"Sounds exhausting," Meiling said.

"You have no idea. Every minute I was not healing, I would be hounded by this one master who would say to me, 'What? Why are you not healing?'" She mimicked his voice, tossing it much lower and thinner. "I finally resorted to handing him my knife and telling him to kill me. Because that was what he was asking me to do. That seemed to shut him up. Though his eyes were on me all the time. Judging.

You know what is one of the worst things in the world? Silent judging. Tell your judgements to my face!" A loud smacking sounded. Presumably her smacking her thighs in frustration.

"The brigands kidnapped you," Meiling reminded her, smiling again in the darkness. "Then what?"

Feiyan sighed in irritation. "Then they hauled me half across the empire and dumped me here. They'd already picked up a guardian on the way by the time they got me. Zuan Wan. The brigands made him set a trap for you. Some other brigands eventually came and took him. I flatter myself by thinking that one of me was handful enough for all of them. I'm not sure where he is. Presumably somewhere around here. Hey, Wan! You in here?"

Her voice echoed off the walls, bouncing and reverberating and dying.

No response.

Were they the only ones in this part of the dungeon, or were they surrounded by other prisoners? She wasn't convinced she wanted to know.

"The brigands handed me off eventually to some others. One of them was so old I am certain I could have crushed every one of his bones with the perfect kick. But he was so strong. Had feral powers and while I hate to admit it, I was no match for him. Always humbling to be whipped by someone older than your grandma. Not the first time I wished I had battle magic."

A faraway door banged. Then another, much closer. Meiling stood, torn between a desire to fold into the corner and a desire to rush forward and cling to the iron bars, begging to be taken out of this dreadful place.

But Feiyan was here. As long as Feiyan was here, Meiling would be fine. And if she wasn't fine, at least she wouldn't be alone.

The closest door opened with such a screech that she startled and hung back. A rocking lantern entered the darkness, and she was simultaneously blinded by and enamored with it. She drank in that painful brilliance through the slits of her fingers like a desert wanderer finding a sparkling oasis of clear, crystal water.

Beyond the light was a beard. There was a jarring clang of metal on metal. A key being inserted into a lock. A roughened voice barked something in another language that sounded like a command at Feiyan.

"I'm not your dog," Feiyan retorted, leaping up and diving to the opposite end of the cell. "Catch me."

Meiling wanted to call out to her, to tell her that such fighting was useless. She would be overwhelmed in but a moment and would only get herself hurt. The lantern was set down, and a frustrated growl reverberated against stone as the guard stomped into her cell, muttering in his language as he went.

Feiyan laughed, swiftly dodging the guard and angling a well-placed kick. The guard grunted. She was trying to maneuver herself to be by the door, moving too fast for the burly guard.

Perhaps Academy training for healers was not entirely useless.

Another banging of the door. More growled words. Only this time, the voice was familiar. Meiling had heard it only a handful of times, but she recognized it immediately, despite the unfamiliar language.

Shuren. The illusionist.

His voice was rich, beautiful like the rest of him as he filled in the doorway of Feiyan's cell. He blocked the light of the lantern, concealing the scuffling and grunts of the healer and guard.

A hard hit sounded.

Feiyan let out a cry. Shuren entered the cell and hauled her to her feet, clamping iron shackles on her wrists.

"Keep fighting and you'll wear these all the time," he threatened in a low voice, gripping her upper arms so high that the candlelight flickered on her grimace.

"I don't care," Feiyan snapped. "You phoenix-scorched dragon-spawn."

Her boots scraped on stone as the two men hauled her out. She turned her face back toward Meiling as the guard bent to retrieve his lantern. "Farewell! I must go heal the tortures they've inflicted upon our brethren. And themselves. I'm not sure how these dragon-blasted idiots manage to hurt themselves so much. Don't have too much fun without me—"

The door clanged shut, the sound vibrating in Meiling's tight chest.

CHAPTER 3

MEILING HUDDLED BACK into the corner of her cell as the clamor of Feiyan's struggles with her captors faded. Eventually, it was quiet.

Drip, drip, drip.

She shuddered, trying to hide from the echoing memory of Feiyan's startled, wounded cry. She leaned her face down, so she pressed her eye sockets into the jut of her knees. Wrapping her cloak around her hardly staved off the cold.

Shang's cold was so different from this. There was an inherent life in his ice. This was death and despair, crawling like spiders to devour her. She shivered. What she wouldn't give to go back to that cave, when Shang had held her in his arms. He hadn't been cold then. He'd been so *very* warm . . .

How long would she be a prisoner here? Would she be rescued? Would someone come for her?

Would . . . would . . . Shang come for her?

She squeezed her eyes shut. Now was not the time to give into girlish fantasies. Shang would be at Liafugen, or on trial—might even be facing execution at this moment—for his failure to deliver the princess safely to the fortress. Fen too. For all she had sacrificed, they would probably die anyway.

If they'd even survived their injuries.

Why did she suddenly feel so weak now that she was alone?

She resonated with more of Feiyan's words than Feiyan probably realized. No magic would be better than having this strange magic of hers, this magic that was not helpful in battle. Shang had called it useless himself.

Not that it mattered what he thought.

What sort of things would Fang Zedong want with her magic? She fought to keep her mind from wandering down that shaded, winding path. It was too terrifying, too oppressive. She sucked in another lungful of dank blackness. And yet, one thought slipped through: *I can enter anyone's mind. Anyone's.* No secret could be hidden from her.

She was such a small piece in the grand scheme of life, of the empire, of war.

That was what this was. War.

If the abducting of magic-wielders was not blatant enough an act of war, then abducting a princess certainly was. It was senseless. Zedong wouldn't have risked the rage of an emperor—of an *empire*—for nothing.

She hoped Feiyan would not be hurt. It seemed a vain hope.

There was nothing to do but be anxious. Or sleep.

With how black this dungeon was, she almost wondered if she was already asleep. Asleep and awake were hardly different here.

She could not bring herself to lie down on the wet and frigid floor. Not when it was covered in something that squished beneath her weight. So she leaned heavily against the wall, pressing her face into a corner of stone. A soft breath escaped her lips.

She was not entirely helpless here. As long as she could sleep, she still had one power available to her. She exhaled again, the darkness swirling before her as she closed her eyes.

In this place, she slowly crept out of her body, sliding with the prowess of a lion on the hunt. Except that she felt more like a kitten, but that didn't matter because no one could see her. She was in another dimension.

Now she could explore her prison and see if there was anything she could learn about her surroundings. Could she even help Feiyan? If she could find her, perhaps she could enter her captors' minds and try to influence their actions. She could prevent them from hurting her too much.

This dungeon was just as dark in the spirit realm as in the waking world. There were no other glowing souls. So they had indeed been alone, unless the other captives held in this place did not possess magical abilities.

She moved through blackness, uncertain whether she passed in between iron bars or stone walls. Eventually, light flared before her. She quickened toward it, desperately happy at the sight.

There were three wielders here, all prisoners. The only light came from their souls. Two of the glows were shades of purple—one was lighter, with a tinge of pink, while the other was a dark violet. The third glow was bright, flaring green. Green, like a sapling. Could he be Zuan Wan, the guardian protecting the territory of Ganhai, who had set the trap of vines for her?

What did Zedong want with his abilities?

She didn't enter their minds. Finding Feiyan was a higher priority. But before she could progress further into the belly of the dungeon or rise to the higher levels of the fortress, her soul tether yanked tight.

No, no, no! she cried as she was pulled—

Lantern light seared her eyeballs. She cried out and tried to shield herself against the bursting pain. Hands groped for her arms, and she was dragged up, her mind still reeling with the shock of her sudden awakening. “What are—”

She tried to scramble to her feet as they dragged her out of her cell. The grips on either arm were so unforgiving they might have been shackles. Stringy, matted hair fell in her face as she tripped over her own feet, struggling to catch her balance.

They dragged her up a set of stairs, through the heavy air and past more chambers of prisons. The lantern only illuminated a few steps ahead, but at least now she could walk without falling.

More light flared. She tilted her head away, processing in a distant part of her mind that this was only the soft, illuminating glows of torches in the upper parts of the dungeon. If they were taking her into the sunlight, she might die from the pain.

The world grew brighter and brighter. She looked up at the two guards escorting her. Their hard faces were set against hers, refusing to glance down at their captive. They wore armor, but it was far more primitive than what the palace guards wore. Their slightly darker coloring, their tight braids, the furs and skins lining their armor—all of it registered in her mind with sudden clarity.

They were barbarians. People of Butagin.

A vague part of her fuzzy mind remembered that they were her enemies, people working with the traitor Fang Zedong to wage war against Zheninghai. Against her Pa. And yet, a tiny sliver of her heart whimpered silently. Part of Ma’s heritage was Butagin. Part of *Ma* was Butagin.

It had been *so, so* long since she’d seen either of her parents or her siblings.

Did Hou and Yun know Meiling was gone, or were they so consumed with Academy things they hadn’t noticed? Did they think she was just upstairs in her room or holed up in the library, instead of captive in an enemy fortress thousands of li away?

She sagged a little lower in the guards' grips.

No, she shouldn't think these thoughts. She ought to figure out her situation. These guards were taking her somewhere. To be forced to use her magic? To be tortured for information?

Her spine quivered. She couldn't handle torture.

Shang, Shang, Shang, she cried inside her mind as panic settled into her bones. What if she couldn't handle whatever she had to face? She needed Shang. His constant strength. His ability to handle whatever came his way.

But Shang wasn't here. Meiling was alone.

The guard on her left kicked open the last door between her and that agonizing sunshine. She let out a cry, trying to bury her face in the arm of the guard. They dragged her up more stairs and before she could prepare herself, before her eyes could adjust to the brightness, she was flung to the ground.

Her palms hit smooth, stone-paved ground. The whiteness was near blinding. The cold harsh against her thin robes.

She squeezed her eyes shut, breathing heavily.

Slowly, the pain in her eyes eased, and she lifted her face from the ground to find a pair of wide-braced feet. She craned her neck toward a black robe billowing in the chilled wind. The brilliance of the sun hid his face and Meiling was forced to look down again, her eyes watering.

"Why do you treat my princess like a dog?" a sharp voice sounded from above her. "She deserves your respect. You are dismissed."

Meiling attempted another glance up at the man's face. She could make out his beard before she had to look away.

"Daughter of Liena," the voice rumbled overhead.

"Fang Zedong," Meiling whispered.

"I'm sorry?"

She lifted her chin, sitting up straight so she did not lay prostrate before him any longer. "Fang Zedong," she said, louder.

A smile crinkled his features, turning his features unsettlingly warm and pleasant. "I'm pleased you know me. Has your mother told you of me?"

She said nothing, only lowered her gaze from his to take in her surroundings.

They stood on the parapets, alone save for guards standing alert at the door to the nearest tower. Over the edge of the battlement, a valley stretched as far as she could see, green and fertile. The wind was stronger so high, and it whipped Zedong's cloak around his neck, held fast by a lotus clasp. A single wooden bead hung from a cord at his throat. Meiling's own hair caught in the wind, sweeping it around her face so she could hardly see.

But even her hair could not hide the phoenixes circling overhead. Her heart thumped at the sight of those *mó guǐ*, their fiery feathers seeming to *almost* consume them, but never quite.

"Have you seen the view? Come, let me show you."

Zedong did not wait for her to rise but strode to the wall, one hand clasping his wrist behind him. His cloak billowed behind him in the wind, legs planted wide. He cut a dominating, imposing figure.

Meiling glanced down at her ragged, soiled garments. She reached up, caught her hair over one shoulder and held it in a fist so it would stop whipping about. When she climbed to her feet, her own filthy cloak pulled hard at the clasp at her throat, joining Zedong's in its fight to break free and fly away.

He has use of me.

As long as he had use of her, he couldn't truly hurt her. It did not matter how much stronger he was than her. She was the one with the rare magic. She was the princess. He could not hurt her.

Meiling squared her own shoulders, forcing away the desire to shrink into herself. She walked with steady steps to Zedong's side and placed her hands on the stone wall, looking out over the forested valley below. Different colors of green painted the countryside, and a long, winding river cut through the midst of the valley.

It was beautiful.

Anything green and sunlit and colorful was beautiful after that dungeon.

"That river is the border of Zheninghai," Zedong said beside her. "This is Butagin."

Meiling pushed back her flying hair, following his pointing finger. Then she turned and found him watching her, his strange blue eyes glittering with movement. Despite the rapid flutter of her pulse, she met his gaze.

He smiled. "May I call you Meiling? I prefer there to be no formalities between us. You can call me Zedong."

Her throat constricted. She said nothing.

"Tell me about your mother. How does she fare these days?" he said, his gaze burning into the side of her face, doubtlessly noting the tensing of her jaw and bobbing of her throat.

Your mother's friend . . .

That was how Shang had described him.

Meiling bit her tongue. Hard. She could not fight like Feiyan, but she could be silent. There was more than one way to resist. She would not give in to this monster's attempts to make her trust him. To converse with her like an old friend.

"I must presume she is well," Zedong said finally, a slight touch of annoyance lacing his voice. "I have heard no news to the contrary. Tell me about yourself, then."

She kept silent and instead peeked overhead at a phoenix flying too close for comfort.

Zedong smiled slowly, his teeth flashing in the sunlight, white and striking like his eyes. "Your silence does not surprise me, little one. Liena was always quiet, too. Quick as a whip, always knew the right answers in class, but let other people answer. Do you know what her best subject was?"

Meiling's resolve faltered. She focused her desperate attention on that snaking river in the distance, a little thread of blue amidst so much green. Her fingernails pressed into the little crevices of the stones forming the wall. Pressed painfully tightly. Gritty dust crunched beneath her nails. A shiver raced down her spine.

"Fair enough." His tone grew brusquer. "Then let us put aside the pleasantries. Tell me about your magic. The vision I was given was a bit . . . hazy."

At least she had expected this question. Despite the alarm bells ringing in her head, she almost relaxed more now. She wasn't even tempted to answer. If he did not fully understand her magic, then perhaps she would be less useful to him than he expected.

Did she *want* to be less useful? Would he kill her if she could not prove her worth?

He would not dare kill the daughter of Emperor Nianzu. Not the daughter of his old *friend*.

Would he?

Zedong crossed his arms, leaning his shoulder on stone and fixing her with his full attention. "I know we started this relationship off slightly rocky. Do forgive me for the kidnapping. You can be sure I only did it because it was of utmost importance. Now, my little princess, I want to have a good relationship with you. You are, after all, Liena's daughter. I would encourage you to be cooperative." He drew out the last syllables slowly, blinking intentionally as he regarded her. "It will go better for you. I promise."

With each word, Meiling's heart sputtered, and her toes curled in her boots. Each muscle in her body quivered with tension. She gripped her hair tighter.

What did he want her to say to that?

She kept silent. Her eyes cast downward to the bright stones under her feet reflecting the sunlight. She swallowed heavily and ground her teeth.

Zedong snapped his fingers.

The nearest tower door—presumably the one Meiling was brought out of—swung open on screeching hinges. Two guards dragged a man heavily between them. She sucked in a gasp, glancing from the chained man to Zedong, who watched her carefully.

Lord Zuan Wan. The guardian of Ganhai.

He was middle-aged. Forty, perhaps, with lines around his eyes and a strong, square jaw. His hair was disheveled as much as Meiling's, but where she expected a spark of defiance in the set of his shoulders, the gleam of his eye, there was nothing. His spirit seemed sunken. Haggard.

Only the most powerful wielders could become guardians of the empire's territories. Only the strongest, fiercest, most experienced. It was the one position never granted to new Academy graduates, only seasoned warriors.

But this man . . .

His face remained downcast, with no trace of rebellion. No trace of the fire that got him his prestigious position. For the first time since arriving, Meiling felt a stab of true fear. If Zedong could break Zuan Wan in such a short time, what could he do to her?

The guards stopped a few feet short of Zedong and Meiling, hands clenched tightly around Wan's shackled arms. The guards saluted sharply with their free hands to Zedong.

Wan hung limply between them.

"Look, my pretty little Meiling." Zedong smiled casually, still leaning against the wall of the battlement. His eyes burned with an otherworldly light. "This is how things are going to work henceforth. I will ask you a question, and you will give me an answer. Otherwise"—he raised his eyebrows with a shrug—"I will have no choice but to threaten you. If you still do not comply, I will make good on my threat." He smiled almost indifferently, like he could yawn at any moment.

Meiling gripped the edge of the wall to keep from swaying on her feet. Dread settled into her stomach, slowly eating away her hope of being brave and escaping.

"Here's my first threat," Zedong said, all traces of indifference and amusement vanishing in an instant. "Tell me about your magic or else I will order this man slow-sliced in front of you. Something tells me you have a compassionate soul like your mother's."

He couldn't mean it.

Meiling's eyes snapped to those gleaming blue orbs. Her lips parted in a silent gasp. Horror and blood stained her vision red, and she blinked quickly to keep herself from fainting.

He did mean it.

His blue eyes were a whirling vortex of . . . *something*. Something very similar to the madness she had seen blazing in the illusionist's eyes more than once. Feiyan's words echoed in her ears, about how she was going to heal the tortures of the other prisoners. More than likely, any wounds inflicted upon Wan would be healed later. Zedong would not kill a prize wielder. He supposedly had use of Wan's unique abilities.

But it was that dejected stoop of his body, the limpness of his limbs, the way he could not muster the strength to even meet her gaze, that ruined her.

She couldn't.

She opened her mouth, struggled to find her voice. "My spirit can leave my body when I sleep," she whispered, barely audible.

Zedong heard her. He leaned closer, angling his ear to catch her words. He nodded. "And?"

"And . . . and . . . enter minds."

"Ah. How useful. It was as I heard. You, my darling, will be very useful indeed." He was smiling again, and the sight made her shudder. "Now, tell me: what is life like as the cursed princess?"

A stone dropped into her gut.

How were his eyes so menacing and captivating, terrifying and beautiful all at once? Why did it seem like something squirmed just beyond his pupils?

And worst of all, why did he actually seem to care about her answer to his very personal question?

Meiling hesitated.

It was so fast she could hardly react. Hardly realized the scream in her ears was her own.

A blade flashed and plunged into Wan's arm. It withdrew almost as quickly as it entered, but blood poured and Wan cried out. He threw his head back, baring his teeth against the pain.

"No! No—stop! Please stop!" Meiling begged, rushing forward. "Don't hurt him!"

"Calm yourself." Zedong reached out and snatched Meiling's wrist, preventing her from falling to her knees at Wan's side. He dragged her backward, toward him, toward the wall and that precipitous drop. "I merely need you to see that I am a man of my word."

"You did not give me a chance to answer!" she cried, too enraged to be silent.

He squeezed her wrist tighter in his fist, and then his face split into a smile. "You look just like her when you're angry. I knew you had fight in you. Somewhere."

She yanked on her wrist, and he let her go, let her catch herself on the wall. Blood seeped from Wan's sliced arm as she panted, staring at his mild face. She choked on a furious sob. "What do you want from me?"

Her anger only seemed to please Zedong more.

"Many things," he said blandly, with a wave of his arm. His eyes sharpened. "Tell me how Liena is faring."

"She is well," Meiling said quickly, her eyes darting between Zedong's predatory stare and the shackled guardian.

"Happy?" Zedong prompted.

She paused, only for a moment as she tried to read the expression on his face, and then said carefully, "I suppose so."

He seemed pleased with her answer. "Now, what about you? Were you happy with your life?"

She gritted her teeth, still leaning heavily on the wall for support. "I suppose so."

Another cry erupted from Wan's lips. Blood seeped through his tunic.

"Stop it! Stop it, I tell you!" she cried frantically. "I answered your questions!"

Zedong blinked, and his voice was more of a growl. "I do not have time for calculated answers. I want honest answers. No games. Only the truth. Were you happy with your life as the cursed princess of Zheninghai?"

Meiling's mouth hung open, her hands trembling like leaves swept up in the autumn wind. She looked down. "No."

He nodded slowly. "I suspected as much. Come, little one, I think this is enough for now."

He snapped his fingers again and more guards came, latching onto Meiling's arms and pulling her roughly between them after the bleeding and stooping form of Wan.

"Be gentle with her," Zedong called after them.

She did not need to turn to know he stood with his legs braced wide, one hand clasping his wrist behind his back, cloak dancing in the wind, with his blue eyes piercing into the back of her head.

CHAPTER 4

IRON CLANGED SHUT behind Meiling.

She fell against the bars, wrapping her fingers around the cold metal and pressing her face between the openings. Her eyes were as wide as they could go, hunting for even the smallest scrap of light.

It was so much darker after the sunlight.

She choked on a shuddering sob, but the tears would not come. There was nothing except cold and fear. So, so much fear.

"You're back," a dry voice muttered from the other cell.

"Feiyan!" Meiling cried, groping for that voice and reaching through the bars that separated them, trying to find her. She touched something warm. An arm. And then small, callused hands found both of hers and clasped them tight. Warmth flowed from those hands into her body, soothing her racing heart.

"Had a little chat with Fang?" Feiyan asked.

"Yes," Meiling whispered. "He started slow slicing Zuan Wan in front of me to get me to tell him about . . . my magic. And my mother."

What *exactly* had been the nature of their relationship?

It was hard to imagine beautiful, smart, and dignified Ma giving a brute like Fang Zedong any attention of any sort. Not when she could have one as good-hearted as Pa.

"Don't worry, those cuts aren't deep, and they're done with precision so the victim doesn't bleed out. I'll heal him tomorrow, likely. He won't suffer much. It only kills when there're hundreds of cuts."

Hundreds of cuts . . .

Meiling placed a hand on her convulsing stomach, willing herself to be strong. "That is not the greatest of my fears," she said, squeezing Feiyan's hands like they were her only hope. "He . . . I see now. He can make me do anything. And I am afraid of what he will make me do."

The words were so paper thin that they seemed to disintegrate the moment they left her lips.

Feiyan's arms moved, like she was readjusting her position. "Meiling," she said firmly, "Everyone is a fool. So, don't worry. Worrying will drive you mad."

Meiling's brow pinched. "I don't . . . I don't understand how those things are related. Much less how it is comforting."

Feiyan laughed and Meiling's ears rang with the strange sound.

"You're a fool, Meiling. No offense, of course. I'm a fool. And the best part—Fang Zedong is a fool too. Which means you shouldn't worry about what he can make you do. Focus on getting out of this phoenix-infested place."

Logical progression notwithstanding, Feiyan's conclusion was right. Meiling had to get out of here.

They both did.

It might have been a thousand years before the guards returned for Meiling. She might have slept once or a hundred times; she might have wrinkles lining her face. It was impossible to know.

Distant boots clanged on stones and doors kicked open before candlelight flared in her vision, so bright and painful. She did not rise from where she was leaning against the far corner, her hand resting on the stones on Feiyan's side of the iron bars. She wasn't touching Feiyan and hadn't heard her speak in hours. Or years. Meiling assumed she was sleeping.

Had they come for her, Feiyan, or both?

Perhaps they would veer down another direction into some other wielder's cell. But the footsteps kept coming steadily nearer and while she dreaded being taken, worse still was the idea of Feiyan being abused again.

The lantern stopped in front of her prison. Her heart lurched as the door swung open.

Two unfamiliar guards entered her cell and stomped toward her. She pulled back as they caught her by the arms and roughly dragged her between them out into the passage.

Scrambling sounded from Meiling's right and Feiyan stuck her face in between the bars, gripping them with both hands. The lantern light struck her full force, but she didn't flinch as she growled at the guards. "If you hurt her, I'll bite off your legs and spit out the bones. Understand?"

Did the guards even understand a word she said?

As they dragged her away, she glanced over her shoulder to hold Feiyan's fierce gaze as long as she could. Feiyan seemed to be trying to will strength into her.

She needed every bit of fierceness she could borrow.

The door clanged shut, cutting off Meiling's view of those raging eyes.

Don't be afraid, she told herself. This was . . . good. Yes. It was good. Every time one of them were taken away from their cell was an opportunity to plan for escape. An opportunity to look for weaknesses in the defense of the fortress, to hunt for any little crevice they might squeeze through to freedom.

Wherever they were taking Meiling, she was not helpless. Fang Zedong might think he could manipulate her and force her to do things she never wanted to do with her magic. But while he held a knife to her throat, she would be looking for any chance. She would not be overcome by her fear, she would be calculating, like Shang.

They did not take her to the parapet again. Instead, she was dragged through dim hallways with windows to the outside world, glaring so brightly she couldn't distinguish what lay beyond them. She tried to note what hallways they took, how many doors they passed, when they took a left or a right—

She was lost.

They entered a small room. The only light came from the single window on the far wall, sneaking around the edges of the curtain and spilling into the dark space. A low bed was nestled into one corner, and that was it. There was no other furniture in the room. No rugs, no tapestries, no murals on the wall, no ornate carvings or decorative dragons.

Fang Zedong waited in the middle, hands clasped behind him and legs planted wide.

In front of him, a man was slumped on his knees, his hands chained behind him. Those wilted shoulders could only belong to Zuan Wan. Immediately, her courage rushed out of her like spilled water as she took in the blood staining his ragged garments on his arm and side. His breathing was stilted.

Please, she wanted to cry. *Please do not torment this poor man further.*

"Princess Meiling," Zedong said coolly as the guards released her. "I thought it would be a good time for us to practice." He smiled.

Meiling took an involuntary step backward, bumping into the armor of a guard. Zedong watched her movements with those sharp, blue eyes. His smile drew into a thin, distant line. His voice was nonchalant when he spoke, but it bore a hard edge.

"Enter his mind. Find what he knows about the empire's military preparations."

She realized it then. In a vague, distant part of her mind, she'd already known—she'd just been hiding from the truth. Now, however, there was no more running and no more hiding.

She could be the downfall of her empire. Of her Pa.

Lu Meiling, the nothing princess, could be the one tool in the hand of a traitor that destroyed everything she knew and loved.

She had to resist. She couldn't do it. The only option was refusal.

And then she looked at Wan, panting beneath his bowed shoulders, bloodstained and weak. There was nothing but the quivering of his limbs, the brokenness of his soul, the fear in his heart.

How could she let him die? How could she let Zedong kill him?

If she resisted, he surely would. And that death would be slow, agonizing.

Zedong would make her stand there until the last shuddering breath escaped what was left of a once powerful guardian of Zheninghai. He would make her watch every stroke of a glinting knife, every flowing drop of blood.

Then he would give her someone else and tell her to enter their mind. No matter whether Meiling resisted or fought, people would die. She raised her stricken eyes from the guardian between them to Zedong. His smile grew.

"I see you understand better than if I'd explained it. I'm glad you are smart. Like your mother."

Like your mother.

She shuddered.

At least . . . at least Meiling had one little smidge of power in all this. Zedong needed her, depended on her to tell him what she had found in his mind. She could lie or conceal the most important information from him.

But how was she supposed to know what would be the one little piece of crucial information that would prove the weakness of the empire? She knew nothing about military strategy.

If Shang were here, he would know. He knew military strategy and how to differentiate between what was important and unimportant. He would analyze this fortress for weaknesses. It wouldn't take him long to come up with a way to escape. He'd certainly be a better liar.

But Shang was not here.

Which meant Meiling had to get herself out of here. It meant she had to discern for herself what things should and should not be shared with Zedong. It meant that she had to be strong.

No one else was going to be strong for her.

"I need to be asleep," she said softly, but firmly.

Zedong made a wide, sweeping gesture to the one piece of furniture in the room. "Please. Make yourself comfortable."

She stepped cautiously around Wan's bent form and stayed out of Zedong's reach. She reached the bed and stopped. It was hardly a foot above the ground, boasting only a flat head cushion and a threadbare blanket. "Surely you could have spared something more comfortable," she growled, flashing a glare at Zedong over her shoulder as she set herself down on the bed.

He laughed. It was a strangely good-natured laugh. The sound might have made her trust him if she didn't know better. Was it his laugh that had fooled Ma?

Meiling eyed the guards, Zedong, and finally Wan from where she sat on the bed. She licked her lips. "Any . . . privacy? It will be hard to fall asleep with all of you watching."

"Don't worry about that, my dear," Zedong said.

With two strides, he was at her side and snatching her hand. She tried to yank back, but before she could, he swept something out of his cloak and plunged a sharp tip into her finger. Blood welled, spilling over her finger, onto her nail, and then dropping to the floor.

"Wait!" Meiling cried out.

He kept the thing held firmly in her finger, gritting his teeth against her struggles to wrench away from his grasp. The blood kept coming, kept spilling.

He pulled it out and, after plucking a suspicious leaf from somewhere on his person, wrapped it and his hand around her bleeding finger, squeezing hard. Painfully hard. Meiling would have cried out again, would have fought harder, but the edges of her vision started to go black. She lost control of her muscles. Her mind screamed for her to leap to her feet and run, but her body betrayed her.

Heat scorched across her skin. She was so tired. Her eyes rolled, closed, opened. She saw darkness.

And then she fell.

CHAPTER 5

MEILING'S SPIRIT CATAPULTED out of her body.

She turned just as Zedong caught her body before she hit her head on the floor and arranged her limp form on the bed.

"Go into his mind," he said aloud into the room. "Find what I'm looking for. I will give you one hour."

With something akin to a whimper, she drifted closer to the defeated guardian. She hesitated, just above his head, afraid—hating herself. What choice did she have? What other option was there?

She would simply have to find enough information to appease Zedong, but not enough to destroy her beloved home. Not enough to ruin her Ma and Pa. But she also could not let Zuan Wan die. It didn't matter that she'd never met him before. She couldn't . . .

She slipped into Zuan Wan's mind.

The world shifted, leaving her standing on a wharf. A wharf that seemed eerily familiar. She looked down the coastline, picking out the familiar flags on these ships. Everything was silent. The wharf, the ships, the beach, the street leading back into the city—it was all abandoned. The only sounds came from the rhythmic crashing of gentle waves on the shore and the squawk of seagulls overhead.

Was this . . . was this home?

Meiling's heart quickened within her. She drank in the sight, hardly minding that clouds covered the sun. A storm brewed on the horizon and lighting flashed in the distance, but all that she cared about was that this was home.

Something like a sob racked her spirit. Could she go to the palace? Would she find her Ma? Pa? Hou and Yun?

No. The answer to those questions was a firm, unforgiving no. This was not her mind. This was Wan's mind. The only places in this city that she could visit were places he had been. Perhaps there would be some places in the palace of overlapping familiarity. Either way, there were clearly no people in this abandoned city. Her family would be the last people present.

A crack sounded beneath her. She looked down, surprised to find flickers of her own limbs standing on a dock. The wood started splitting, burned black along the edges of the crack. Strange: there was no fire. She hesitated only for a moment before running down the dock toward the shore. She could almost feel the rough wood splitting under her bare feet, sending splinters into her flesh. The cracking continued until she threw herself into the sand, and an ear-splitting break behind her made her roll in time to watch the entire dock plunge in burned and broken pieces into the shallows of the ocean.

More whining cracks sounded. Meiling whirled as the ship nearest her started cracking like the dock, the same burned spidery lines scaling the sides to its proud mast.

She only had an hour. And this mind was crumbling to pieces around her.

Lord Zuan Wan? she called as she ran away from the wharf, becoming more spirit and less physical the faster she moved.

Don't call me lord. I am no guardian.

The voice was dejected, disheartened, and utterly defeated.

We're going to be rescued, Meiling assured as she plunged into the familiar city streets. Streets she had only traveled often at night. *And then you will get your position back.*

A huge wave crashed behind her, overwhelming the breaking ships and swallowing the beach where she had just been. Saltwater stretched like reaching fingers into the city streets, flooding around her ankles and then higher, until she discerned the emotion trying to pull her into its watery darkness and drown her.

Despair.

I can never go back, Wan said.

Another wave crashed, and the water was to Meiling's waist. It pulled at her hungrily. She closed her eyes, forcing away her physical projection of herself and flew into the air above the flood overpowering the city.

The ships were gone. Completely gone.

She was running out of time. As much as she longed to comfort Wan, to give him even a kernel of hope, she couldn't. *Where is your knowledge stored?* she asked, instead of trying to respond to his desolation. *I need to give Zedong something. If you could just tell me something I can give him without hurting too many people, it would . . . simplify things.*

No response.

The tides of the flood seemed to retract, however. They sank lower into the ocean, and the thunderstorm on the horizon seemed slightly more distant than before.

Wan sank into a stupor. She felt it. There would be no help from him.

He did not care. He had given up.

She was not about to give up with him. She gritted spirit teeth and looked around at the mountain rising behind the city, behind the palace. In the other direction, the ocean went on forever until the storm's darkness swallowed it. Her heart ached for a moment.

Then she shook herself. Minds could not be navigated like the physical world. People were not merely physical. They were spiritual beings, with thoughts and feelings.

She remembered how she had found Shuren's memories. Feiyan had betrayed their location, but even then she could not sort through them without finding a guiding rope of some sort . . .

She closed her eyes, trying to shut out her broken home and the frustration gnawing at her soul. If only there was someone to teach her. If only she had been able to attend the Academy and learn how to wield her magic in the safety of a master's supervision. If only she had more time to figure these things out. If only each mind was not so infinitely different and complicated.

There had to be links. Everything was interconnected. Memories, emotions, knowledge, thoughts. They all twisted and twined together until they were nearly inseparable.

There had to be a more efficient way of finding things . . .

She tried to block out everything else of this mind, focus on the blackness behind her eyelids. She reached out with her hands, feeling for something she wasn't entirely sure existed. But she reached anyway, and then, when her frustration was too much, she began drifting slowly, waving her arms and searching for *something*. Anything to guide her to what she needed.

A brush against her fingertips.

Meiling gasped and opened her eyes. She floated in the middle of a street, by a doorway to what seemed to be a shop of some sort. No trace of what she'd felt was visible, no matter how hard she looked. Growling, she snapped her eyes shut again and felt for that thread.

It vibrated when she accidentally plucked it.

She snatched hold of it and opened her eyes. Now that she held it, there was the faintest glimmer of spider silk trailing from the doorway of the shop down the street. With a cry of excitement, she hurried down the cobblestones, keeping her hand firmly latched around that string. It was so wispy in her grasp she feared she'd break it.

But this memory thread—or whatever it was—seemed strong. Like it was something he was very familiar with. Perhaps Wan had walked these streets frequently, or perhaps something significant happened here. Meiling was about to find out.

She suddenly stopped short.

How did she know where this thread went? The chances of this leading to the information she needed was so, so incredibly slim. She plopped down in the middle of the street, a puddle of spirit, and shoved her face into her hands.

How much longer did she have?

Perhaps not being able to navigate minds would work in her favor. Could Zedong punish her for not knowing how to wield her magic?

He could. And he would.

She pulled herself to her feet, grabbing the thread. If there was one thread, then there were others. If she could only quickly eliminate unnecessary ones . . .

An idea flashed through her mind.

Where would Zedong have learned information about the empire's security? Probably not in the streets of the city. Probably in the palace.

Finally, she had a reason to race to the palace. She lost her physical projection of herself as she sped through the air to that familiar, towering palace at the highest point of the city, situated right into the base of the mountain. The lifting eaves of the red and gold roofs made her heart sing.

The floodwaters had not reached the palace, so it remained mostly unscathed. She flew up the long, long stairs to the entrance of the red palace, past places that were distinctly devoid of guards, and onto the threshold of the palace.

She stopped and closed her eyes, reaching out with her hands.

Just as she had expected, many threads of spider silk stretched into the palace, reaching in different directions. Their delicate strands slid between her fingers, their weight and vibrations giving varying impressions of strength.

That made sense. Some memories could be recollected with perfect clarity, while others were foggy and confused. The same was true about knowledge—not everything was known with certainty.

How could she know which string to follow?

She closed her eyes again, feeling the strands. She tried to concentrate hard, to see if there was any way to differentiate between the threads. They sure felt similar, except for their strength. Meiling could feel that easily enough.

That thought made her pause. What if . . .?

She stopped thinking about how they felt, but tried to *feel* how they felt. It was a subtle shift in how she perceived the threads she held.

It was agonizingly tedious.

The wave of frustration rolling through her was stronger than the spiderwebs, making her lose more of her mental projection of her body. She gnashed her teeth and clenched her fists around handfuls of threads.

Patience, Meiling, she told herself. Her nerves frayed thin, her anxiety threatening to overwhelm her. She needed to stay calm and keep trying.

She closed her eyes again and focused on feeling the threads. Her mind kept reverting to thoughts as she continually forced those away and channeled all her perception into her hands. Why was this so difficult?

She would never—

There!

She could *feel* the difference between the two threads she held. One was a positive association, while another had a negative association. She concentrated harder, knitting her brow. The positive one . . . it was less accessed than the negative one. It was weaker, older. It had a strange sense of youthfulness to it. She discarded it and picked another one.

Now that she had begun to notice the difference, it started to come easier. The next thread she held felt *routine.*

Its destination flashed before her mind's eye. It led to memories of Wan's yearly guardian report and inspection. When she plucked it, this one thread's vibrations split into many others—each a different trip. She almost gasped in relief. She was finally making progress!

But then, did she *want* to make progress?

The thought made her stop short, her fingers only barely shy of grasping another thread. What choice did she have? She had to find the information. She did not need to share everything with Zedong. But if she found nothing—

Something jolted painfully along her soul tether.

Meiling cried out, trying to grasp at the memory threads or the palace pillars or anything to prevent herself from being dragged away. But she couldn't fight it. It was like when Shang had kissed her to wake her.

A sudden bolt of alarm shot through her. Was she being kissed?

She clawed at thin air with spirit hands as she was pulled at a dizzying speed out of Wan's mind, back into that dimly lit chamber, and back into her own mind.

The violence of her spirit's return threw her from the bed. She blinked awake, her hands braced instinctively against the wood floor. Sweat poured in rivulets from her nose and the tip of her upper lip. The ground shook as though from an earthquake. She braced herself to keep from falling.

As her awareness returned to her, as her mind struggled to catch up with her body, it became clear the ground wasn't shaking at all. *She* was shaking.

Someone was speaking. The voice was as distant as a faraway land, but it still roared in her ears.

"What did you find, little one?"

CHAPTER 6

MEILING STRUGGLED TO calm her gasping inhales. She had never returned to her body like this before, and it took several minutes for her to collect her mind and her body enough to stop trembling so violently.

Finally, hands still planted on the floorboards, she lifted her eyes through a curtain of matted hair to find Zedong staring down at her with fierce blue eyes.

"What did you find?" he repeated sternly.

"Nothing," she blurted, and then vomited on the floor between her hands. She gasped, shaking all over again. "Nothing. I did not have enough time."

Zedong lifted his chin, casting a lazy glance back to Zuan Wan. He muttered something in that barbarian language to the guards and then turned to sweep grandly out of the room as guards gripped Meiling's arms and dragged her to her feet.

"Perhaps . . ." Zedong stopped in the doorway, his long black cloak seeming to fill the entire space. "Perhaps you were not motivated enough."

Meiling could give no thought to planning an escape while she was hauled through corridors that seemed much dimmer than before. The sunlight weakened, casting long shadows through open windows. She tried to keep pace with the guards, tried not to stumble over her own feet, tried to shove back the surge of helplessness.

I will escape this place. I will escape this place. I will escape this place.

Those words became a chant in her head. She could give no attention to practical ramifications; she could only latch onto it as her one hope and comfort.

This was not how she would spend her days. She would not be threatened like this. She and Feiyan would find a way. They'd escape together.

A pang stabbed her heart. What about Wan? The other wielders held captive here? To escape with all of them would be nigh impossible. Darkness descended heavily around her as she was dragged back to the dungeon. Thick, so thick, so foreboding. But Meiling could not think of that.

I will escape this place.

It was not until she was flung into a heap of trembling bones into her cell that she could finally wipe her mouth on her filthy sleeve. It was not until her cell door banged shut and the guards stomped away that she could process where she was.

"Meiling?" Feiyan's voice cut through the fog in her brain. "They left food while you were gone. It should be under your door."

Despite having just vomited, Meiling practically threw herself at the door, feeling along the wet ground for anything edible. Her hands found a cup of water, which she nearly knocked over in her hurry, and a hunk of bread. She inhaled both. They didn't help the pulsing weakness of her limbs.

A hand brushed her arm. With something like a sob, she grabbed that hand with both of hers and clutched it to her chest. Healing warmth flowed from it and the other hand that came to rest on the bend of her elbow. Her trembles eased and her weakened muscles seemed to knit themselves back together.

"I know, I know," Feiyan whispered.

"How are you so strong?" Meiling cried. "Why am I so weak? If I had gone to the Academy, I would be stronger. I would know how to fight."

Feiyan tightened her grip on Meiling's elbow. "This place will break the strongest of people."

"It hasn't broken you."

She chuckled mirthlessly and said with a sad sort of voice, "Oh, but Meiling, you forget. I am a fool."

"You are no fool," Meiling said.

Silence and a soft thumb stroke were Feiyan's only answer.

Meiling drew a steadying breath. "Did they come for you while I was gone? Are you doing all right?"

"No, I haven't moved. And I'm fine."

"Are you bleeding?"

"Not anymore."

"Feiyan! Do you need me to bind your wounds? Is there anything I can do? Here, my clothes are dirty, but I could tear off some of my undershirt. It should be cleaner—"

Feiyan barked a short laugh. "No, keep your stinky clothes. I'm fine. They dare not injure me too terribly. I'm too valuable for them to be careless with me. Isn't this a fun feeling? Knowing that you are so important that they can't hurt you?"

"It only means they will hurt others instead of you," Meiling mumbled. "We need to get out of here."

There was more shuffling on the other side of the bars, and it sounded almost *wet*. When Feiyan spoke again, Meiling expected her to whisper in a hushed tone, but her loud volume indicated she wasn't worried about being overheard.

"I have a plan. I think I can overwhelm a guard, steal his clothes, and take the keys to let you out. Then I'll take you as my prisoner and escort you out of this phoenix-infested place. And then we run for it."

Meiling pinched the bridge of her nose, wrinkling her forehead. "You think that could work?"

"Pfft! Of course not! But everyone knows the rules of escape. You form a stupid plan and then you don't follow the plan, you improvise. If you don't have even a stupid plan, then you're dead. People are silly that way. What's the point of a plan that's meant to be followed? Rules are for breaking."

Silence fell.

Drip, drip, drip.

"You're cynical," Meiling said. It was not an accusation, merely an observation.

"I prefer to think I'm realistic." The tone and sound of crinkling lips indicated a grin accompanied those words.

"So . . ." Meiling began, scooting so she could lean against the cold stone wall. "The next time a guard comes, you'll . . . knock him out?"

"If there's only one, I should be able to incapacitate him," she said nonchalantly. Like she waved her hand at the ease of overwhelming a guard.

"If there are two?"

"Then we wait until there's one," she said, like it was the most obvious thing ever. "Unless you can tear through the iron with your bare hands and take out the other guard. But if you could do that—"

"We wouldn't need to wait for anything," Meiling finished, almost laughing despite herself.

"The problem is that dragon-blasted illusionist. He always seems to be lurking around every corner, just waiting for another opportunity to slug me in the face. As much as I hate to admit it, he's too strong for me. These barbarian guards are one thing. But him . . . The fire-brigand and the wind-brigand—they thought they were so strong, you know? And they were, of course . . ." Feiyan trailed off, her incomplete thought hanging in the air.

Meiling knew what she wanted to say. There was something different about Shuren. He was powerful, but subtly powerful. It was the sort of power that was even more deadly than brute strength, because the art of illusion could bypass even the strongest defenses.

What Feiyan wanted to say was that Shuren was insane. Actually insane. He did not view the world as it was. He viewed it through the lens of possibility. What it could be—and not necessarily how it could be improved. He sold truth for beauty until he was so enslaved to hope that he could not see the despair and deceit clouding his vision.

Meiling had been in his mind. She knew. She knew better than Feiyan what she had been trying to say. What she was afraid to say.

"I know," Meiling whispered softly.

There was a pause. Had Feiyan even heard her?

"I'm hungry. Before we escape, we'll need to stop for a snack."

"They're coming. You ready?" Feiyan whispered, poking at Meiling's shoulder through the bars. "I'm ready. Ready to crush some skulls."

Meiling stood quickly, her heart thumping wildly in her chest. Doubt plagued the back of her mind. Could this work? Was it possible?

The thought of Feiyan's half-brained plan made her limbs melt into a puddle of quaking muscle and bone. Surely, they could come up with something better. But try as she might, she couldn't think of anything else.

Shang could have. He could have planned and executed a flawless escape. If only he was here, in the cell next to hers. She wouldn't have to be strong, not if he was here.

What was she thinking? She didn't want Shang here! The last thing she wanted was for him to be captured and tortured behind enemy lines.

But . . .

No. She would never wish other people were trapped here, too. It did not matter how comforting their presence would be. It did not matter how much stronger she would feel if they were here. She would never want them in a dungeon next to her.

For a split second, the memory of his arms around her flashed through her. If only she could go back to the moment when she'd laid her head on his chest and listened to his heartbeat. How her own heart had thrilled when he'd asked her to stay!

The door opened with a painfully loud bang and that cursed lantern screamed in Meiling's eyes. When would she get used to adjusting to the light? Likely never, so long as she was kept in such permeating blackness.

"I think there's only one," Meiling whispered.

"Sweet," Feiyan said, cracking her knuckles.

But the guard came to Meiling's door, not Feiyan's. She tried to look over at Feiyan, to see if the lantern light might cast upon her face, but she didn't get a chance. Arms slid through the bars, swift and silent, snatching the surprised guard and yanking him against the bars.

"Punch him!" Feiyan cried. "Kick him! Do something!"

Punch him? In the face? Or . . . somewhere else?

It was too late.

The element of surprise was lost, and the guard wrenched free. His hand shot through the bars, trying to catch hold of Feiyan's arm, but she was too quick for him. He called something in his own language and footsteps sounded down the hallway, through the open door.

The guard latched onto Meiling's arm and yanked her so hard after him that she let out a cry of pain. He dragged her out of her cell and nearly rammed her straight into Shuren, who turned a key in the lock of Feiyan's cell. Presumably to administer punishment for her insubordination.

"Don't hurt her!" Meiling cried as she was dragged past. "Please! Please don't hurt her!"

Eyes rimmed with emptiness met hers, his hand stilling on the key in the lock. There it was again—that gleam of strong emotion mingled with so much fear.

"Don't hurt her," she said again, softer.

The door slammed shut behind her. She squeezed her eyes shut, her heart clenching in pain at the thought of him beating her. Or worse.

Feiyan could handle herself.

But Feiyan would run headlong into disaster if allowed. She'd seen the illusionist's rough treatment of her in the past. His duty apparently outweighed his feelings.

Was she being taken to hunt through minds again? Was the betrayal of all she loved right around this next bend? It was hard to tear her attention away from the memory of Shuren's eyes and the sick dread in her stomach. Would he heed her words? Would Feiyan even be conscious when she returned?

He could not kill her.

Somehow, the thought was no longer so comforting.

It was evening. Sconces lined the length of dark hallways, casting eerie shadows on the bare walls. There was not even a rug to cushion the clicking of boots on stone and the scuffling of Meiling's tripping feet.

A door opened at the far end of the hallway and a girl stepped out, her back to the open window. The last rays of the sunset caught on her dark hair, illuminating every stray piece and lining her silhouette in gold.

She curtsied stiffly.

Her robes were a muted red, wrapped around her slight frame and tied with a colorful patterned sash lined with furs. Her hair was bound in two braids, falling over her shoulders and down to her waist. A beaded circlet wound around her forehead—a small but pretty decoration. One that wasn't worn anywhere in Zheninghai.

Why her people called them *barbarians* was beyond Meiling. This girl was just a regular girl.

The guard loosened his hold on Meiling's arm, and she almost fell at the unexpected removal.

"Come," the girl said with a strong accent. "Help you."

Meiling pulled back warily, glancing back down the hallway at the retreating guard. "Help with what?"

The girl gestured at all of Meiling and her face seemed to say, *"Um . . . with your filth, of course."* Instead, she said, "Clothes. Clean." She smiled and nodded, her beads clacking pleasantly. "Clean."

She gestured toward the open door.

"Clean?" Meiling repeated and hesitantly followed the girl inside. It was a small room, but compared to the bareboned furnishing of the rest of the fortress, it was comfortable. A bed was arranged next to a window where skins hung, ready to be tied down to keep out the chill. There was a wardrobe on the opposite side of the room and next to it, a mounted mirror and a seating cushion. Finally, beside the door was a wooden bathtub, already full of steaming water.

She almost gasped at the sight.

"Clean," the girl repeated, smiling and nodding at the bath. "Clean you."

It was a trap. It must be, right?

Meiling could not care.

She shed her filthy garments as quickly as she could—not caring about the servant girl watching—and slid her grime encrusted body into the tub. The water was the perfect temperature, just slight of scalding, and for a moment, there was no such thing as empires at war, imprisoned wielders, her own torment at what she would be forced to do. Nothing except the heat of this bath that soothed away her cares and worries.

If she closed her eyes, she could believe she was back home.

The water was brown with dirt by the time she had finished, but she'd never felt so clean as when she regretfully emerged and was greeted by a warm towel in the arms of the servant girl.

She looked sadly back at her own dirty clothes, but then the girl quickly motioned to the wardrobe. "You wear!" she said brightly. "You wear!"

Meiling opened it to find three clean sets of robes. She touched one, the soft texture sliding between her fingers. These were robes fit for a princess—in the Zheninghai style she was accustomed to. She stared at them, baffled beyond words.

Guilt stabbed her.

Here she was, clean and bathed and about to don fine clothes again while Feiyan was likely lying half-awake in that dark, disgusting dungeon with a black eye.

What was going on?

Once she was in a dressing gown, her maid pulled a note from her sash and handed it to Meiling with another sweet smile and bow. "You!"

"Thank you," Meiling said back in her language, trying to ignore the pang of guilt that she didn't know any Butagin except the blessing Ma always spoke over her food when she wasn't in public. She shouldn't have spent so much time studying constellations in the palace library. If she'd focused on the far more valuable skill of learning their neighbor's language, she would have an advantage now.

She'd just never dreamed she would actually leave Zheninghai.

The paper was crisp, and the seal made a little *crack* when she broke it. Unfolding it with unsteady hands, she found neat, well-formed characters.

Dine with me tonight, Princess.

It was only signed with the stamp of a lotus.

She dropped to sit on the bed, suddenly overwhelmed by a tumultuous flip of her stomach. What did he want from sharing a meal with her? Perhaps he wanted to win her over, so she'd be more cooperative.

Well, *that* was not going to work on her. It would take a lot more than a bath, fine clothes, and a meal to change her opinion of Fang Zedong.

At the thought of a meal, her legs wobbled. As much as she wanted to be stubborn and resist his invitation, she didn't want to provoke his wrath unnecessarily.

But the real reason: she was absolutely starving.

The girl clucked and hummed as she brushed out Meiling's hip-length hair until its gloss returned. Her hair hadn't looked this nice since she left the palace. When the girl helped her into the robes, saying scattered, "Yes!" "No, no!" and "You!", they were just a smidge too large on her frame, even though Meiling could have sworn they were the right size.

Too quickly, the girl stepped back, nodded, and said, "Yes!"

She was ready then.

A guard awaited her in the hallway. Instead of snatching her arm in an iron grip, he held out his elbow to her like an escort. A chill ran down Meiling's spine as she looped her arm in his and let herself be led to whatever awaited her at supper.

CHAPTER 7

"WELCOME, MY LOVELY princess. I knew you would look ravishing in bluc."

Meiling said nothing, quietly meeting Zedong's gaze as he greeted her at the door and ushered into the dining hall. It was large, but sparse. A long, slender table—that was shockingly high—ran most of the length of the room, covered by a crimson tablecloth and dozens of candles. Large windows rose along either side of the hall, blocked to ward off the night cold. Most notable, however, were all the thrones arranged around the table.

Meiling stopped, brow wrinkling. Before she could stop herself, she blurted, "So many thrones!"

Zedong glanced down at her, a line appearing between his eyes. Then he surveyed the table and thrones again and burst out in an unexpected laugh. Meiling stiffened.

"You've never seen a chair before!" he said, grinning. "I'd almost forgotten that everyone sits on those little mats and cushions in Zheninghai. It's been so long."

Meiling tested the word on her tongue skeptically. "Ch . . . air."

"Chair."

"Ch-chair."

He grinned again, and there was that disarming warmth she'd glimpsed before. If she wasn't careful, she'd forget he was the same person who had ordered Zuan Wan's torture only hours ago.

"Come, let me show you the way of chairs. I think you'll be converted before too long." With that, he stepped ahead of her and grabbed a chair by its back, pulling it out and gesturing for her to sit in it.

Head swimming, she forced her feet into action. It went against every instinct to turn her back to him as she sat. He pushed her chair toward the table, and she sucked in a surprised gasp. "It's so . . . *high*! Am I supposed to put my feet on the ground or hold them up?"

She would never get used to this.

Zedong was giving a quick brush of his immaculate garments, but at her words, he snorted, as though choking on a laugh as he sat at the head of the table, to her left. "You put them on the ground, darling."

Slowly, she lowered them until her slippers touched the cold floor. The wood was unyielding beneath her—not nearly as comfortable as a cushion. This dinner was already going to be long without having to sit on a throne for the duration of it.

Was *this* why her people called them barbarians? If so, the term was deserved. Thrones for everyone at meals! It was so ridiculous she couldn't help shaking her head.

Zedong, having suppressed his amusement into a polite smile, fixed those blue eyes on her. "I have decided to amend my ways. It was unfair to keep you in the dungeon, princess as you are. You must forgive me. My home is your home. Your birth will be honored here, and you will have everything fit for a princess from now forward. Please, I want you to be comfortable here."

He gave her another charming smile and then shifted his gaze to the empty table, raised his hands, and clapped loudly. Servants like the girl who had aided Meiling bore dishes of food out to the table.

To her shock, Zedong bowed his head, closed his eyes, and spoke a blessing over the food. The very same blessing Ma had always spoken over her food.

Meiling stared, her mouth falling open.

"Please tell me," Zedong said as a woman set a bowl of watery soup in front of him, "more about your family. I knew both of your parents during my Academy days and haven't heard any personal news from them in many years."

Would he threaten her if she did not tell him? Would he bring in Zuan Wan or another wielder—her heart balked at the idea of Feiyan—and order him slow-sliced before her eyes?

She delayed by taking a sip of the soup. It was salty, brothy, and had a slight fishiness to it. Ravenous hunger burst through her body with a force that almost made her dizzy. She tried not to devour the soup in one huge gulp. "They are well," she offered tentatively. "My parents are well."

"So you have told me." He grinned, looking almost handsome again despite the lines of age scoring his face. "What keeps them busy?"

Each question needed to be handled with the utmost care. Meiling chewed on her words before saying, "Hou and Yun are at the Academy. Ma sees to the running of the palace. Pa . . . mostly runs the empire."

"Mostly?" Zedong grinned again, lifting his wine goblet to his lips and taking a large draught.

"He runs the empire," she corrected.

"Ahh. And what do you usually do each day?"

She shrugged. Her soup, finished, was whisked away. It was replaced by steaming bowls arranged between her and Zedong, full of rice, pork, broiled bamboo shoots, and an assortment of vegetables. She was so hungry she nearly whimpered at the welcomed sight. She had not had a meal like this since she'd left the palace weeks ago. Nevertheless, she tried to slow her greedy reach to fill her bowl.

"I read," Meiling said hesitantly. "I study."

"Books? Do you not attend events at the Academy with your siblings? No responsibilities in the upkeep of the palace?" His frown seemed genuinely surprised.

The fluffy, savory rice in Meiling's mouth turned to mush as she tried to swallow the knot forming in her throat. She gulped hard. "Not usually."

"Hmm," he said to himself, wrinkling his forehead and looking down at his own plate. "You did not go to the Academy. What has it been like? Being a powerful wielder and yet being . . . disregarded by society?"

Meiling did not want to eat anymore. She knew she should, however, so she kept slowly shoveling bites into her mouth, chewing halfheartedly and swallowing thickly. Her food lost all its taste.

She dared to raise her gaze to his and was taken aback to find something like sincere understanding shining in his strange eyes. A locked away part of her quivered, an old scab ripped away from her heart. She wanted to speak, wanted to share. No one understood her. And something about the look on his face . . . *he would understand*. In a way that no one else ever had.

But she clamped her mouth shut. She would not trust him.

Her silence was useless. Apparently her face had given away enough of her feelings, for he just nodded once, silent.

"It's a lot of disgrace for one person to bear," he said softly, almost whispering.

She closed her eyes tight and focused on shoving down the welling emotion. She forced her thoughts toward Feiyan. How if Feiyan were here, she'd be fighting. The healer wouldn't let Zedong manipulate her.

She could not think about the truth of his words.

"Perhaps . . ." Zedong continued quietly, watching her with keen interest. "Perhaps society could use some . . . *reform.*"

Meiling stared at her bowl, not seeing its contents. She hadn't lifted her chopsticks to her mouth with a bite in several long minutes. She gritted her teeth.

"I thought you might agree," he said, almost contemplatively.

A hot flush spread across her cheeks. She could not let him fire attack after attack, leaving her struggling to defend. She needed to strike out herself.

"You have not told me about your time at the Academy," Meiling said.

He seemed surprised that she had spoken. He smiled. "Indeed. I prefer not to recollect those days."

"You met my mother."

His smile remained exactly as it had been, not twitching the slightest bit. "So I did." His eyes trailed past her to the end of the otherwise empty room.

She tried to read the strange expression on his face. If she was not mistaken, it was a complicated jumble of conflicting emotions, too tangled for her to discern. What *had* happened between them at the Academy? Where did Pa fit into all of this?

"I hope you found your chamber satisfactory," Zedong said at long last. "I'm sure that you've noticed that luxury does not characterize our standard of living. We prefer severity."

"You need the money to fund the troops," Meiling interpreted.

His eyelids slid lower while one brow rose. "It seems nothing slips past you," he said with a wry twist of his mouth.

Absolutely nothing, she thought, with no lack of ire.

She returned her attention to her neglected food. Whereas before she had been shivering with hunger, now she was almost sick. She took another bite anyway.

When she was escorted back to her new room, she expected the distinct thump of a bolt dropping, of an iron key in an iron lock after the door closed. *Nothing*. After the loud footfalls of the guard echoed down the hallway and faded into silence, Meiling checked the door and was surprised to discover it was, indeed, unlocked.

Only a few minutes later, a pair of tromping steps returned. They stopped in front of her door and did not move. She bent to her knees and peeked under the door to find boots on either side of the door.

Guards.

Well, that was probably more effective than a lock anyway and had the appearance of protection rather than restraint.

Meiling blew out a puff of frustrated air. Why was she here while Feiyan was in the dungeon? Why had Zedong been so *strange* over dinner?

And *why* couldn't she get his words out of her head? They permeated her mind, sinking into her subconscious like poison. Or perhaps they had always been there; she had simply refused to give voice to them.

Reform . . .

She was hot. So, so hot.

She strode to the window and untacked the skin, pushing it aside so she could lean over the edge and stick her flushed face out into the night. She breathed deeply of clear, cold air. It was intoxicating—the fresh wind in her lungs, her hair, on her cheeks. Even the memory of the dungeon was not enough to mar her enjoyment of this beauty.

Except . . .

Feiyan.

Feiyan was probably worried about her, wondering what horrible thing had happened to her. Yet here she was, being treated like a princess and fed until she was fat and happy. She told herself it was not her fault—and it wasn't—but it still sat wrong in her bones.

The guilt was relentless.

And then her knees almost buckled at the realization that she would likely not get Feiyan's reassurance, companionship, and comfort for a long time. Ever? When *would* she see Feiyan again? How could they escape now—now that they were separated? Now that Meiling was guarded so heavily?

Unbidden, Shang's hard face flashed before her vision. She tried to scrub it out, push it away, but it was insistent. His eyebrow cocked, and he crossed his arms over his chest. She wanted to bury her face in that chest and cry until dawn. Then he melted away, replaced by Fen's snarling face. It seemed to look at her and say, *"Pathetic."*

She was alone. Her against Fang Zedong. She had no means or methods now to escape. As if to confirm this, she peered down at the sheer drop of several stories into a barbarian infested courtyard.

Escape may take time. But she was determined. She would not stay here complacently, letting Zedong fill her mind with lies.

But surely . . . surely effort was being made to recover her? Surely she would be rescued. She was the princess, after all.

Surely . . . surely . . .

Meiling undressed and eased herself slowly into the bed. It was so soft and foreign after these last several weeks, but especially after sleeping against the dungeon wall. Which was what Feiyan would be doing now. She chewed her lip until it bled, warring with herself over whether she should get up and sleep on the floor instead. She stayed, heart throbbing painfully.

How long would she be here?

Not long, if she had a say.

What in the seven valleys?

She stood in a familiar corridor, surrounded by the wealth and luxury she had grown accustomed to at home—at the palace. The colors of the rugs were brighter than she remembered, catching vividly in the blinding light that came from everywhere and nowhere at once. Torches along the walls burned sharper than ever.

It was more colorful than Suguan under the noonday sun.

Her room was just down that corridor. Was her family here?

Meiling peeked down the corridor at the familiar door, something tugging her toward it. As much as she longed to run and fling herself down on her own bed, stare out her own window, she ignored the pull and walked quickly away from it. Toward her family's rooms.

Why was she going there? They were not there. She knew it instinctively.

No one was here. No one but her.

Why in this phoenix-infested world was she *here*? She recognized it. Not as her palace home, but as what it truly was. And why was she here? The question brought so much angst to her soul that she was pulled again, back the way she had come.

She held her ground.

She had power here.

Looking down, she found her toes poking out from under the hem of her sky-blue robes. The robes she had been wearing earlier, not anything she owned at home. Something was very, very wrong.

Something was *incredibly* wrong.

She should not be here. She needed to get out.

Turning on her heel and trying to keep her pace controlled and dignified, Meiling swept through the hallways toward the main entrance to the palace. Overhead, qilins battled phoenixes in a vivid mosaic on the ceiling. Sapphire scales on a deer-like hide gleamed; red, orange, and blue flames licked the trim on the walls. She passed the hallway leading to the throne room. Reaching out her hand, she felt the tiny threads vibrated beneath her fingers. Not many. One in particular hummed the loudest, strongest. The sensation sent a pang to her heart.

The palace was so empty.

There was no one to enjoy its unreal beauty except Meiling. And the sight of this beauty made her stomach twist into knots.

Don't panic, she told her mind, trying to restrain herself from reaching out for each of those threads that surrounded her. One touch was all she needed to know where each led. Visions flashed in her mind when she touched them. If she were not careful, the palace around her would shift, leaving her to be lost in the memory.

She focused on the door.

She needed to escape this place.

There was no time for a dignified pace. She broke into a run, breaking through threads that reknit immediately, racing down hallways in a manner that would make her mother frown. Ma was not here, though. Not like Feiyan had been present in Shuren's mind. No one was here.

The panic continued to mount, making her gasp as she ran. At first, soft rugs tickled her toes, followed by the chock of cold marble, but eventually her feet disintegrated into spirit as she flew.

Straight into an angry, ferocious black wall of magic.

Pain ripped into Meiling's soul, rattling her tether. She cried out, and the sound echoed louder and louder through the palace. She tried covering her ears, but the sound wasn't physical. There was nothing she could do except listen to her own voice crying out over and over, until at long last it reached a crescendo, and slowly died away.

She lay on the ground at the threshold of the palace, staring without understanding at the flaring black magic. It was like the fat, messy brush strokes of paint, swiped across the door, prevented her exit. The edges gleamed with a color she couldn't describe. Something like if black was a shade of light, rather than the absence of it.

She leapt to her feet, rage surging through her limbs. She approached the door again, more carefully, but this time, she tried to slip her finger into one of the small patches where the black binding had not fully covered. Her finger slid through, free to the other world beyond, but she could not even fit her hand through.

Size should not matter! She was spirit, not physical. And yet, here she was, too big to fit through the small openings.

Maybe a window was open somewhere.

Meiling raced at breakneck speed, terror scraping like a dagger down her spine. She flew to every window, every door, in the entire palace.

Every single one was blocked. She checked all—except one.

With a cry, she finally tore down to her room, ignoring the flashing memories as she brushed silken threads. She burst through the door, not bothering to open it but merely slipping through it.

There was her own window.

It glared horrible black gashes of magic paint.

On the windowsill so close to that ragged sorcery, a soft, golden glow emanated. It was no thicker than any of the other silk memory threads, but it throbbed with life and pain and everything that made Meiling herself. It was beautiful, especially standing in stark contrast to the ugly hue of black magic.

It was her soul tether. And tangled in with it were threads of black, raging magic. Restraining, confining. *Binding*.

Meiling let out a burst of wild emotion. Anger, frustration, fear, panic. It coursed from her to her soul tether, making the converging threads tremble.

She was trapped. Bound.

Zedong had imprisoned her in her own mind.

CHAPTER 8

MEILING WOKE WITH cold sweat streaming down her back, her face, her armpits. She sucked in one ragged breath after another, afraid to return to that dream that was not a dream at all.

She moved an arm. Then a leg. She drank in the feeling of autonomy.

Not that she was free, but the only other time she'd been so panicked by imprisonment was when she had hung above sharp rocks, suspended with Fen and Shang by spelled vines. A trap that Zuan Wan was forced to set for them.

Her mind had always been a place of freedom. Sleep was respite.

But now, while she lay awake in her bed, early dawn light staining her bedclothes, sleep was a prison. She tried to calm her racing mind and heart.

Then she threw off the covers, practically leaping out of bed, and hurried to don a new set of fine robes. These were pale pink, embroidered with roses and gold thread. She spared one guilty thought for Feiyan as she fastened the sash around her waist and quickly braided her hair.

With a deep breath, Meiling approached her door. Would the guards stop her?

Zedong had said his home was her home.

Squaring her shoulders and trying to control her anger—something she was not used to struggling with—she turned the knob and pushed open the door. The guards eyed her sidelong, but otherwise ignored her. She strode past them, barely keeping from slamming the door in her wake.

She needed air. She needed to escape.

Her slippers padded almost silently down the hallways. Only her fury made them audible. How dare he imprison her like that? How dare he be so kind to her, fill her head with treason, and then bind her?

How *dare* he?

Early sun streamed through the open windows. Those windows would be boarded up soon to prevent the winter cold from seeping too deeply into the fortress. For now, they let the cool breeze of the autumn dawn waft through Meiling's sloppy braid and ruffle her embroidered sleeves.

She passed more guards, and none made a move to stop her.

By all the lights above, she would go straight down to the dungeon, find a key, let Feiyan out, and the two of them would escape.

"Out for an early morning stroll?"

The dark, amusement-tinged voice cut through Meiling's thoughts. She whirled at the top of the staircase she was about to descend. Behind her, striding down the corridor, adjusting the sleeves of his close-fitted, all black attire, was Fang Zedong. Morning light caught in his strange eyes and he smiled.

"Allow me to serve as your escort," he said smoothly, quickly reaching where she stood frozen. "There is much of the fortress I wish for you to see."

He held his arm out to her.

Her anger evaporated in an instant. *Most of it*, that is. A little kernel of it still smoldered in her breast, waiting for the perfect opportunity to ignite into a roaring blaze. Terror filled the space left behind.

With a thick swallow, she looped her arm in his and let him lead her down the stairs. She kept her eyes downcast, trying to focus on taking each step carefully and not losing her balance. Trying not to lean too heavily on him.

If Ma were Zedong's captive instead of her, she would know how to behave. She would be strong, bold, gentle. She would know how to draw out his secrets, would know how to defeat him. Somehow, she'd be brave while still being good.

Meiling could not deny the hatred that burned in her core.

"Let me show you the training," Zedong said pleasantly, like any kind father showing his child something. "It might look familiar."

He brought her through a heavy door into the rising sunshine of a large courtyard. Wielders—*brigands*—were already practicing. There were dozens of them, exercising their magic and perfecting their technique. It did remind Meiling of the Academy fights, with so many different powers. Overhead, in the clear sky, red flaming phoenixes circled. More were perched on the towers, peering into the courtyard or out into the valley.

Meiling's attention was diverted by scuffling down the portico. Two Butagin maids carried baskets of laundry between them. Beyond them, a few men dressed in similar servant attire wrestled a fat hog in another direction.

She looked away, suddenly lightheaded. She had no stomach for slaughter. Perhaps the Academy would have cured her of her squeamishness. Shang's sharp gaze flashed through her mind, the memory returning of how he'd looked at her while preparing rabbits for them to eat.

"Here, power is earned." Zedong's contemplative voice interrupted her thoughts, jerking her attention back to him. "Not bestowed by the whims of the fathers."

She glanced up at his face, catching the expression that vanished almost immediately. She remembered the black sorcery chaining her to her own mind, the way that Fen and Shang had described the brigands' magic as being *enhanced.*

Black magic. Zedong used black magic to make himself and his wielders more powerful.

What sort of magic did Zedong wield?

"You bound my soul," Meiling accused.

He glanced down at her, tearing his attention away from his brigands. "Hmm? Oh yes, do forgive me. I had little choice."

Right. Because Meiling was so *dangerous* when unbound. She took a different approach. "How did you do it? Bind my soul, that is?"

He crossed his arms over his chest, watching as Ruogang—one of the brigands who'd captured her—threw a fireball and nearly decimated another whose abilities seemed to be some variation of feral strength. "When you limit magic to what you were born with, you can never experience the fullness of the power you are capable of. Power you were meant to wield."

Several retorts came to mind, but she said none of them. Let him sidestep the question. She glanced up again at her captor, trying to catch a glimmer of what lay behind his eyes.

Instead, there was a flicker of . . . of . . .

That light . . . He seemed almost drunk with power. With his own potential. When he turned back to her, however, it was gone, replaced by a cordial smile. "Come, let me take you further."

Meiling fell into step next to him, the brigands glancing at them in passing and trying to not look overly curious. She forced herself to hold her head high.

"You remind me so much of her. Everything about you is so like her. Even the way you move. Liena was always dignified, even before . . ." He trailed off, covering it with a warm, glittering smile down at her. He placed his other hand over Meiling's on his arm. "Sometimes I can make myself believe that you are her."

"I'm not my mother," Meiling said with a little more vehemence than she intended.

He nodded, smiling still. "Indeed. You are right; there are some differences."

Besides the fact that Ma was more than twice her age?

"Your complexion is lighter, and you are shorter. Your voice is a little higher, too. She always tried to hide her accent. Only occasionally, when you say certain words, do I catch a hint of her accent that you picked up." He glanced at her sidelong, briefly. "You're more scared of me than she was."

She could not keep the tension from shooting through her body into the arm he held. She knew he felt it, and that only made it worse. It took everything in her to not hang her head in shame. No, she wasn't as brave as her mother.

They continued walking under the cover of the portico alongside the practicing brigands. Morning brightened around them, bringing more color into the bleakness of the fortress.

Suddenly, the door ahead burst open and two barbarian guards pushed through, hauling a third guard after them. Zedong stiffened next to her and pulled his arm free of hers, striding forward a few steps out into the sunlight.

He barked something in another language to the guards as they deposited the miserable man at Zedong's feet. One of the standing guards replied, gesturing to the kneeling man and pointing in the direction of the palace portcullis.

Meiling's heart plunged into her stomach. Had the guard been trying to escape? He'd been caught doing *something*. What would happen to him? Would he be thrown in the very dungeon he had guarded?

She crept forward, wishing she understood the exchanges, wishing she could do something.

Could she do something?

Zedong targeted a question at the groveling guard. The guard looked up, eyes wide and mouth sagging open, speechless. Terror ringed the whites of his eyes. He glanced past Zedong, caught sight of Meiling. She instinctively reached out her hand just as Zedong turned to follow the guard's gaze.

The guard hung his head.

Then he leapt to his feet and swung a kick at one of the guards, throwing a punch at the other. Fast as an arrow, he dodged a blow, then grabbed and twisted the other guard's arm to a painful angle.

Zedong stepped back, lifted his arm, and snapped his fingers.

A phoenix, poised ready on the nearest tower, spread its flaming wings and rose into the air. Horror dragged Meiling's jaw open as panic and dread flooded every inch of her body.

The loyal guards saw the phoenix and threw themselves to the side.

Meiling threw herself forward.

"No!" she screamed, rushing for the prone guard lying on the ground and staring up at his fate. "No, no!"

Zedong grabbed her arm and pulled her away, his grip harsher than iron. So hard, she feared her bones would break. But her bones didn't matter. She writhed and twisted in his grip.

"Call off the phoenix! Don't kill him!" she screamed. She clawed with her nails, overcome with the desperate need to *hurt him* and make him stop. But the harder she struggled to get free, the firmer his grip became.

She closed her eyes just in time before the phoenix opened wide its mouth. The cries of the guard cut off abruptly.

"No, no, no, no, no," she was saying, repeatedly, wetness streaking down her cheeks. "No, no, no."

When she opened her eyes, the sight that met her made her scream again. She shut her eyes fast, hiding her face in Zedong's chest without recognizing it as him. Her body shook violently, her stomach churning.

There had been nothing but a blackened spot on the ground where the guard had been.

"Shh, little one," Zedong said, loosening his painful grip on her arms so he could hold her close. "I have no appetite for bloodshed, either."

Her head whipped up, tear-streaked and flushed. Her lips parted in horror, her brow furrowing. "You ordered his death!" Fighting his arms around her, she tried to pull away from him. "You did this!"

He didn't let her go, his grip and gaze hardening on her face. "Those who are strong do what needs to be done, despite their own qualms. You are quick to pity, little girl. Be careful; it will be your downfall."

He released her, and she fell hard against the wall.

Zedong growled something in Butagin and then two guards were at her sides, pulling her to her wobbly feet and guiding her back to her room.

Behind her, Zedong's heavy footsteps stormed in the other direction.

Tears streamed in furious, heartbroken rivulets down her cheeks. The sun had barely risen, and she had just watched a man be murdered before her eyes. A man who only wanted to be free of this horrible place.

Something compelled her to lift her eyes.

Standing on the shadowy edge of the courtyard, a tall figure's eyes burned into hers.

Shuren stared at her. His frame emanated power, but it was an utterly helpless power. Hopelessness flashed across his sorry face. He seemed to say, *"You see why I can't flee this place? Why I can't help Feiyan?"*

They were both trapped. Neither of them could be free of Fang Zedong. Every which way she turned, he seemed to anticipate. He blocked even her most basic attempts at escape. He manipulated her mind, ensorcelled her soul, bound her to himself so he could wield her as his weapon like Shang wielded his ice.

Meiling tore her attention from Shuren, shifting it instead to the guards escorting her, the brigands training in the courtyard, the people from Butagin running his fortress. Her thoughts returned to the sweet girl who'd brushed Meiling's hair. All of them were Zedong's weapons. They were not people—not to him. Nothing mattered except him having power.

She was afraid of that power.

Why couldn't Feiyan be here with her? Why must she face this demon alone?

The guards deposited Meiling in her room in a flurry of crumpling robes. The door shut behind her as she burst into fresh sobs, burying her face in her hands.

Would she ever be free? Would she live out all her days locked here? Even if she *could* get out, what then? She couldn't survive on her own in the wilderness. She'd die one way or another.

Was this . . . was this what the rest of her life would look like? Her and Shuren trapped beyond rescue, and Feiyan eventually being beaten to death for her stubbornness? Would she be a slave to the man trying to conquer her beloved people? Would she be the very tool that would guarantee their downfall?

If only sleep held respite . . .

CHAPTER 9

SHANG GRITTED HIS teeth, bracing his core, and slowly lowered himself out of the tree's branches. It seemed word of Meiling's capture had traveled swiftly to Suguan, and the emperor wasn't about to play nice when his daughter was on the line. Either that, or the Secret Service's spies had tracked down this fortress as the one holding the missing magic-wielders captive.

He wasn't the first one here, despite the swift pace he'd maintained since he'd escaped Liafugen a week ago.

A small army was just setting up an encampment on the Zheninghai side of the border, not far from Fang's fortress. This would make some things way simpler—breaking into a fortress solo was a bold and risky move—but it would also make other things far more complicated.

Silently, he dropped to the ground and pulled off his mask.

The scouts were close. They'd find him any moment now.

He didn't touch his weapons, instead leaning against the trunk of the tree and lifting his hands in the air. Making himself vulnerable and unthreatening.

Hardly two minutes later, a human shadow fell between two trees ahead. It stopped abruptly, then dodged behind shelter. The familiar click of a *jiaun* hit Shang's ears. He lowered his brows but didn't move.

"Who are you?" demanded a roughened male voice. "What are you doing so close to the Butagin border, alone?"

"Tan Shangdi," Shang replied cooly. "Bodyguard of Princess Meiling."

"Some bodyguard," came the icy retort. "Convince me you're not a brigand spy or I'll shoot."

"Who is your lieutenant?"

"Answer my question."

"It's Lieutenant Jadaala, isn't it?" Shang replied, lifting his chin. "Tell him the son of former General Tan Cheung is here and wishes to speak to him."

The scout kept his face and body hidden, but after running his eyes over the area, Shang finally found the double pointed tip of *jiaun* arrows in the foliage. Pointed right at his heart.

"You didn't answer—"

"Ask Lieutenant Jadaala if I'm a brigand," Shang challenged, his chest rising and falling with his slow, measured breaths. "He knows my name. Ask him."

"And I'm supposed to believe you haven't given me a false name?"

Shang didn't allow his irritation to penetrate his mask. Meiling was in real danger, and this idiot was wasting time. It almost made him want to take the man in combat, knock him out, and go find Lieutenant Jadaala himself. But if he didn't play this carefully, he'd lose his chance to save Meiling. "He also knows my *face*. Hold me at *jiaun* point and escort me through the encampment if it'll make you feel better. I will show you that I do not lie."

At last, the *jiaun* lowered. A man not much older than Shang, with a rather pitiful excuse of a beard and wormlike eyebrows, stepped out from behind the tree. "Very well. I will take you there, but the moment you do anything funny, I'm shooting. Now walk that way."

Shang lowered his arms. "Let me get my horse."

The young man waited impatiently as Shang retrieved his horse from where it was tied up.

It was strange walking into the encampment, the scout keeping his *jiaun* loaded as Shang led his horse through the throng of wielders. There were a few familiar faces, but not many who would recognize Shang in return. He'd made it his business to know who many, many people were. Especially those in the military.

After all, he'd been destined for the position of military strategist.

Until Meiling had tip-toed into his life with her sweet goodness, oblivious to the havoc she wreaked on his life. A few short weeks, and everything had gone from perfect to disaster.

It was strange, but Shang wasn't most anxious about his appointment back in Suguan, or going on trial for failing his duty to the crown. Those weren't the things that had driven him like a madman half across the empire, despite his partially healed injuries.

He'd been driven by the image in his mind of Meiling, shoved to her knees, her hair whipping around her grimacing face as her wrists were bound behind her. And him—unable to stop it.

Controlling himself hadn't been a struggle most of his life. He'd always kept his emotions and impulses under tight rein. But it took every ounce of control he had to keep walking through that encampment like nothing was wrong, like he wasn't burning up with anxiety on the inside, like he didn't spend every moment of every day fighting to *not* imagine what Fang could be doing to her right now.

I'm going to get you back, he swore in his mind to her. *I will get you out of there. Just be brave a little longer.*

"Lieutenant Jadaala!" called the scout.

Shang had already recognized the sharp lines of those shoulders even before the lieutenant turned, revealing a frowning face and a long, pointy nose.

"What is it?" As he said the words, the lieutenant's gaze swept over Shang. His black clothes couldn't hide the last week of grime and dust, but Shang didn't care. The lieutenant's frown deepened. "Tan Shangdi. What in the seven valleys are you doing here?"

The scout glanced between them, then made himself scarce.

Shang met Lieutenant Jadaala's stare evenly. "I was one of Princess Meiling's bodyguards. I came to aid in her rescue."

His eyes narrowed. He flicked his fingers in a quick gesture to follow him, then made his way to a private tent, away from the prying eyes and ears of the wielders setting up camp around them.

Shang ducked beneath the tent flap after the lieutenant into the sparse interior. The low table, mats, and the partitioned sleeping quarter was illuminated only by the dim light of two red papered lanterns. He sat on a mat when beckoned, but didn't touch the proffered tea. He had no intention of engaging in pleasantries.

Lieutenant Jadaala sat cross-legged across from him, folding his arms over his chest. He seemed equally disinclined toward pleasantries, despite being an old friend of Shang's father. "Well," he said in those growling timbres of his, "tell me. Everything."

Without hesitating, Shang launched into his tale from when the emperor's summons had come early the morning after Graduation, keeping his voice low. He told . . . *almost* everything. When the lieutenant pressed about why Meiling was being pursued, Shang lied straight to his face that he suspected Fang wanted her as hostage to force Emperor Nianzu's hand. He didn't regret it one instant.

He would guard Meiling's secret to the grave.

Everything else, however, he told the ugly, raw truth of his and Fen's failure. Meiling's capture. The lieutenant listened silently, his face dark and serious. Until—

"You snuck out of *Liafugen* undetected?"

"I did."

"Stars above, boy! You cannot be serious. That fortress is armed to the gills."

Shang said nothing.

"And you managed the journey from Liafugen to here—in a week. One week."

"I did."

The lieutenant shook his head. He unfolded his arms, planting his palms flat on the table between them. "I must give your father his due credit. I always said he was too hard on you, but he said all you needed was motivation—and when you had it, nothing could stand in your way." He gave a short chuckle, oblivious to how his words struck Shang like a blow to the face. "Seems the old man was right."

Shang clenched his jaw, fighting the sudden rattling of his composure and the stupid way his heart lurched at this unexpected praise. Father had said that . . . about *him*?

If Father knew where he was now and what he'd done, he'd disown him in a heartbeat. Just before he likely suffered a stroke from shock. He'd scream at him for days, telling him he wasn't worthy of the Tan name, that he'd made a mockery of the line of ice-wielders he'd come from.

It was only a matter of time before Father found out what happened.

Up until now, Shang had shoved those thoughts out of his mind. Even now, beneath the table, he clenched one hand in a fist. Getting Meiling out of that fathers-forsaken fortress before it was too late was his priority. He wouldn't think about anything else.

"I understand your plan," said Lieutenant Jadaala. "If you'd waited much longer at Liafugen, you would have been escorted back to Suguan for trial. This way, you have a chance to prove your worth and competence before the trial. I'm not sure it'll work, considering the protocols you broke getting here, but it cannot put you in a *worse* position."

Shang remained silent.

"So. You're here to fight."

Shang inclined his head, once.

"Very well. I will put you with the special forces. It'll be higher risk for you, but also a higher potential to prove yourself a worthy warrior before your trial. And should the risk be too much . . ." The lieutenant's eyes met Shang's, a grim severity limning his face.

He didn't have to finish.

Dying here would be far more honorable than facing trial.

Shang ignored the unsettling of his gut and spoke. "Thank you, lieutenant."

"Very well. Go find some place to settle yourself for now. It won't be much longer until we attack."

Shang inclined his head in a respectful bow, then drew himself to his feet and marched out of the tent. It was an effort to bring his breathing back under control and calm his racing heart. At least that conversation had gone better than expected. He'd been prepared to strongarm the lieutenant with his father's name and some carefully timed challenges if he'd refused Shang's request.

He'd have stooped to blackmail if it was the only way. Which could always end with Shang finding an *accidental* knife in his back on the battlefield if he wasn't careful.

But at this point, he'd break any rule if it meant getting Meiling back.

Meiling was strong—stronger than she or anyone else knew. Fen was too blind to see it, but Shang had, especially during those last few days of their journey. She'd pushed herself to her very limits, and she'd stayed strong.

Until the cave. She'd broken then. Not completely, but *enough.* Enough for Shang to know she buckled under pressure just like everyone else, despite how serene she might appear on the outside.

Don't break, Meiling. Don't break. Stay strong a little longer.

"Shang?"

That familiar voice fried Shang's thoughts in an instant. He whipped his head to the side, trying to squash the sudden hope filling his soul at that sound.

But no. He wasn't wrong.

Hardly five paces from him, wearing an expression of mingled shock and concern across his honest face, was Cao Renshu. He had his hair tied up in a knot on top of his head, a dark line of scruff on his jaw, and he wore light armor over his dark red robes and tall, bulky frame.

"Renshu?" The word came out like a croak.

A wide grin burst across his face. "Shang, my friend! What in the seven valleys are *you* doing here?"

Before Shang could respond, Renshu pulled him into a bear hug and nearly squeezed the air out of his lungs. If it had been anyone else—or, well, *almost* anyone else—he would have shoved away and scowled. But with Renshu, Shang returned the embrace, a tight coil in his chest relaxing just slightly. It had been too long.

If Renshu had come from the beginning instead of Fen, we wouldn't be in this mess at all.

Shang shoved away the bitter thought, though another realization quickly followed it. The entire dynamic of their journey would have been so very different. If Renshu had gone, he would have been far kinder to Meiling than Shang had been, and vastly kinder than Fen. He would have had the princess laughing the entire way, and there was no one else Shang would have trusted with his life like he trusted Renshu.

Though if Renshu had come, they would *still* have that stupid panda with them.

"I could ask you the same question," Shang replied, pulling away. "You were appointed to Emperor's Guard. Why are you *here*?"

"The emperor nearly lost his mind when he heard of the princess's capture. There was a whole scene. His council barely kept him from jumping onto a horse and riding straight here himself. The compromise was that he sent his entire guard here—along with everyone else—to fight. But what of you? I haven't seen you since Graduation."

Shang glanced around at the wielders setting up camp. He nodded toward the forest, silently suggesting they talk elsewhere. Renshu's face hardened. Together, they slipped away, and when they were a safe distance, Shang told him everything.

Except, of course, the truth about Meiling's magic.

CHAPTER 10

"WE WILL TRY this again." Zedong's voice boomed in the bare chamber.

Meiling kept her head down, her hands folded deceptively demurely in front of her. She refused to meet his eyes when he tried to catch her gaze. He seemed to sense that after this morning's incident, she was even less inclined to be cordial than before.

"I want this guardian's knowledge about what the empire has done to prepare its military for attack," Zedong said briskly, indicating Wan slumped on his knees in the middle of the room. "You will want to comply, little one."

Meiling bit her lip. The choice presented itself before her yet again. Let Wan die and try to protect her empire for another day or two, or save Wan in exchange for her empire? She had seen what

Zedong was capable of. As much as she did not want harm to befall Wan, would it not be more noble to try to save her people from this monster?

Someone had to stand up to him. *Someone* had to try to stop him.

Zedong sighed. "Ah, my pretty one. I did not want to do this, but you continue to force my hand." He snapped his fingers, and the door opened behind her.

She should not look. It was probably Feiyan and she would not be able to let Feiyan die. They would bring her in bloody and bruised, unable to heal herself, and Meiling would break.

She turned.

Nothing could have prepared her for the horror before her.

Meiling screamed, her eyes going wide as panic gripped her throat, her chest, her entire body. "What have you done to them?" she screamed, whirling on Zedong. "I will kill you!"

Before her, beaten and wounded, bound and gagged, forced to kneel on the ground—

—were Hou and Yun, her brother and sister.

Hou's little body quivered with fear and the fire was gone from Yun's once brilliant gaze. Neither of them met Meiling's gaze.

How in this dragon-blasted world had he gotten them? *How?*

He's taken so many.

"Now, now, my princess, there is no need for bloodshed if you will only behave."

Hou—fierce, tough, little Hou—wept, tears dripping off her nose.

Blood boiled in Meiling's veins. She leapt for her siblings, prepared to wildly tear apart their captors with her bare hands. She wasn't thinking—couldn't think. All she could do was act.

And then a knife glimmered under little Hou's chin.

"Don't make another move," Zedong threatened darkly, pulling back Hou's head with a fistful of her hair to expose her neck more. Hou's eyes squeezed shut, and she rapidly gasped over and over, tears coursing down her cheeks.

Meiling froze.

It dawned on her then.

Zedong had full power over her. If he had Hou and Yun . . . She could not fight. She could not resist. He held her in the palm of his hands. He was the puppeteer and she was the mindless, stringed puppet.

Zedong smiled a mirthless, tight-lipped smile. He removed the knife from Hou's neck, letting her head fall forward. "I want your cooperation, not their blood." He strode to Meiling, crossing the distance between them with one long-legged step. Gripping her arm tightly, he forced her to look up at him and touched the point of the knife in the hollow of her neck, lightly, but enough to sting. Enough for it to freeze her chest. "Unlike you, I have no use of these two." His breath was hot, and he snarled each word between clenched teeth. "I *will* kill them unless you give me your complete obedience. No tricks, no stubbornness."

Meiling stared up at him, meeting his gaze despite how she trembled in his grasp. She was afraid of that knife tip, even though her mind tried to reason with her that he would not kill her.

Her helplessness flooded her bones, washing away the last of her strength and resolve. Her eyes traveled to her two siblings, bound and beaten and ragged. Then to the defeated Wan.

So she would become Wan. Broken, miserable, despairing.

She would be the knife in an assassin's hand; the poison in the emperor's goblet. Lu Meiling, Princess of Zheninghai, would singlehandedly orchestrate the downfall of all she knew, loved, and hated.

And there was nothing she could do to stop it.

"One hour," Zedong said. "If you do not find the information I seek, Princess Hou and Prince Yun will be slow-sliced to death in front of you." His eyes met hers, blue and mad and completely serious. "One hour."

Before he could grab her and drag her to the bed in the corner, Meiling stepped around Wan's form and laid down on the bed. She cast one last glance at her siblings, gritting her teeth, trying not to allow her heart to break inside her chest.

Zedong was at her side in a swoosh of black cape. With one swift motion, he snatched her wrist and plunged the tip of his knife into her finger. Blood welled. He pressed something into that wound.

She was too angry to feel pain.

Blackness wrapped around her vision, and she fell into the dream.

Meiling did not stand on the wharf this time. Violent ocean waves had swept away it. She stood on the sand, overlooking the deceptively still depths. The storm had come closer. Now that this was her second time in this mind, she recognized the storm for what it was.

It was Wan's death.

Imminent. Swiftly approaching.

Spirit shuddering, she turned on the beach and found the streets that threaded into a sea of rooftops. The once-colorful city was bland, gray, dull. She glanced to the side, to her favorite overlook, desperately wishing she could go sit and think.

That did not matter anymore. Freedom did not matter.

Only surviving. Only saving her siblings from Zedong's clutches.

At least now she was familiar with Wan's mind. She was learning, too, and Meiling now knew to find the spider silk threads connecting everything in this mind. She closed her eyes, felt along with her hands. As soon as she caught hold of one, she concentrated on it.

It was easier having done this in her own mind. The memories flowed much faster and easier into her fingertips, into her conscience. This thread connected Wan's memories of him and his father. They apparently had come to the beach often—sat on that outcropping over there—when he was a young boy.

This was not the thread she needed.

She broke into a run, away from the shoreline, into the ghost-like streets of Suguan. There was no need to open her eyes to watch where she was going; she penetrated barriers with ease. So, she kept her eyes closed and hands out, searching for more threads.

There were many of them, but when she touched them, she only caught glimpses of his childhood.

Wan, clinging to his mother's skirts in the marketplace. He loved the towering bowls of colorful spices. Could he take the bowl home? One time he had poked his finger into the bowls, managing two eyes of a smiley face before his mother yanked him back and scolded him.

Wan, discovering his magic by accidentally sending a mass of vines tangling into a wagon's wheels. He was so young; he didn't want to leave his family to go to the Academy! Could he stay at home a little longer?

Wan, sitting on his threshold with his Pa, being told that he had to go to the Academy because it would bring their family honor. Wan, deciding he *really* wanted to bring honor to his family. His mother, packing up the few things that the Academy would let him bring. He needed no clothes; those were provided.

This was not what she needed. She needed to go to the palace.

Meiling rushed ahead, becoming no more than a streaking blur heading for that grand, towering building. Her home. The closer she got, the more her heart raced. How long had it been? She redoubled her pace.

Finally, she stood above the thousand-step ascension to the palace. Finally, she stood at the threshold. She caught fistfuls of strands, touching each to get a glimpse at their memories.

That strand led to his appointment to the role of guardian. Those to his yearly inspections. Another few for festivals—

Aha. A meeting with the general. Meiling grasped that thread and followed it down into the bowels of the palace. Past the corridor that lead to the wing where her chambers were, past the corridor that led to the throne room, outside to the next complex, and the next. The Academy was lodged adjacent to the palace and when she finally reached the meeting room in one of the far buildings, its window overlooked more Academy training grounds. These were eerily vacant.

The room was dim, the trim made of dark wood. Fine woven tapestries of battles in centuries long ago, the battles they were all taught as children, lined the walls. Each one hung in the middle of the wall panels. A low table made of a light-colored wood rested in the center of the room, surrounded by red-dyed cushions. Maps were laid out on the table, along with ink wells, stamps, and long, gold finger-pointers.

Meiling kept her hand tightly gripping the threads. They split into many and converged again at one spot at the table. Had he always sat there? Some of the threads seemed to twine together, as if the memories were hard to distinguish from each other.

She gave the room another glance and spotted, in the corner, a large wooden cabinet. That wasn't part of his memories. The shadows were off, as if it had never belonged here.

His knowledge. So organized.

She flitted to the far side of the room, to the cabinet. It was etched with qilins, spearing each other with their horns. She grasped the golden handles and pulled the doors open. Inside were drawers with round, polished knobs. A pang hit Meiling's heart, a wracking of guilt. She quickly suppressed it. There was no other choice.

She wrenched open the first drawer to find documents arranged under the topic of *General's Orders.* The next was labeled *Ganhai Improvements.* The third drawer had *Suo Guanting's Jokes During Meetings.*

Then she pulled open another. Her eyes fell on the characters.

War.

Meiling shoved the others closed. No doubt, information was filed under multiple headings, but this seemed like the most efficient option. With a grunt, she heaved the contents out of the drawer and dumped it all on the table.

The papers sprawled out, their black-ink characters drawn with the precision of a scribe. For a long moment, she stared blankly at the immense amount of parchment. She was *not* going to read everything. It would take far too long.

This was a mind, after all. A mind did not read its own knowledge off a sheet of paper.

Meiling planted her hand on one sheet of parchment. She closed her eyes. Winced. She had no practice with this, and her siblings' lives depended on her proficiency? Her heart throbbed in her throat. She shoved down the panic and pushed her weight onto her hand, onto the page. Perhaps this wouldn't work, or perhaps it was a horrid, lazy shortcut her masters would have balked at if she'd been trained at the Academy.

Yet, beneath her hand, the characters seemed to twist, dissolve, and float around her own mind. *Solid!* she thought frantically. *None of this fuzziness!*

Slowly, the information coalesced into something that made sense to her.

This was a catalog of the wielders who had gone missing. Zedong probably had the same catalog in his own mind. With a growl, she moved to the next page. The information still resisted, but it came easier this time. This was—*oh*. More missing wielders.

Next.

The next page contained information about Butagin military strategies. What they had done in the past, how the empire had fought them back, what their weaknesses were. It was so technical that she struggled to grasp enough of it in her mind that she could transfer it.

But Zedong probably did not care about this.

Following that, she found a document detailing how the information they were receiving about the barbarians amassing in the north were not following their typical behavior. The page contained traces of emotion. Concern, an attempt to reason away why things might be different this time. An attempt to hide that concern.

Then, she found Fang Zedong's profile and information from when he had been a student at the Academy. Her curiosity piqued, and she drank in the information.

He had been a late bloomer with his magic, so he had come when he was ten years old. Already behind and lacking battle magic, he struggled. His magic was of a rather unique type; he possessed a variation of mind reading, but it was so strange it was nearly useless, and he could gain no control over it to wield it properly. He could hear the non-articulated transfer of information between people.

Sometimes.

The problem was that magic was not needed to understand most nonverbal communication. His report cards showed failing grades in all his subjects. Except his report cards started improving after . . . after he became friends with one of his classmates. One Song Liena, from the north, with barbarian blood. The current queen of the empire. Her magic had bloomed even later than his, revealing her to be a seer with no control over her magic. She struggled to catch up. They were both taunted, teased, frowned upon by the other students. And they bonded.

The nature of their relationship was uncertain. As Meiling moved her hand from one paper to the next, more information became clear. Queen Liena herself had a vision about Fang Zedong and warned the general. She confessed to them that while she had been forming a growing attachment to the then prince of the empire, now her husband, Zedong had formed a similar attachment to her.

Meiling paused only briefly. This made so much sense. And . . . and . . . it meant Ma had never been in love with Fang Zedong like Meiling had feared.

He had run away from the Academy and had never been seen again.

Until he showed up as the leader of the barbarians.

The next document was exactly what she was hunting for. It held information about the measures the empire was taking to prepare for war against Zedong and his barbarian forces. Again, it was so technical that she had to absorb the information a few times before she was sure she could remember it and explain it.

Finally, she finished going through the stack of papers. Apparently not a moment too soon. She stood, planning to pick up the pile and return it to the drawer, but a sharp jolt pulled along her soul tether.

She couldn't even brace herself for the violent waking. One moment, she was in the room with the dark wood trim and a low table with maps. The next, she was vomiting on the floor of Zedong's fortress. She wasn't supposed to move this quickly! It was almost like there was no travel.

She was simply in a different place. Her body could not handle this brutal awakening.

Over and over, she retched until her stomach heaved with emptiness.

"What did you find?" Zedong asked.

She hardly had the strength to raise her head, but when she managed it, he was holding his knife to Hou's throat again.

Meiling spewed every single thing that she found. Even about his own time at the Academy, his own relationship with her mother. She could do nothing except tell everything. When she was done, she leaned against the stiff wood of the bed's edge, trembling and breathing hard.

"My, that was fast," Zedong said, chuckling and releasing his grip on Hou. "I'm glad we've reached an agreement."

Meiling's eyes shifted from his triumphant face to her bound and bleeding siblings. "Now that I've given you what you want," she growled, the words coming out jumbled. "Don't hurt them. Please don't hurt them!"

She was groveling, and she didn't care. She'd grovel until he ended her sorry life.

He smiled a soft, understanding sort of smile that only served to terrify her even more. "I know, I know you love them."

A shiver raced down her spine. A dark thought seeped like poison into the farthest, deepest recesses of her mind.

If I didn't love anyone or anything, he'd have no control over me.

She dropped her head to dangle between her bracing arms. Zedong turned and strode out of the room.

What would they do with Hou and Yun?

Meiling glanced up, wishing she could encourage them somehow. Tell them it would be all right. The guards pulled them to their feet, and she desperately tried to catch Yun's eye.

They were gone, pulled out into the hallway, before either looked up. The door remained open like a wound behind them, beckoning Meiling to shove to her wobbly knees and race after them.

She would hurt anyone who hurt Hou and Yun.

She'd . . . she'd . . .

A form shifted in the shadows, and she barely noticed it through her spinning vision. But no, she wasn't alone in this room—there was someone else. Someone whose silent gaze locked on hers.

The illusionist.

The . . . *illusionist.*

Profound relief flooded Meiling, making her whole body turn to water. She collapsed to the ground, weeping. Shuren strode across the room, bending down and lifting her up into his arms. Wordlessly, he carried her out of the room, down the hallway, and toward her own room.

The tears kept flowing, but no longer from terror. She was almost mad with joy; her tears were almost laughter. She buried her head in Shuren's chest, delirious but for one conscious thought.

He doesn't have them. He doesn't have them. He doesn't have them.

Shuren shifted her in his arms so he could open her door, and with a few more steps, placed her gently in her own bed. He didn't even look at her before he turned on his heel and fled.

CHAPTER 11

AFTER MEILING HAD composed herself and cleaned up, she knelt to peer under her door for guards.

No booted feet.

Perhaps Zedong thought she would be too emotionally exhausted to try anything. But he didn't know that she knew her siblings were still safe at home. He thought he knew her because he had known Ma.

He had said himself that she was more afraid.

Meiling might be frightened out of her wits, but she was not stupid, and she was not going to sit around waiting for someone to come save her. Whatever sort of rescue was being attempted was taking too long, and she simply did not have the time. Not if she wanted to keep from going insane and committing countless treasonous acts against her empire.

Zedong underestimated Meiling. He overestimated his influence on her.

He could bribe her with fancy meals and clothes and a comfortable bed, and he could threaten her with the blood and tears of her siblings. But she wouldn't stop fighting.

She would *never* stop fighting.

Twisting the knob carefully to avoid making a single sound, she drew open the door and glanced down the end of the hallway. Afternoon light gleamed brightly through the window to her right, making the rest of the hallway seem so much dimmer.

No guards. No maids. No one.

She slipped out, reaching down to remove her shoes and carry them as she crept down through the darkness to the stairwell opposite the big window. She peeked out the smaller windows lining the wall of the hallway, down into the courtyard. Most of the training had ceased, but brigands, guards, and servants milled about. Search as she might, she could not glimpse that tall, black-clad figure anywhere.

A small, but monumental blessing.

She reached the stairs and quickly descended them, glancing over her shoulder repeatedly to ensure she was not being followed. At the bottom floor, she hesitated before the door. Was sneaking really the best approach here? Or should she throw her shoulders back, jut out her chin, and stride through this fortress like the princess she was?

If she were caught sneaking, it would look worse.

Especially if she was barefoot.

Meiling leaned her elbow against the wall for balance as she reshod each foot. She straightened her robes, narrowed her brow, and pushed open the large door.

She immediately felt the burning gaze of busy wielders and stone-stiff guards. At least the servants seemed to ignore her. She briefly wondered about the little maid who had helped her bathe. Then she was striding down the flagstone, avoiding the central courtyard and trying not to be self-conscious about all the eyes following her. Did she look as terrified and uncertain as she felt?

No one stopped her.

There was no point in clinging to shadows, despite how much she longed to do just that. She paused, suddenly unsure if she should open the door in front of her or turn to the left, following down another covered corridor to the doors there. Why could she not remember where the dungeon was?

Taking a deep breath and squaring her shoulders, she moved by instinct to the door she faced. If she were wrong and walked straight into Fang Zedong's arms, the worst thing that could happen was . . . She shook her head, gritted her teeth. With a tiny, low-pitched growl, she pushed open the door.

Darkness fell like a shrouding cloth.

This must be the right way.

She stood still, silent, for a long moment. Her eyes took painfully long to adjust to the dimness. She was glad she waited, however, for she soon could make out steps before her. A chilling image of plunging down those dark stairs into the blackness below made her shiver. Moving tentatively, she placed her hand along the wall. Dust fell onto the stone stairs, making quiet pattering noises.

Each step was agonizingly slow. Though her nerves jumped like the children in the streets of Suguan during a festival, Meiling forced herself to be patient. She sucked in damp air through her teeth, tasting the growing foulness.

At the bottom of the staircase, she snuck down a dark corridor and spied first a single lantern hanging from a hook on the wall.

Then the jailer.

He was a potbellied man with a long, scraggly beard, sitting on one of those thro—*chairs*. A second lantern hung over his head, illuminating the furs lining his shoulders and belt. No sign of keys on his belt.

He was asleep.

Or he *seemed* to be asleep. He didn't stir a muscle, didn't give any indication he'd heard Meiling come down the stairs.

Doors lined the corridor on either side, set into the forbidding stone. Somehow, she had expected the dungeon to be one open room, with cells everywhere, but from her vague memories of being dragged out of her cell, she knew if she opened one door, she would find more doors. And more, the further she went.

Was it a labyrinth?

It was probably as good as one.

If she stepped around the corner, she'd be in plain sight of the jailer. Would he hurt her if he caught her? Drag her back to Zedong and dump her unceremoniously at his feet? Or would he take advantage of the fact that she was alone and vulnerable, and that no one knew where she was?

Meiling swallowed hard.

Then she gritted her teeth, and as quietly as she could, she slipped out of her hiding place and tiptoed to the nearest door.

The jailer didn't stir.

She pushed open the first door. To her shock, it didn't make a sound. But a draft of cold air blasted her in the face, sweeping into the confined space. Deeper darkness met her. Hurriedly, she slipped back out, reaching up with hesitant fingers and snatching the lantern down from its hook. She slid through the open door with a last look over her shoulder.

Still, the jailer slept on.

The door closed behind her with a thud.

The putrid stench of despair coiled insistently around her nostrils. She covered her nose with the edge of her fine, embroidered sleeve. It was strange to be in such a terrible place in such expensive robes. She held the lantern up high, trying to peer into the gloom while her heart hammered in her chest.

Candlelight flickered, danced on iron bars. Tremulous. The light seemed so small, so insignificant against that devouring darkness.

She stepped forward, holding the lantern closer to those iron cells.

They were empty.

She gagged at the sight and smell of the previous occupation. She quickly retreated and briefly moved her hand from covering her nose to press against her stomach. When the stench was almost unbearable, she covered her nose again. Clean linen was hardly a barrier against the moist, penetrating odor of excrement.

There was another staircase. With each descending step, the sputtering candle jumped erratically on the walls and low ceiling. She hunched instinctively, though she was nowhere near being too tall for the space. She huffed in frustration when she reached the bottom, finding herself presented with three doors.

What was the point in picking a random door each time? She took the first. She might have a hope of finding her way out of here if she kept her choices consistent. How in all the seven valleys was she supposed to find Feiyan in here?

The floor grew wetter and slicker the further she went.

She walked through several more doors, finding more empty cells, before she began despairing. “Feiyan?” Her voice teetered like a thin memory-thread, threatening to break at the slightest provocation. “Feiyan?” she called, louder, firmer.

Was that a groan she heard?

On the other side of that door?

She hurried forward, almost slipping in her haste. She shoved her shoulder into the door, grimacing when it seemed to stick. Huffing, she set down the lantern and threw all her weight at the door. It creaked loudly, but it finally gave.

When she lifted the light to peer into the darkness—was it thicker, heavier here?—there were two eyes gleaming, reflecting the light of the fire. “Feiyan?” she asked, hopeful, despite knowing those eyes weren’t Feiyan’s.

“Who are you?” a masculine voice rasped.

She hesitated, but then whispered, "I'm Princess Meiling. Who are you?"

"Does it matter?" the voice croaked, and the form seemed to sit back on his haunches.

"Yes, it does matter," she said, bending and shining the light closer to that face.

The man cried out and shielded his face. His body was thin, boney, and clad in rags. His hair was matted and long, his beard tinged with gray. Beyond him, another form huddled in the adjacent cell. Another man, she guessed.

"Who are you?" Meiling asked gently. "Why are you here? Are you a wielder?"

The first man grimaced and still covered his eyes, but he answered in that grating voice of his. "I am Du Liuxian, and yes, I am a wielder."

"Kidnapped? By Fang Zedong for use?"

He only nodded. He parted his knobby fingers, trying to let his eyes adjust to the brightness. Meiling, after pausing, stepped back a few paces and set the lantern on the ground. She returned to the first cell, hoping it helped to lessen the strain of the light in his eyes.

"What powers do you wield?" she asked. She wanted to reach out and take the cold iron bars in her hands, but she could not bring herself to. She never wanted to feel the sting of freezing iron in her grip ever again.

"Is this how you always start conversations?" Liuxian muttered.

She flushed.

"What are you doing?" he continued, gesturing to the darkness of the world surrounding them both. "Why are you here? Did Fang send you here to manipulate me?"

She shook her head vigorously. "No! I am trying to find my friend."

"Friend? What, are you the rescue party from Zheninghai?"

"I'm kidnapped too," Meiling said.

Liuxian raised one pale eyebrow, the hard line of his lowered brow relaxing enough that two dark eyes gleamed in the shadows of his face. "Convincing."

Something about him was vaguely familiar . . . She was almost certain she had glimpsed his soul before. A glowing, violet soul.

Meiling cocked her head. "You're an evanescer, aren't you? You were the one in my room."

He shrugged.

"How long have you been here? A prisoner?" The cold of the floor seeped into her knees, but she ignored it.

"A long time," he mumbled, lowering his head. Just as quickly, his head snapped up. "How old is the prince?"

Meiling blinked, then understanding dawned. "He is not yet twenty."

Liuxian nodded slowly, closing his eyes. "Then I have been here nine years."

Her eyes widened and horror dropped like lead into her stomach. "Nine years?" Her gaze flicked from Liuxian to the second huddled form. "And you?"

"Twelve years," a deep voice returned. That voice was too deep for the smallness of that body. "I am Pen Tao, high seer."

She pursed her lips, tugging her heavy robes around her to ward off the impending chill that threatened to percolate into her bones. "Were you the one with the vision of me?"

"I was."

"Why are you here?" Liuxian demanded, letting his arms dangle off his knees. "Trying to rub your special treatment in our faces?"

Meiling jerked backward, biting her lip hard and tasting blood. She controlled her voice and pushed away her own hurt. It didn't matter. "I'm trying to find Feiyan, the healer."

"Fathers above be with you," he snorted. "You'll find no one in this prison."

She refused to let her spirit drop, refused to be discouraged. She stood. "I can still try. How many wielders are held captive here?"

Liuxian barked a laugh. "There's no knowing that."

"Twelve," Tao muttered.

Meiling and Liuxian both turned to Tao. He did not even twitch, so still he sat.

"There are twelve wielders," he repeated. "Me, Liuxian, you, the healer, Zuan Wan, Ye Min, Cai Fu, Kang Lei, and four others. I do not know their names or their abilities."

"The last three you spoke," Meiling said, standing and turning to retrieve the lantern. "What are their abilities?"

Silence hung for a long minute.

"Cai Fu is another high seer. Kang Lei . . . she is a siren. Ye Min is dead."

"Dead?" she gasped. "But—but Fang Zedong kidnapped us to use our magic, not to kill us! How . . .?"

"Death isn't always intentional," came Liuxian's bitter growl. "And Fang can be very . . . *unhappy* when someone tries to thwart his plans."

She retreated a step without realizing it. Liuxian's hands turned up in a sort of shrug.

"Don't mean to scare you," he muttered, strangely penitent. "But it's the truth. Whatever fancy he's set on you, letting you roam about like *that* . . ." He gestured at her soft, well-spun robes. "Don't fight him. He'll break you harder and then he'll kill you. It may be accidental, but it'll happen."

Meiling stared at Liuxian until he lowered his head. For a long moment, the only sound in her ears was the soft puffs of her breathing.

Resolve gripped her heart. "I'll bring you food," she whispered. "Later. As soon as I can."

"Don't bother," Liuxian snorted.

Tao said nothing.

She gripped the warm handle of the lantern as guilt stabbed her chest and retreated out the door she had come. There were, thankfully, no further doors after Tao and Liuxian's cells.

Did they fill the deepest, darkest cells first? Would she have to follow every last trail down to its bitter dregs before she found Feiyan? She remembered how long it had taken her to be dragged to the bright, shining world above this dungeon. So many doors had slammed before the door to their cell finally opened.

She wished she could leave the lantern with Liuxian and Tao. They could use a small glimmer of hope. But then she would never find Feiyan. If she never found Feiyan, they could never escape.

Meiling wanted to shield her face from the repugnant odor as she pushed open the next door. She forced herself to resist the urge. If they had to live in it, she could endure it.

Another guilty pang rammed through her heart.

Here she was, dressed in robes embroidered with gold thread, eating her fill of satisfying foods—food like she'd loved at the palace—sleeping in a comfortable bed, with the freedom to go as she pleased. Mostly.

Being favored, if that was what she was, tasted sour in her mouth.

Liuxian's words hummed ceaselessly in her ears, tormenting her. *Don't fight, don't fight, don't fight.* It would go easier for her. If she complied, she could sleep in her comfortable bed and never go hungry. She could bring about the destruction of her empire while wearing fine linen robes, while picking at gold hemming. She would never have to see the face of another victim kneeling before Fang Zedong's towering form. Never have to hear the screams as they were tortured before her. As their blood flowed red over worn, dirty rags and skin darkened with grime.

She could ignore the tormented eyes of people like Zuan Wan.

She would not be killed. Her days would not be spent growing old and weak in the dungeon like Liuxian and Tao. She would not wilt and wither.

She could surrender, could stop trying to escape. Perhaps after Zedong did his worst and decimated her lands, killed all she loved—for how could he leave a single member of her royal family breathing?—then maybe he would give her the freedom to do what she wanted with her life. Perhaps the *reform* he spoke of for society, perhaps it would be good.

What if she was fighting something that was good?

Don't fight, don't fight, don't fight.

Give up, give in—the tantalizing temptation whispered in her ear. If two powerful wielders such as Tao and Liuxian could not free themselves in the many years they had been held prisoner, then how could Meiling be so bold as to presume she could escape?

Perhaps Feiyan was right.

They were all fools.

Door after door, Meiling found not another trace of human life. Only remnants that suggested former occupation. When she opened one door, grunting with the effort, the foul stench of death immediately assaulted her. She coughed and gagged, quickly leaving.

Years passed.

So it felt in this darkness.

Her lantern flickered dangerously low. Would it sputter, die, and leave her abandoned in this labyrinth? She had to move faster.

Suddenly, doors slammed open and shut above and behind her. Footsteps started stomping down a staircase. Her heart shot straight to her throat. She glanced around wildly, holding up the lantern to look for any hiding places.

But she couldn't hide the lantern.

As much as she hated to admit her cowardice, she would rather be caught than snuff out the only light she had. She propelled herself forward, stumbling a little against the door. Surely it was the final door on this long stretch. She pushed it open, accidentally grunting. She froze as the sound echoed in the air, and then she redoubled her efforts, forcing the heavy door open. The following chamber was empty save for two iron cells and no other escape.

They would not come to an empty chamber, surely. Unless Zedong had noticed her absence, or the jailer had noticed the missing lantern. They *could* be coming for her, or . . .

Could they be fetching Feiyan?

The thought made her lungs freeze, halting her intake of chilled, wet air. What if, after all this, Feiyan was dragged out of here and Meiling lost her chance to speak with her?

The heavy footfalls grew louder. They seemed to be on the other side of the wall to her left as she faced the door to this deep chamber. Then, suddenly, the sounds began fading away. Meiling decided it was safe enough for her to leave this innermost room. It sounded like the guard took a further door, one that departed from hers two levels up.

Why did the door have to be so dragon-blasted loud?

And why was Meiling suddenly so used to cursing in her mind? Before she knew it, she would be spewing expletives that would make any member of her family blush with shame.

Not that they would ever hear her speak such ways unless she escaped.

Thumping, clambering sounds resounded dully through the thick walls. Was that a shout? Were those more footsteps running, taking the stairs two steps at a time?

It had to be Feiyan.

She had been so close!

She was certain those heavy boots pounding just outside her chamber belonged to Shuren, taking the middle door and plunging deeper into the labyrinth. He had always hovered nearby when Feiyan was summoned, ready to force her fiery temper into submission. Or rather, compliance.

It had to be Feiyan.

Meiling stuck the lantern in a corner, hoping the slight cracks under the door were not enough to leak the traitorous light. She waited, listening with bated breath.

Sure enough, more diminished shouts seeped through the stone walls. Growing louder. And then, the door next to hers burst open with a bang and she could clearly make out Shuren's grunting and Feiyan's unmistakable yelling.

"Dragon spawn!" she shrieked.

"Stop struggling!" Shuren growled, then said something in another language. A third pair of feet entered the chamber. The guard.

The guard said something that sounded harsh.

"I'm giving you one more chance," Shuren said. "Stop fighting."

"Stop fighting, my elbow!" Feiyan cried. "Let me go, you qilin-stabbed brain!"

There was a strange muffling, and it was far worse than the shouting. Meiling's limbs quivered with the effort to stay and not burst out into the fray. But what could she do against them? What help could she possible offer?

"What?" Feiyan raged. "What are you putting over—" There was a last, protesting grunt, and she fell silent.

Try as she might, Meiling could only discern two pairs of footsteps taking the stairs. She strained and strained, but it did not matter. Only two pairs of muted, thick-soled boots.

Her heart fell straight to her silver-edged slippers.

At least . . .

At least she knew where Feiyan's—and her own—cell was. If she could come back again later, she could find it within minutes now. But what if the jailer was awake next time? What if there was no lantern? Could she stumble her way through the dark?

They were far enough away that Meiling deemed it safe enough to shove open the door and follow after them.

How long had it been? How long had she been down here?

Had Zedong noticed her missing?

It was so unlikely she would be able to come back. Zedong would lock her in her room for her insolence—probably saying something about how she forced his hand or whatnot—or something else would prevent her. Guards, their alert higher now that they had seen her slip in once before, would probably stop her next time.

But Liuxian and Tao . . .

She promised them food. She had to come back.

CHAPTER 12

THE JAILER WASN'T asleep this time. Meiling peered through the slight opening through the door as he quaffed something from a skin and settled back in his chair. Could she sneak past him a second time? She could leave the lantern behind this door, if necessary, but it seemed like risky business.

Then again, what were her options?

Planting the lantern on the floor, she eased the door open, her heart about to fly out of her ribcage. The jailer didn't look up. Refusing to breathe, she slipped out of the door and shut it behind her, willing the shadows to wrap her up in their concealing wings.

The jailer's head shot up. Their eyes met.

Meiling froze.

Not knowing what else to do, she gave a little wave and smile. "Thank you."

Then she burst into a run toward the stairs.

A clatter echoed behind her—like the jailer had just fallen off his chair in his effort to get to his feet quickly. Small and untrained though she was, she pumped her legs hard, racing up the stairs, not wasting any second of advantage.

She threw open the door and burst into the blinding brightness of sunshine.

"Princess Meiling," a familiar voice rang with a curious lilt. "I've been awaiting your return."

She whipped her head upward, around to where that sound had come. A gasp caught in her throat. There was Zedong, only a few feet away, leaning casually on the wall. His blue eyes roved the length of her.

"I'd say the dungeon is a rather peculiar place to spend your free time," he drawled, eyes settling firmly on hers. "Why, my darling—have you done something wrong? You look as though I've caught you committing some filthy sin."

Don't fight, don't fight, don't fight.

"I . . ." She cleared her closing throat and tried again. "I did not know if you would want me in the dungeon," she answered honestly.

His smile raised gooseflesh on her arms. "I did tell you this place was yours, did I not? How comforting to know that your conscience is stricken, nonetheless." He turned away, gazing over the much emptier courtyard and fixing on the southern tower. Three phoenixes perched atop its edges.

She could not suppress the shudder that ran down her spine.

Feeling Zedong's attention burning into the top of her head, Meiling looked up. She wanted to growl, *"What do you want from me?"* But she held silent.

"Walk with me," he said smoothly, holding out his arm for her to take.

She hesitated, then ducked her head as she complied.

He led her to the east tower door, opened it for her like she was a dignified lady, and brought her up the stairs to the battlement. Cold wind greeted them at the top. Autumns must be more bitter here, so much farther north than the capital city. The season was only barely turning, yet Meiling wished she had grabbed her cloak before setting out on her daring escapade to the dungeon.

Zedong brought her to the edge of the battlement to stare out at the beautiful valley and the ribbon of blue threading through the healthy green. He released a small, satisfied sigh, not seeming to notice how stiff her arm was in his.

"Where are all these wounded people that Feiyan must heal?" Meiling asked abruptly.

He glanced down at her, surprise lighting his face for a moment. He shrugged. "In the infirmary." A bare note of condescension slipped into his words.

"Where is that?"

"Perhaps some other adventurous afternoon, you should find it. You found the dungeon easily enough."

So he *was* irritated that she had delved deeper into the fortress. Somehow, this made her feel better. Though she didn't know how she'd sneak into the dungeon again if he didn't want her to.

"There are no battles happening," Meiling said quietly. "Why are there wounded?" Feiyan had off-handedly mentioned the wounded as *their brethren*. The twelve captured wielders?

"These do not make up the entirety of my forces," he answered easily. "Wounded soldiers arrive at the gates nearly every day to be healed."

Yet she never saw them. "You torture the other wielders," she accused, carefully watching the side of his face as he turned back to gaze into the distance.

"If you would not fight me, then there would be no need for such things. No more needless bloodshed."

"I do not fight you," Meiling said. The earnestness of her words surprised her. "I cannot fight you."

She regretted the admission as soon as the words left her lips.

Was that a glow of pleased accomplishment emanating from him? She turned to follow the winding road leading to the fortress portcullis until it disappeared into the valley, too small to see. The lowered sun cast golden rays on the green, making the world glow with light and shadow.

Zedong was quiet for a long minute. Eventually, he spoke. "I do not wish for you to lose all your fight. I merely prefer to channel it into something worthwhile."

"Worthwhile?" she blurted incredulously. How blind was he? "I cannot fight you," she repeated, instead of responding. She almost added, *"But I won't fight* for *you."*

"Yet you try," he mused, turning so his back rested against the edge of the battlement and crossing his arms. "You cannot fool me, sweet one." The words were not cruel, or even accusatory. They were *almost* kind. Or . . . indifferent. As if he were calculating some sort of mathematical problem in his head and was puzzled about the solution. "If you would stop *trying* to fight me, I would have no need for bloodshed. I would have no need for torture."

Another well-aimed strike at Meiling's soft heart. Her mind reasoned with her that if he sent Feiyan to heal them, was it so terrible to let them continue being tortured and healed?

What a horrid existence: bound up only to be broken again and again.

"I do not want to be your tool," she whispered.

"Pardon me?"

"I do not want to be your tool," she repeated, grinding her teeth.

He sighed, blinking into the setting sun. The wind whipped at the ends of his scalp-tight braids and the black cloak pinned against the wall with his back. "There are worse things in this world to be, Meiling."

So she was to be grateful?

"I was nothing at the Academy, but here I am now," said Zedong. "I've allied Butagin's tribes into a single formidable force. They haven't forgotten the way they were pushed so far north, losing their land to your people. Now I'm helping them return to the land they once had. I've given Zheninghai brigands something to fight for. They're not all rebels, you know. Some of them were born into these networks and have no hope of being accepted into society."

He paused, tapping his fingers on his forearm. His face hardened. "I was the boy who lost every arena battle. I couldn't stand up for myself, much less anyone I cared about. And now I've kidnapped, subdued, and restrained Zheninghai's most powerful wielders. Did you know the siren down in my dungeon, Kang Lei, humiliated your mother in front of hundreds of students? And now look at her. Wasting away to nothing. What happened to *her* so-called power?"

A familiar shriek sounded from below. She hurried forward to the edge of the battlement overlooking the courtyard below—anything to distract herself from the way Zedong's words assaulted her. "Feiyan," she breathed, spotting the form she had not seen in full daylight since Fen had tried to rescue her ages ago. Feiyan was doing the exact thing she had been doing then—fighting Shuren's hold on her and hurling insults into his face. Meiling wanted to call out to her, but her throat closed tight.

Zedong stepped to her side and watched with her.

Shuren gripped her elbows behind her hard, holding them so high that there was no doubt Feiyan was in pain, despite her struggles. She tried to kick him and he gave a wrench on her arms. Feiyan cried out—wrenching Meiling's heart—gasped, and he relented.

As if sensing their gazes, Feiyan's eyes snapped upward and met Meiling's. For the space of a heartbeat, she stood frozen, confused. She glanced from Meiling to Zedong at her side and her head cocked to one side, a puzzling set to her chin.

It was enough for Shuren to whip out a cloth from his cloak and shove it over her face. She swore, renewing her futile efforts. Too quickly, her head lolled, and she dropped. Shuren barely caught her, lifting her up in his arms. His eyes darted to Meiling's—hopefully too quickly for Zedong to notice—and he swung Feiyan's limp body over his shoulder and marched toward the door that led to the dungeon. Her loose hair flung down his back, swaying with each of his movements.

Don't fight, don't fight, don't fight.

By all efforts of reason, Liuxian was right. Yet here Feiyan was, doing the seemingly stupid thing. Fighting for all she was worth, despite the odds stacked against her. Should Meiling be fighting like Feiyan? Should she refuse to be broken until she was dead? Should she scrape with bloody fingernails at every shred of independence and autonomy she could find?

But Feiyan had gone to the Academy. She was only a year from graduating herself. Moreover, she only fought Shuren and nameless barbarian guards. She was not forced to endure the manipulations and targeted, tailored threats from Fang Zedong himself.

It was so easy to make the excuses. They curdled bitterly on her tongue.

Meiling looked up, finding Zedong's gaze leveled down at her. His mouth twisted.

"Come," he said, holding out his arm again. "It is nearly time for supper. We ought to freshen up. I've ordered more clothes made for you. Until they are finished, my servants have been instructed to return your cleaned garments to you promptly. You need not worry about anything under my care."

She said nothing as he led her back down the tower staircase. She felt very cold and very, very weak. It took every ounce of willpower to keep from shrinking against him for a shred of warmth, of dependability.

If only it were true that she needn't have worries here!

If only . . .

If only she dared trust Zedong.

Or, if only she was more like Feiyan. Strong, unyielding, faithful against all temptation.

He had threatened her with the murders of her siblings. She *needed* to fight against him. But what use was it when he was so much more powerful than she? What could she possibly hope to accomplish when she would lose, no matter what choices she made?

Zedong left her standing in the evening-dimmed corridor, pointing to her room at the end, near the big window. He strode off toward his own chambers—she assumed—to find a new suit of black. Or retie his braids. She had no clue.

She stood still as a statue for a long time in that corridor. Was it her imagination that the shadows lengthened from the small windows lining the corridor, from the one window glaring at her at the end of the corridor? Why did the wind slipping through feel like grasping fingers, trying to propel her forward when she did not want to move?

"I know you're there," Meiling whispered.

Warmth coalesced behind her, made of shadow. She did not turn; not when she knew who it was.

"You see why?" that slightly accented voice whispered.

Meiling nodded. "I see why." Still, she did not turn. She faced that window at the end of the hall—so far. It seemed to shrink under her scrutiny. "Is there no hope?" Her voice was just barely audible. Even the echoing stone could not catch hold of it.

But Shuren did.

"For you."

She closed her eyes, shutting out the creeping twilight. Faces and boney bodies and broken spirits swam before her eyelids. "Is she . . .?"

"She will be fine," Shuren said. "I am always . . . careful."

Careful while he slugged her in the face, drugged her, and slung her over his shoulder like a sack of rice to be bought and sold in the marketplace. Her throat tightened, but she did not press him.

"I need food to take . . . below," she said instead. "Bread. And water."

Silence.

Had he left? She tilted her head slowly, and her periphery caught sight of that shadowy bulk.

"I might be able to," he said, his voice adopting a tense edge.

"And . . ." She drew in a deep breath. "Help. Getting in."

Would she ask Shuren to stretch his neck out on the chopping block for Liuxian and Tao? To volunteer his flesh for slow slicing? When he already risked so much by this tentative relationship they shared and his own care for the wild healer? She could still tell him that it was too risky and that she could not ask it of him.

She held silent.

When the silence lasted too long, she twisted her head around, moved her feet.

The length of corridor leading to the stairs was aglow with brilliant, flaming, orange light reflecting on the hewn edges of stone.

It was empty.

"I almost despaired of you coming."

Meiling, wearing the last of her robes—this one a pale yellow embroidered with more gold thread and decorated with rich green accents—slipped into the banquet hall without a word. If only more people were here, she could blend in. Like she did at home.

Ma had told her once that princesses usually did not escape notice so well as Meiling did. It seemed to be something that both pleased and bothered Ma. But here, with Zedong, it was as though a trumpet heralded her coming.

She should apologize for tarrying, for making him wait. As if he did not owe her a dozen apologies to her one. More than a dozen. Meiling kept her mouth shut as she seated herself at Zedong's right hand.

Zedong scrutinized her face. "You seem tired, my dear."

"I'm not your dear," she wanted to spit. She held her tongue and only nodded once.

Silence reigned supreme as the servants set bowls of soup down before them. Zedong ate first, tucking in heartily. Meiling hesitated, her hands clasped on her warm bowl. Would she ever be free to eat without thinking of those who could not eat like her? Would she ever be able to return to her blissful ignorance that was her former life at the palace?

Yes, she had been unhappy. But she'd had her Ma, her family, the small pleasures of day-to-day life. A wild impulse almost burst from her lips, but she clamped them shut only just in time to avoid asking Zedong if he had any books she could read. The topic hardly mattered.

She had been happier at home than she'd realized at the time.

"Something you should know about me," Zedong said suddenly, setting down his bowl of soup. He gestured with one hand, almost a flick. "Our earlier conversation made me think of it. I think you should know it. Blood—not my preference. Never has been. Too messy, too *forced.* I mentioned that you and I, that together, there could be another option."

"Blood is not my preference either," Meiling said dryly.

He cracked an amused smile. There was that *movement* behind his eyes. The movement that disconcerted her more than anything else about him.

Servants whisked away their soup dishes—Meiling's only half-eaten—and replaced with heaping bowls of roasted venison and fluffed rice. As much as she wanted to resist the lure of the food, she could not. She ate hungrily, piling her bowl with bites from the side dishes spread between them.

"Do you know what wins wars, little one?" Zedong asked after he had slowly chewed and swallowed. He gathered another bite on his chopsticks and paused before lifting it to his mouth. "Do you know?"

She had a fair number of guesses, but she kept silent.

"You may think blood wins wars. Most do." He shrugged. "I cannot blame them. But blood does not win wars. Wars are won with *information.* Information, Meiling."

The way he said her name made her throat tighten around the mouthful she had just swallowed.

"And information, as you have discovered with your skill, is stored where?"

He wanted her to answer. Her bite was still lodged in her throat. She took a swig of the only liquid available to her on the table spread—ruby red wine. Strong and heady, burning. She barely kept her composure as tears sprung to her eyes. "Memories," she croaked.

He grinned, delighted. "Indeed, my dear. Memories." His gaze went glassy as his thoughts seemed to turn inward. "Memories," he repeated, musingly. His gaze snapped to her. "Memories, my darling, are treacherous. Never trust them."

How did he manage to always ruin her appetite with a few words? They rang in her ears, so loud and pressing that she stared down at her food without moving until they settled on her mind like a coat of dust.

CHAPTER 13

FOLLOW ME." Zedong stood and reached down, raising her to her feet with one large, cold hand. "I have something to show you."

Meiling let herself be led away. Her lips parted slowly and the cold air bit at her teeth. She drew her soft shawl closer around her shoulders. One hand gripped the silk tightly to her chest, the other rested, tense, on Zedong's arm.

The sun had set when they left the banquet hall. Sconces were lit, few and far between, flickering dangerously in the cold wind. Zedong was so tall and his clothes so black that she might not have seen him in the darkness. Might have thought him nothing more than a shadow.

But no darkness could hide the unnatural brightness of his eyes.

His strides were purposeful, despite their leisurely, unrushed pace. His footsteps were strong and firm on stone, while hers were light and hollow. She walked two steps for each of his. The sound of every footfall was like a head-pounding hammer in her skull, banging a nail into the lid of a coffin.

Why was she so sick with dread? Why did she feel so stupid, so dragon-blasted helpless? Couldn't she be like Feiyan? Or Ma?

"Here," Zedong said, his low voice a hum in the darkness. He pushed open a door and motioned for her to enter.

It was even thicker with darkness than the sparsely lit corridor had been. Meiling immediately shrunk under the closeness of the room, her hackles raising as she backed away defensively. The door thudded closed, sealing them in darkness. Her throat was so dry. She swallowed, licked her lips, trying to find some moisture in this terrifying place.

She did not want to let her mind guess what he might have planned for them.

For her.

A strange sound, like fumbling, met her ears. Then a long, frustrated exhale.

"Forgive me. Please wait one moment."

In a whirl of dark cloak, Zedong exited the room and closed the door solidly behind him. She shivered in the stillness, in the pitch blackness. She should feel around, try to catch some semblance of what this room might be.

But her limbs would not move.

She stayed still, her arms wrapped tightly around herself. A long breath escaped her lips, shuddering a little at the end. She would wait. Wait like a lamb for the slaughter.

No, no. She would wait like a tiger, ready to pounce. A sudden thought flared brightly in her mind. Could she . . .? No, there was no possible way.

But—was there? Could she do it?

Despite her growing fear and racing heart, she forced her arms to unwind themselves from her middle and start searching around in the darkness. Anything sharp or hard would do. A knife was preferred.

Her hands were trembling so hard she knocked something off a table. She knelt to retrieve it.

The door opened and light burst upon her. Meiling blinked up into that glow, her hands closing around something cold, small, and smooth. She rose as Zedong entered the room with a candle.

"I told them to leave this room lighted," he growled in frustration. He quickly set to lighting all the candles about the room. She finally was able to take stock of where she stood.

It was . . . an office, of sorts. There was only one piece of furniture in the entire room: a large table that filled most of the space, with room to circumvent it comfortably. The table was completely covered with maps and parchments with wild scribbles. Nothing like the neat, tidy characters she had seen on the note he had sent to her.

Meiling looked down and found she held a smooth, glossy black stone. A paperweight. She set it down slowly on the table when his back was turned as he lit another candle.

Finally, Zedong set his candle down on the table. Half a dozen tiny flames flickered around the room, illuminating it enough for her to read what was on the page closest to her. She frowned. Was it . . . school curriculum?

He stared down at all the papers and maps. He was beaming, unable to help the smile that spread across his face as he said, "I'm planning my new society." His voice was eager. Too eager.

It made Meiling glance around the room quickly, back toward the door, and then focus intently on Zedong's own flashing eyes. She glimpsed it again. Not the wriggling that was always there. No, that glimmer of insanity. The insanity she had seen in his eyes when he watched his brigands training, their abilities magnified unnaturally.

"Come," he said, his excitement almost painful. "Come and see it, little one."

She took one obligatory step closer, pretending to peer down at his work while she darted glances up at him through her lashes.

"Strength and power—it can be for anyone who wants to work for it. Gone will be talent. This magic I've been exploring . . ." His soul glowed so brightly through his eyes that Meiling could almost see it without her magic. "It's ancient, and it is magic that can be learned. Performed by anyone."

"Black magic," Meiling said. "Wungfao."

Her tone seemed to snag him out of his enthrallment just slightly, enough to make his mouth quirk with that flavor of unintentional condescension. Or maybe it was intentional this time.

"I prefer to think of it as *enlightened* magic," he said, his lips pulled apart in a patronizing smile. "I will bestow it upon my most loyal and devoted subjects. People like you and me, my dear young one, and your mother, can have the power we deserve."

He had not spoken of Ma in a while, but the way he mentioned her now made her suspect she was never far from his thoughts. After all these years, how was such a thing even possible?

His words were whispers, soft and tantalizing and low. "We need not be bound by shame and disgrace."

Meiling turned away at that, his words piercing her heart sharper than any iron-wrought knife. Lies, a huge heap of lies! He could not make shame and disgrace vanish from this world.

But he could make my *undeserved shame vanish.*

She nearly gasped at the treacherous thought. She sucked in a tight breath through her teeth, only barely keeping herself from snarling at the wall, at the smooth rock that pinned a map of her home to the table.

Suddenly, Zedong stepped in front of Meiling and, before she could back away, snatched her face in both of his hands. He dragged her closer to his face and, for a wild, terrifying moment, she thought he intended to kiss her. Her voice clogged in her throat, but her hands grappled with his, trying to peel away his grip.

"No more shame, Lu Meiling," he said forcefully, his fingers digging into her scalp. "Look at me!" he growled, tightening his grip against her prying, resisting hands.

She obeyed, opening her terrified eyes wide and trying not to cry as his face filled her vision.

"No more shame. Think of the life you could live! The friends you could have. Meiling, they would see *you*, the real you. They would not despise you because of your blood. Because of your magic." He spat the last words and spittle landed on her cheeks.

She let out a whimpering cry, grimacing and fighting and trying to escape his grip. But suddenly, he seemed much stronger than a mere mortal, much, much stronger indeed. His pupils rounded and dilated as he clutched her face, his eyes pinning her gaze.

"You and I, together, Meiling. We can build this. This is why I need you and your abilities. With your help, I can set up a new society. One of equality, a beautiful place for all souls. For you."

Finally, she wrenched free as he let go. She stumbled against the opposite wall, crashing into the table and causing a few papers to flutter to the floor. She gasped in a ragged breath. A sob caught in her throat, making her choke. She shuddered as she closed her eyes for one blessed moment where she was free of those living blue eyes.

She opened them again, and his face darkened. Hardened.

"Perhaps . . ." he said, softly, the words edged with sharpness. "Perhaps you need time to think."

Instead of offering her his arm, he opened the door and beckoned her to leave. Meiling stared at him for one second and then hastened to obey. The door pulled shut with a reverberating thud behind her.

She stood in a dark corridor, very like the one where her room was, with only half the sconces lit. Little pools of yellow tried to reach into the darkness, tried to force it just a little further back. But the darkness was insistent, crouching and prowling around the little spheres of light.

Harsher light—burning light—caught her eyes through one of the windows. She forced her cold limbs to move and peek out the window, her fingers barely brushing the icy stone.

Phoenixes.

Several circled overhead while others perched listlessly, seemingly harmless, on the tops of towers. Their feathers were burning flames, yet the fire didn't consume. It was the strangest sight to see so feral a creature bound to be so docile, to see the blazing wildness of their souls gleaming in orange eyes, as they sat like snow-white doves on stone.

Meiling pulled back her fingers and turned in the corridor. Which way was her room? She pulled her thin shawl tighter to ward off the cold. Her teeth chattered.

"Are you there?" she whispered.

Silence.

She thought she had sensed Shuren's presence in the shadows, but apparently she was wrong. He would not dare watch her so closely. She was even more lonely than she had been before. How was she supposed to do this on her own? She had hardly enough strength to stand on her own two feet.

She did not even know where her room was.

Well, it was about time that she learned.

She picked a direction and strode down the length of the darkness. Being alone at night was what she had always craved, but this was different. Nevertheless, she tried to focus on how she was mostly safe here, how the wind tickled and frosted her ears until they stung.

Her soft footfalls were nearly silent. She pushed open the door at the end of the hallway and found diverging corridors. She picked the one that felt right and followed it. Only two torches gleamed in the quiet. Meiling poked her head out a window and found herself overlooking the courtyard. Which meant she could probably find her way easily enough from here.

Moonlight streamed like milk onto her face when she slipped down a flight of stairs, opened the door, and stepped out into the night. She stopped, startled. This was not the courtyard. Maybe the other direction would prove more efficient.

But in the silvery light of early night, she thought she could make out—a garden? Puzzled, she closed the door softly behind her and glanced around for any sign of prowling guards. None.

A covered walkway stretched between her and another door. The left was a wall, like the back of the many small chambers dotting this fortress. The right was what she suspected was a garden. A large, twisting tree she could not name rose at the edge of a tall, great wall. Between the path and the tree was a plot of dirt, not very big, full almost to bursting with plants. Some plants she recognized, like lettuce and cucumbers. Most, however, she did not. Curiosity plucked at her mind. She glanced over her shoulder, but there was no sign of guards. No light, save for the stars and moon. Not even the burning of the phoenixes reached here.

She crouched on the walkway, reaching toward the closest plant. A compulsion to touch it nearly overcame her. She could make out the edges of sharply cut, purple leaves. There were several of these small, low plants. She leaned forward so her knees fell into the soft earth. Her fingers brushed one leaf.

That one touch sent small sparks flying into the air.

She should be scared, but her eyes widened in fascination. Her fingers hummed strangely where she'd touched the plant. She glanced down and found a glowing imprint on the pads of her fingertips.

Magic.

A magic she did not understand. A magic that Zedong definitely did understand.

Her eyes flitted over the other plants. Some were taller, some were thin, tangling vines, and some were supported by wooden terraces. Now that her fingers had tasted of the magic, now that it stirred her blood, she could make out the faintest traces of different colored auras around the plants.

She should find her room.

And then what? Go to sleep, only to be trapped in her mind again? Twice imprisoned?

She certainly could not feel the dark magic binding her soul, but it was there. Could these plants undo that magic? Could she free herself?

Meiling hesitated to touch any of the plants again. What if some were poisonous, but she did not know? She wanted to grab handfuls of each different type, fill her skirt with them, and then race back to her room to try to find the right one or the right combination to break the spell binding her.

The thought of a combination made her heart falter. He might have used some complicated mixture to cast the spell. How did one even use a plant for this?

She might be curious, and she might be desperate, but she would not be foolish. Best not to trifle with magic she did not understand. Nevertheless, the one plant she had touched seemed harmless enough . . .

Meiling plucked a leaf free. It sizzled at the severance and a drop of acid landed on the ground, smoking in the dirt. Carefully, she held the tip of the leaf so no noxious drops burned her hand through to the bone.

Now she *really* needed to get to her room. Before Zedong took a midnight stroll to his garden and found his prisoner raiding his secret black magic.

She ducked her head and slipped back through the door she'd come through just moments ago. Her jaw firm, she set at a quick, but still dignified pace, down the corridor, past the first hall she had come down, and through to the other, far door. It spat her out into the starlit courtyard.

Strange how empty a place was after dark.

Perhaps it was a good thing Shuren had not been hiding in the shadows to escort her safely to her room. Here, at least, guards stood watch. They were still, black, and almost formless lumps of shadow. She tucked the leaf out of sight and held her head high as she strode toward the door that would take her up the stairs to the wing where her chamber resided.

Silence, laced with dread, permeated the air with its clinging fullness.

She slipped like a phantom into her room. A waxing moon gleamed through her window. She looked back and saw her own shadow, lined with silver, twisted and roiling. Angst rose in her chest, her hands humming and vibrating softly where she held the little leaf. She set it on her windowsill and withdrew her buzzing fingers.

As much as she dreaded it, she should sleep.

CHAPTER 14

SHE STOOD IN a more colorful, more beautiful version of her father's throne room. The dais shined as though recently polished. Colorful dragons crawled up the pillars. The throne was empty. No Emperor's Guard lined the hall.

It was just Meiling, standing alone amid shimmering memory threads.

With a guttural growl that echoed through the bare space, she turned and ran out of the throne room. She flew through silk curtains and painted ornate doors. She was focused on her destination like a *mó guǐ* stalking its victim. Nothing could distract her, not the tugging threads, the promise of windows or other doors.

No, she had one goal.

She realized suddenly that there was another shadow beside hers. She whirled, stopping abruptly. There had never been another person in her mind before. Never, ever. She ground shadowy, boneless teeth. Bit fleshless lips.

The shadow was gone. In its wake was a humming sort of magic. Meiling's heart picked up its pace. She hastened forward again. She should not let herself be distracted. Gold and red and white and green gleamed like flashing rainbows of color, begging her eyes to feast upon their beauty.

This was her mind, after all. She had constructed this place. Or, perhaps, the barebones had always existed since her birth, but she had painted and decorated it to the radiant, clean beauty that spoke of home. The only place she had ever lived until Liuxian had been forced to kidnap her.

Meiling focused, redoubling her pace. Through cavernous, exquisite halls she flew, faster and faster, until she stopped suddenly and whirled.

Who are you? Meiling called. *Show yourself.* Magic hummed where she had sensed the shadow's presence. *I know you are there.*

Do you? a familiar voice whispered.

Her heart lurched. Her voice stuttered, caught on strings of strong emotion. *Sh-Shang? Is that you?*

The nonexistent shadow laughed, but it was not Shang's laugh. Then again, had she ever heard Shang laugh?

Why are you here? she demanded, wishing she did not feel suddenly wispy with weakness.

You invited me, Shang's unmistakable voice returned, coming from behind her.

She whirled, barely catching the slightest darkness before it dissipated again in laughter and humming. *I invite no one into my mind,* she growled. Before she could prevent it, a piteous mewl poured from her throat, escaping her lips and flooding her mind. *Why haven't you come for me?*

Why would I come for you? That unfamiliar, strange laughter resounded again. *You were my interruption. Your helplessness plagues me. I weary of you! I weary of saving you! Save yourself, for once. Then, maybe I shall consider you as more than an inconvenience.*

Meiling jerked back, gasping with pain.

His voice seeped into the floor, swallowed by humming. That humming was starting to make her ache as though she had a headache, but the sensation was different while standing in her own mind.

She needed to get to the palace entrance. But as soon as she started forward, the shadow reappeared.

Go away, Shang! Meiling cried.

Who is Shang? a very different voice mumbled quietly. *Shang, as in Tan Shangdi? Your protector?*

Ma! She gasped, turning and trying to grasp that shadow. It vanished between her formless hands. *Ma! Why do you run from me? I need you! I miss you!*

Mei, my sweet, do not try to find me. I do not wish to be found by you.

But why? Why, Ma? She whirled round and round, clutching for a shred of that shadow, of that warmth and comfort. *I need you! I need your strength!*

Do you love me only for what I can do for you?

A knife, as real as any in the waking world, plunged into her heart. *Ma—what could you possibly mean? Of course not!*

I've long known that you only love me because no one else does. Meiling, my darling, you only love those who love you. It is your greatest fault. You think you are only misunderstood. You do not consider that you, yourself, are unlovable. You think the fault is with everyone else, never you.

Everything froze for just one instant, as though her blood had halted in her veins. Then she crumpled into a pile on a red, woven rug with white tassels and gold threaded embroidery, sobbing. Those harsh words, spoken with such melting tenderness, could not have cut deeper.

Why do you weep? A completely different voice replaced the gentle whispers of her mother. *Get up! Fight, you fool! Unless you are as weak as I have always feared you to be. Unless you cannot fight. Then you are a greater fool than the rest of us.*

Mirthless, bitter, biting. A cold version of Feiyan's voice.

The humming was almost overwhelming now. Yet, it could not drown out those insistent, crushing voices.

Two spoke together—*You bring us shame, sister.*

A third voice, lower and stronger with a tinge of fire and smoke—*You disappoint me, daughter. You weaken under affliction. Have you no spine, daughter-mine? Will you trade all you love because you do not understand the meaning of sacrifice?*

And another—*I can remove your disgrace before the people. No more shame.*

Round and round, the voices hummed until they were buzzing, combining, twisting into a thorny crown of bloody roses. The crown pressed down on Meiling's brow, its agony falling heavy—

But those were not roses that Meiling saw. They were purple, sharp-edged leaves. They dripped acid, sizzling carpet and wood in their wake.

For one single instance, the humming quieted. Enough for her to have one conscious thought—

Get to the door.

She burst into a run, tearing off the crown and flinging it into the burned rug behind her. It seemed to sputter, pop, and crackle. The humming grew louder, but the voices were now indistinguishable. Gasping through sobs, she ran and ran until she was no more than a zipping line of awareness.

Black flared before her vision.

She stopped just one moment before she plunged headlong into that ugly, glaring magic blocking her exit. Imprisoning her. She looked down and there, at her feet, was the crown she had discarded. It lay, glowing purple and black and other ugly hues for which she had no name.

The crown of her worst nightmares and fears.

She picked it up and ignored how it burned her flesh. She was not physical; she could not truly burn here. So she gripped it in her fist and squared her shoulders against the exit of her mind.

I can free you from your shame, the crown whispered. *From your shame, your weakness, your sins, your disgrace.*

With a cry of rage, Meiling swung the crown and struck the hideous bar on her mind. The blow sent her reeling backward. Sparks flared and a strange, throbbing noise banged through her awareness.

She threw herself back at the barrier, wielding the crown for another strike. Again and again, she raked claws of thorns across the blackness. Again and again she was thrown back. But this was her mind. Again and again, she got to her feet again and charged forward.

Slowly, the magic shredded before her vision. Her room in Zedong's fortress clarified beyond that blocked door. The magic weakened, bit by bit. If she had to be here all night to break the spell, then she would be.

She was so close! The magic was mere tatters of what it once was. But in her determination, she did not notice that the room beyond her mind grew brighter.

She did not notice until the door in front of her and the thorny, poisonous crown in her hand started to blur and dim before her. That was when she blinked and looked through the door at the dawning of the waking world.

That was when she opened her eyes and stared at the rafters overhead.

She gazed vacantly at the ceiling, at the streaming pink sunlight. Her breathing was heavy—almost rasping. Her body was slick and dampened with sweat, her muscles quavering as though she'd run halfway across the world.

Then, with a cry, she lurched upward in bed. She sprang toward the window where a single purple leaf lay, fluttering slightly in the breeze. It had blackened throughout the night, but still retained its distinctly purple hue. She pulled her sleeve lower so she could fling the leaf out into the world below, away from her, without touching it with her skin.

She shuddered, covered her face with her hands, and sank to the floor. The bare skin of her calves and feet slid along the smoothed wood.

What horror had she unleashed in her mind? True, she had almost broken through Zedong's enchantments, but at what cost? She had almost lost her soul to that . . . *fear.* Even now, those poisonous words, spoken from the mouths of the people she loved the most, ran like dripping water through her mind, finding every porous surface to sink into. Those words found homes in her mind.

Could she ever be rid of them?

Could she ever look at her father and not hear his disappointment? And Shang—could she face him now, feeling his disgust? Would she be able to embrace her mother without a whisper in her ear, that nagging feeling that she would never be as good as Ma?

But there was no guarantee she would ever see those people again. There was only one person who she very much intended to see again.

Feiyan.

The healer, who was stronger than her. Feiyan, who was good-hearted and yet a fighter. Those noxious words filled like a toxic perfume in her nostrils, voicing the very thing she had feared from the moment she had met Feiyan.

Would Feiyan discover how weak Meiling actually was? Did she see it already?

Day had dawned. A new day.

Meiling breathed in the chill air, the warmth of the rising sun on the back of her head. She listened to the sound of her own inhales and exhales. Soft, reassuring.

Notably lacking from the accusing voices had been Fen's. Was that because she had long given up on winning Fen's approval? Was it because she had already heard every unkind thing from her lips? It seemed that Fen's opinions held no sway over her. Not in her heart of hearts.

But Shang's did.

That thought terrified her.

She'd had enough terror, though. It was time to face the day. She drew herself to her feet, walked to her washbasin, and filled it with water from the pitcher. The frigid cold was a slap in the face, in a good sort of way.

Meiling would not let this defeat her.

She still breathed. There was still fight left in her soul. She had still accomplished a daring feat in her mind. She had wielded dark magic against itself.

And she hoped she never did it again.

The icy water dripped off her nose and slid down her neck. She kept her hands braced on either side of the washbasin, face bent down to stare at her own barely visible reflection.

What a terrifying thing that magic was. This was why dark magic was forbidden. It was too dangerous, too destabilizing, too volatile. It was like a parasitic malady in need of curing.

One could lose their soul and their life with this magic.

And Zedong wanted to teach this explosive art to everyone? To anyone who was *willing to work for it*? Anyone who proved his loyalty to him?

This power could not be wielded. Not without driving the wielder to the brink of insanity.

Meiling pursed her lips grimly. She had tasted of this power. She wanted no part in it. Ever again.

As Meiling was summoning enough courage to leave her room, she noticed a little sack on the ground by her door. She frowned and crouched before it, her blue robes trailing on the wooden floor. It was a lumpy, coarse knapsack with a bit of twine securing it shut. She pulled open the twine and let the cloth fall back to reveal three hard lumps of bread. No water, but even having the bread was a relief.

She knew where she was going first. If she could make it there without being diverted by Zedong or his guards. Would he try to stop her this time?

Maybe another day she could sneak a knife to Feiyan. Tonight, perhaps in her sleep, she could escape the restraints he had placed on her mind and then she could search Shuren's mind for the keys to the cells, whether they were with the jailer or somewhere else. The thought of entering his mind again made her shudder. But she would do what she needed to do. Maybe she could call his memory of Feiyan to guide her again.

Memories, my darling, are treacherous. Never trust them.

Never trust her own? Or others?

This was if Zedong didn't discover how much damage she had done to his barriers. She had no idea when he placed them, or how, and for all she knew, they'd be strengthened and renewed the moment her head hit the pillow. She could only imagine how furious Zedong would be if he knew she had found his garden of black magic.

She needed to take this one step at a time. First, give two loaves of bread to Liuxian and Tao. Then, find Feiyan and give her the third. And tell her everything and ask what they could even do to escape at this point.

Meiling pushed away the memories of Feiyan's words in her mind as she shoved open her door. She tucked the bread into her skirts to hopefully evade notice.

The morning was already escaping quickly as she hurried down the empty corridor, blinking when direct sunlight blasted her eyes through the windows. She tried to not walk *too* hurriedly; tried to walk in such a way that she appeared leisurely and graceful without betraying how fast she was actually moving.

Ma had always been good at it. Meiling had been a little *less* good, but certainly better than Hou. She could still hear Ma coaxing

Hou to be something of a lady, to which Hou always retorted that she wasn't a lady, she was a warrior. And Ma would smile and tell her that part of being a good warrior was being a ladylike princess. Hou never was convinced.

Familiar sounds of practicing battle clanged in Meiling's ears. Why were they still here, practicing? Why were they not taking over the world?

Not that she was going to rush them.

To her surprise, not a single person glanced her way as she walked straight toward the dungeon. There was no prickling sensation of eyes following her movements.

In fact, it was almost as if . . . as if . . .

There.

The shadows were a little deeper in that corner of the portico. Her awareness sparked, even as her heart lifted.

Shuren was helping her after all, despite the risk to himself.

She opened the door to the dungeon, slipped through, and shut it behind her.

Would she ever get used to the sudden blackness?

Descending those stairs took even longer than yesterday. Dirt crumbled under her fingers as she braced against the wall to prevent herself from tumbling headlong. Finally, she jolted her knee when there were no more steps. She walked further and turned to see the corridor lined with doors. And the lantern she'd taken yesterday had been replaced on its hook.

The jailer sat on his chair like yesterday, hands folded across his belly, staring wide awake into the passage.

Please, Shuren, let your illusions hold. Keep me invisible for a few minutes longer.

Stomach knotting, she hurried forward, snatched the lantern off its hook and slipped through the door that would lead to Liuxian and Tao, without a glance toward the jailer.

When the door closed behind her, she paused, waiting, expecting to hear a crash of sound as the jailer came after her. Her heart still thrummed, too scared, and she wondered when something like this would ever *not* scare her.

But nothing happened.

So she took one step, then another, into the depths of the dungeon.

She loved the idea of being able to plunge into this darkness with nothing but a dying lantern and not be frightened, but she was terrified by the road that would lead her to such courage.

Meiling might have been one of the most sheltered children in the empire growing up, but even she knew that courage was forged in adversity. Not in the silken sheets of a safe, luxurious home.

Soon enough, she opened a door and found herself peering into shielding hands. Liuxian grunted.

"I brought bread," she whispered, setting the lantern down quickly and stepping in front of it to protect them from the brightest of its glare. She dug around her skirts for the loaves and produced them, handing one to an eager Liuxian who shuffled forward.

"So you *did* bring bread," he mumbled, tearing into the food immediately. "I doubted you."

"I don't blame you." She stepped past him to hand the other loaf to Tao, who hadn't moved an inch from his position yesterday. "Here," she said, holding it through the bars.

He slowly lifted his head from his knees and blinked at her. He was younger than she had originally guessed. Probably thirty or so. Liuxian must be around sixty, and she'd assumed Tao would be close. With a groan, Tao shifted himself close enough to take the bread. But unlike Liuxian, he did not immediately shove it into his face. Instead, he clasped Meiling's hand tightly.

"Thank you," he whispered in his low voice, squeezing hard on her hand.

"I wish I could do more," she said. "I *hope* to do more."

He didn't let her hand go for several long minutes. Not wanting to deprive him of starved human contact, she did not pull away until he did. He shuffled back to his spot, pulling his knees up to his chest again, and started eating slow, savoring bites.

"I can't stay," Meiling said, getting to her feet. "I cannot promise that I will come back, but I *will* promise that I will try. I'll do whatever I can."

"He'll stop you," Liuxian muttered, picking crumbs out of his beard and popping them into his mouth. "He won't let you help us. He'll find out!"

"He already knows," Tao said.

Meiling's heart faltered.

"He knows you are here, helping us," Tao continued quietly, keeping his head down. His voice reverberated through the small space, bouncing back on the stone walls. "This is the last time for a while that we will see you, Princess Meiling."

"What?" she sputtered. "What do you mean? He has not stopped me yet. I could probably come again tomorrow—"

"Thank you for the kindness you have shown us," Tao said, firmly, with the conviction of a soul who had *seen*. Who knew.

Her heart rate increased, and a cord of dread tightened around her lungs. "Do I still have time to see Feiyan?"

"If you hurry," he answered. "They are . . . coming."

Meiling snatched up the lantern and flew out of the room, hardly caring how loud the doors banged behind her. She tripped up two staircases and finally tumbled out of the last door before she turned and plunged back through a different door, this one leading to Feiyan.

Perhaps she should have thought to ask *who* was coming. The brigands? The guards? If it was Shuren, that was one thing. If it was the red-eyed brigand who had manhandled her all the journey here, that was another. What would they do if they caught her? Part of her mind reasoned that she should be trying to escape the dungeon before they found her. But she *needed* to see Feiyan.

She needed to talk to a friend. Feiyan probably needed the extra bread as well.

Meiling almost pitched forward down unexpected staircases a few times before she finally flung open the last door and held up the lantern to glare in Feiyan's face.

"Grrraaa!" Feiyan cried, throwing up her hands. "I *told* you to stop shining that dragon-blasted thing in my face!"

"Feiyan!" Meiling gasped, immediately lowering the light and shutting the door behind her. "Feiyan! Are you all right?"

"Meiling?" Genuine shock colored that tone. "What—what are you doing here? Why aren't you here? Where have you been?"

"Here, quickly, eat this." She shoved her last loaf in Feiyan's face. "They're coming, so hurry!"

"Who's coming?" Feiyan asked around a mouthful. "You're acting a little weird, you know that? You've *almost* managed to scare me."

"Are you all right? Are you injured?" Meiling persisted, reaching through the bars and grabbing Feiyan's arm. "I saw you struggling."

Feiyan waved a hand. "I'm fine. I do prefer the drugs to the slugs. I wake up very happy after he drugs me. Makes it a little hard to fight, but so does a pounding headache. I'll take the happiness, thank you. Why are you dressed up like someone's queen? They forgot to give you a crown."

It was a genuine question, without malice, but Meiling did not fail to catch the confusion underscoring the words.

"I don't understand anything," Meiling blurted, and her words came tumbling out, explaining everything that had happened since they had last spoken. How she was given her own room, how she now ate with Zedong, how he bound her soul so she could not wield her magic except at his beck and call, how he forced her to hunt for information and give it to him, how he had arranged for Shuren to make an illusion of her siblings to make her think he had captured them too.

Meiling told her about the phoenix incinerating the escaping guard. How she had tried to visit her yesterday but could not find her before the guard and Shuren came to get her. She shared about the other prisoners she had met, how there were twelve wielders in all, how Tao had said she would not see them again for a long time.

"I think they will prevent me from coming here at all, so we cannot plan our escape!" *So your strength cannot comfort me.* "I do not know what to do. I do not know how we are to ever escape this place!"

Feiyan had finished eating, and she gripped both of Meiling's hands in hers. Warmth flowed into her body.

"I found his dark magic too," Meiling whispered. "There's a garden hidden against a wall. I don't know if he uses other things too, or if it is only the plants. But whatever it is, it's . . . it's . . ." She trailed off, unable to describe the horror she'd experienced in her own mind.

"Sounds like you've gotten all the excitement between the two of us. Unfair," Feiyan said dryly. "The plan is still the same. I'm going to try to overwhelm the guard so I can escape—I *almost* had him last time! I'll come get you and we'll climb over the wall or something."

"But Shuren always comes to help subdue you. You cannot fight them both. And how are we supposed to climb over the wall? What'll we do after we escape? And who is going to stop Zedong from doing all the horrible things he's planning to do?"

"Stop overthinking things." Feiyan squeezed Meiling's hands with a little smile. "Remember what I told you? Plans are for breaking. We could walk straight through the portcullis in the end for all I care."

What about Liuxian and Tao? What about the rest of the wielders? They could not all escape, could they?

Meiling clung to Feiyan's hands, hating herself for wanting to burst into tears. Feiyan was the one who had been in the dungeon. Feiyan was the one who should be asking for comfort, not her. Yet Feiyan did not seem weakened in the slightest.

For a long few minutes, they sat there, holding hands through the bars of Feiyan's prison. Silent. Waiting for something they did not know. Or perhaps they were simply savoring the warmth of friendship.

Perhaps Feiyan needed more comfort than she let on.

"I am going to find where the keys are," Meiling whispered. "I'm going to get you out. You, and . . ." She trailed off at the sound of a clanging door.

"Hurry!" Feiyan jerked her hands away and gestured at the lantern. "Snuff that out! Hide behind the door!"

"Snuff it out?" Meiling balked.

"Do it!"

Fingers trembling and fear roiling in her stomach, Meiling unlatched the lantern and blew out the candle with one small puff.

The room plunged into darkness heavier than night.

She groped for the door and barely had time to plant herself and the lantern safely behind it before it swung open and nearly banged her nose. She threw up her hands to stop it in time and hoped the guard did not notice how oddly the door swung.

He was not given a chance to notice. Feiyan immediately began hurling insults. Insults in her tongue that he most definitely could not understand. The meaning, however, was unmistakable. Another pair of boots followed him. *Shuren.* He wasn't even waiting for Feiyan to give the guard trouble before coming now.

Perhaps if she hadn't fought so much, she could have surprised the single guard instead of contending with the guard *and* Shuren.

"Already going to drug me?" Feiyan spat. "Won't even let me prove I'll be obedient this time?"

Shuren only grunted. The sound of scuffling ensued, followed by a strange bang, and another grunt from Shuren, and two pairs of heavy boots left the room.

Meiling huddled in the darkness as the door banged shut. Feiyan was so strong—and so utterly outmatched. How did they stand a chance of escape? The only chance seemed to be if Shuren helped them, but would he be willing to help after what he'd already done today? If Zedong knew she was down here, helping the prisoners, then he would have known that *someone* had let her come down here. It wouldn't be hard for him to connect this to Shuren.

And then she'd lose her only ally.

Hours passed. Probably only minutes; one never knew in a place like this. Without Feiyan's comradeship or even the lantern's attempts to drive away the permeating despair, this place was so much more *hopeless.*

Surely that was why she was thinking these negative thoughts. Perhaps their possibilities would look less dire in the sunshine.

Everything around was silent. She pulled herself to her feet. She knew how to get back. The dark should not make it that much more difficult, right?

Apparently it could.

By the time she had left the burnt-out lantern in the hallway beside the empty chair where the jailer usually was, mounted the last flight of stairs, and pushed open the door, it was evening, and she was weak with hunger.

The sound of battle met her ears.

CHAPTER 15

AT FIRST, MEILING thought it was still late morning. At first, she thought Zedong's brigands were still practicing in the courtyard. But when her eyes adjusted to the painful light after hours stumbling through the dark, there were flames.

Burning fire.

Phoenixes flew overhead, blasting brigands on the wall. They were either incinerated immediately or they fell with a sickening thud to the ground. Why would the phoenixes be burning Zedong's own wielders?

And that was when realization hit. These weren't Zedong's wielders.

These were the empire's wielders. These were . . . these were . . .

Meiling collapsed against the wall, suddenly overwhelmed with sheer joy and utter horror. They came for her. Pa had come to save her. They were here to rescue her. She would not have to fight Zedong, would not be his puppet any longer.

But her burst of hope was soon crushed as she whipped her head around, watching countless wielders fall. They could not get over the wall—not with those phoenixes. How big was the force they'd brought? Would it be enough? How could these wielders fight the phoenixes *and* the barbarian guards *and* the enhanced magic of the brigands?

What if it wasn't enough?

Her instincts warred within her. Self-preservation urged her to run from the fighting and find a safe place to hide until she could be rescued. Another part of her urged her to run straight into the fray and scream for her people to save her.

But one thought threw both of those options to the wind.

"Feiyan!" She lurched to her feet, bracing them wide as her eyes darted around the courtyard, the entrances to the towers, the brigands collecting on the battlements with their array of weapons and magic. Had Shuren brought Feiyan out of that door yesterday? Was that where the infirmary was?

Before she could burst into a run, a hand gripped her arm in a painfully tight grip. She cried out and glanced up to see Zedong, his face a mask of fury.

"Take her!" He flung her into someone's chest. "Your life is forfeit if she dies."

His unspoken words rang in the air between them: *Or she is rescued.* Hands closed around her elbows, lifting her back to her feet, as Shuren dragged her away, positioning himself between her and the fighting.

"Shuren!" Meiling cried, whirling on him. His grip tightened on her, almost painful. "Shuren! Where is Feiyan?"

His face was hard. "To the vault."

"But Feiyan!" She was practically screaming, and the surge of adrenaline in her blood was almost enough to strengthen her so she nearly broke free of Shuren's grip.

"She doesn't matter!" he shouted back into her face, wrestling her into submission.

His words sliced Meiling's heart. Even more than his words, the look in his eyes seemed to drive a knife straight to her soul. "Yes, she *does,*" Meiling cried. "You know she does!"

"What I know doesn't matter."

All her fight fled her limbs. She did not want to give up. She did not want to leave Feiyan to be caught in the crossfires of battle. But really—would Zedong let harm befall her? Surely she was on her way to the vault as well. Meiling should not be afraid for her.

A scream cut through the din of battle. It broke off abruptly.

That was it. Meiling roared, twisting with all her might, and wrenched free. Shuren tried to pounce on her again, but she was running. She ducked into a stairwell and raced upward into a throng of guards. She had the element of surprise and managed to squeeze through them before Shuren could follow and sound the alarm. Before the guards could realize what was happening.

She emerged on the battlements, opposite where the brigands and phoenixes defended their fortress. A few wielders were starting to break through. One phoenix was shot down, trailing a bursting explosion of sparks, followed by another.

Maybe . . . maybe there *was* hope.

She raced as fast as she could, afraid that at any moment Shuren would slam open the door and chase her down. For the moment, and that moment only, she had a head start on him. She flung open the door to the next tower, hardly caring how she practically fell down the stairs.

Straight into the burly chest of a barbarian guard.

His hands closed like claws around her arms as he shouted something in Butagin—to the guards with him. Meiling yelped, trying to scramble back, to pry her arms free, but his hold was unbreakable. In a second, more guards swarmed around her, unfamiliar words sailing in furious tones over her head as the first guard grabbed the back of her neck, squeezing painfully as he dragged her down several stairs.

She dragged in short, shallow gasps of air, her whole body tense as a rod with his hand on her neck. If he squeezed even a little bit more . . .

Her foot slipped on the stairs.

The guard reacted, tightening his hold on both her arm and her neck. Black colored the edges of her vision as she screamed. The nearest guard's head swiveled toward her, his beard and bushy eyebrows contorted.

Then there were arrows.

Protruding from that head.

Blood spewed everywhere.

Horror rendered Meiling utterly immobile, and she couldn't even brace herself before she was slammed face-first into the stone wall of the tower.

Pain. Shouting. So much shouting. So much pain.

That horrible hand hadn't left the back of her neck, forcing her into the wall. The *shing* of a blade behind her.

They were going to kill her, weren't they?

Then, one voice cut through the din around her. A language she knew.

A *voice* she knew.

Its tone, however, was completely unfamiliar. It was snarling, low, *lethal.*

"Get. Your. Hands. Off. Her."

Thwump. A startled cry sounded from just behind her. The hand gripping her neck fell away—and *kept* falling down the rest of the stairs. Meiling's vision swam, full of stone and black spots. It ran down her face, her clothes, and she didn't know if it was hers or someone else's.

Somehow, she managed to twist. Her foot stumbled to the next step, but she threw out her arms and caught herself, dragging her eyes open and blinking against the darkness.

Just as a sword plunged straight into the chest of another guard.

A foot landed on the chest, shoving the body backward as the crimson-stained blade was yanked back.

Then a hand grabbed her arm. Dragged her up half a dozen steps and deposited her in a heap. Her rattled mind tried to catch up to what was happening as she blinked and blinked, struggling to make the world swim into focus.

At last, moving shapes coalesced into people.

And there—

There was Shang.

She'd recognize him anywhere. The long, black queue, the broad shoulders, the trim and muscular body, the cut of his sharp jaw. His back was to her, his sword flashing in a deadly arc against the remaining barbarian guards. Four bodies already littered the stairs, blood dripping down the walls, pooling on the stairs.

Then Shang whirled toward her, black eyes flashing as he yanked his *jiaun* out of its holster, lifted it—and fired it straight over her head. Meiling didn't even have time to scream before a guard she hadn't seem coming up behind her fell, two arrows protruding from his neck. She scrambled away from the body, her heart pounding so hard she didn't have room for a rational thought.

She pressed her sleeve to her nose, wiping away blood. *Away, away, away.* She had to get out of this screaming nightmare.

Abruptly, it stopped.

Only one man still stood amid all those bodies and all that gore.

He turned.

Black eyes met hers. Time froze.

His mouth was drawn in a tight, grim line, his jaw clenched, his face spattered with blood. The blade in his hand dripped. He wore full armor, the plating dented and dulled already, which only served to make him more terrifying in that moment.

She could do nothing but stare, her body sagging against the stone wall.

He came for me.

Then he was kneeling before her, prying away her hand from her face. The cold, lethal glint was gone, instead replaced by wide, half-frantic eyes. "Meiling! *Meiling, Meiling, Meiling.* Hey, look at me. Yes, that's a good girl. Stop touching your face. Let me see it." The moment she let her hands fall to her lap, he hissed between his teeth. With a quick rip, he tore the end off her sash and leaned in close. He cupped the back of her head in one hand, his jaw flexing, as he dabbed away the worst of the blood.

She was just staring at him stupidly, expecting him to vanish at any second.

Suddenly, he grabbed his *jiaun*, shot up to his knees, and fired behind Meiling. A sharp cry. Faster than thought, he reloaded. Shot again. Reloaded. Shot. Thumps followed each shot.

This wasn't happening.

Shang bowed over her again, breathing hard. He laid his palm over her nose and sinuses, and the familiar ice of his touch soothed something deep inside her.

He was saying something.

". . . got to keep moving. I'm getting you out of here. Once you're out of the fortress, our warriors can pull back. Can you hear me? Meiling, look at me. *Look at me.*"

She blinked. His handsome face was lined with blood, sweat, and desperation, one of his wide hands gripping the back of her head, fingers tangled in her hair. His other hand still iced her face.

"Shang?" she croaked.

"Yes? What is it?"

His eyes seemed to swallow her whole, and for a second, she wasn't here in Zedong's tower, surrounded by bodies. Instead, she was in a cave, Shang's arms around her, his breath on her forehead. She was *safe.*

She reached up with one tentative hand and brushed a stray lock of hair out of his face. His eyes widened. "You came back for me."

His expression hardened. He pulled away from her, taking the blood-soaked piece of sash and wrapping a chunk of ice in it. "Of course I did," he growled, pressing the ice into her hand and guiding her hand to her face. "Hold this here. You're still bleeding. It's a miracle your nose isn't broken, but you might have a concussion from that hit. Come on, we need to get out of here before it's too late. I know you're in shock, but we must keep moving."

With that, he grabbed her under her arms, hauled her to her feet, and tugged her down the stairs after him. She clung to his elbow, her knees shaking as she tried to dodge around all the bodies. Arms and legs sprawled in puddles of viscous crimson.

It was so . . .

They'd been *alive* mere minutes ago. Now they were gone. Dead. How many children were orphans now, how many women left as widows?

"Don't look," Shang growled, as though sensing the panic bubbling up inside her. "Close your—"

He shoved her against the wall before he could finish his sentence. She hit the stone hard, a gasp choking her, as a Butagin soldier burst through the door at the base of the tower, yelling and running up the stairs toward them. Shang's bloodied sword flashed as he grunted.

His free hand flung back—covering Meiling's eyes just before his sword made contact with the soldier.

He couldn't block the sounds, however. The clang of metal on metal, the swoosh of air, the abrupt severing of a cry, a horrid *thump* that continued thumping down the flight of stairs. Was that sound . . . a *head*? Did Shang just decapitate someone?

His hand whipped back from her, no longer obscuring her vision of his flint-like jaw and blood-spattered cheek. His shoulders prevented her from seeing *most* of the body, but—

He yanked a loaded *jiaun* from its holster at his hip. "Close your eyes," he growled, aiming the weapon with his left hand up the staircase.

She didn't.

And was granted the horrifying sight of arrows hitting another guard she hadn't seen. He fell off the staircase, and Meiling barely slammed her lids shut before he hit the lower level with a nauseating thud.

Shang reloaded and holstered the weapon in half a second. Then he scooped an arm around her legs, lifting her straight off her feet as he ran down the rest of the stairs. She wrapped both arms around his neck, burying her face in his shoulder as he made a jostling leap.

Maybe she *was* in shock.

Death cries and clashing weapons rang in her ears, smothering every rational thought. She was a tiny child, helpless, unable to fight, unable to even keep herself alive—

Shang squeezed her tightly, and his voice in her ear was strained, but still steady. "We're at the door. I need to put you down because I don't know what it looks like out there. Stay close to me. I swear I won't let anything happen to you. I swear it. Just trust me and do as I say, understood? Meiling?"

She nodded against his neck, felt his thick swallow against her forehead.

Then she was on her own feet, Shang's sharp eyes roving over her face. A muscle in his cheek flexed before he turned away, unholstering his *jiaun* so he held it in his left hand, his broadsword in his right.

She pressed her palms against her ears, then her temples, shaking her head. *Snap it together, Meiling. Snap it together. You need to survive this. Be alert!*

The words didn't magically make the fog disband from her brain, but she still managed to not scream when Shang flung open the door, and ducked behind the wall. His arm guarded her body against the stone, preventing her from moving into the opening.

When no phoenix fire or arrows came shooting through the doorway, Shang leaned out. Just as quickly, he pulled back, chest heaving.

"Is it that bad?" Meiling asked.

He glanced down at her. With the edge of his sleeve, he brushed a trickle of blood away from her face. "I *will* get you out of here."

So yes, it was that bad.

"Get ready to run," he growled. "You can hold onto my belt if you need to, but not my arms. I need full range of motion."

Her numb fingers wrapped around his leather belt between his *jiaun* holster and a knife sheath, her heart beating so fast she was afraid she'd simply drop dead from sheer terror.

"Now."

Shang bolted through the door, whipping Meiling after him as she tried not to let go. A blast of heat rolled over her, smoke clogging her nose and eyes as shouts and screams ripped through the air left and right.

They'd hardly made it a few paces before Shang's blade rang against an enormous battle axe. He deflected the blow, lifted his *jiaun*, and shot the Butagin soldier before he had a chance to recover.

Then they were running again, Shang frantically reloading and Meiling gasping for air.

Suddenly, a name flashed through her mind.

Feiyan.

CHAPTER 16

FEIYAN. THAT NAME shone like a beacon into Meiling's stunned senses. Feiyan was here. Feiyan was in trouble. What had Shang said just moments ago? That once they got Meiling out of the fortress, they could retreat?

No—no, no, no, *no*.

She *couldn't* leave Feiyan behind. She *wouldn't*. And what about the rest of the captured wielders? Would they be left behind to rot in their cells? They were *dying*. At least one was already dead.

Meiling couldn't live with herself if she fled this fortress, thinking only about herself, and leaving behind the others.

Finally, her mind cleared enough for her to see through the smoke obscuring the fortress and take stock of their situation.

Dead bodies from both sides littered the main courtyard. Black scorch marks pocked the ground, the walls, as phoenixes flew overhead, incinerating Zheninghai warriors with deadly flames. Battles waged everywhere, and it was almost sickening how few Butagin soldiers were still standing, unarmed with magic as they were.

Zedong had lied, hadn't he? He'd lied to the people of Butagin—manipulated them with unfulfilled promises as he maneuvered his way into power. He claimed his magic was for everyone, and yet he withheld it so starkly from the very people he claimed to be fighting for.

Now it was *their* bodies lying on the ground, while the brigands fought on.

It wasn't just Zheninghai that needed saving from Zedong; it was also Butagin.

From her vantage point, she could have sworn that between clouds of smoke, those were *vines* at the far end of the fortress, wrapping around warriors and squeezing while they tried desperately to hack them off. Was Zedong forcing Zuan Wan to use his magic? Or . . . or . . .

Meiling ducked behind Shang just as something came flying in the air toward them. He cursed, flinging her further out of the way as a fireball crashed into the wall behind her.

"We need to get to that tower ahead of us," Shang said between firing and reloading his *jiaun*. "It's the retreat point. Our wielders should have held the spot so we can get over the wall."

Meiling was almost sprinting to keep up with him, dodging around bodies and struggling to breathe. "Shang! Feiyan is still here! And the rest of the wielders! We have to get them out!"

Wind rushed in her ears, blowing her hair out of her face.

She looked up.

A phoenix flew straight toward them, a streak of fire against the darkening sky. Eyes like charcoal fixed on Shang. But then they shifted to her, and Meiling's world tilted.

It was obviously bound to Zedong through black magic. And yet, there was something more in that gaze. Something more than a curse.

Something that called to the depths of her soul and resonated with her heart.

It wanted to be free.

That snapping beak opened.

She hit the ground hard, a snarling curse in her ears as a heavy, muscular body pinned her. A wave of intense heat blasted over her as Shang rolled them both out of the way. It took her mind a few hiccupping heartbeats before she realized what was happening, that she clung to Shang as he kept rolling, that it was the frame of his *jiaun* digging painfully into her shoulder blades.

Finally, they came to a stop, Shang on top of her, his chest heaving in time with hers beneath his breastplate. "Your lack of self-preservation instinct will be the death of me!"

She stared up into his face as beads of sweat trailed down his forehead, his temple, and said stupidly, "I'd be dead if you weren't here."

"That's what terrifies me," he growled. A second later, his head whipped up, another vicious curse springing from his lips. He yanked his *jiaun* up, bracing his knees on either side of her as he cradled her head to his chest. "Hold still, Princess."

She squeezed her eyes shut, tasting copper on her tongue as the sharp *twang* of the *jiaun* sounded in her ears. A muted cry followed the shot. *Enemy, enemy, enemy,* Meiling told the part of her that wanted to cry.

It couldn't drown out the louder voice that insisted: *human, human, human.*

A brutal killer held her in his arms right now, protecting her. She was the reason he killed. It both comforted her and utterly shocked her the violence Shang was capable of, and in this moment, when he held her to his chest while he dealt another deathblow, she couldn't be more aware of that juxtaposition.

But all this bloodshed was Zedong's fault. Not Shang's. Not Butagin's.

Zedong's.

He had to be stopped. Someone had to tell him this was enough. Someone had to stand up to him. But *who*? Who was strong enough? Who dared?

Pa could—if he was even *here*. Shang could—if he wasn't so busy trying to keep her alive.

Shang's hand slid to her waist, sweeping her up with him as he rolled to his feet. His gaze darted left and right through smoke, his eyes frantic every time he glanced toward the tower they were trying to reach. "I'm going to get you out of here." He said it through gritted teeth, as though trying to convince himself it was still possible. Meiling's gut dropped to her feet.

A shadow fell over them, wind pummeling hard.

She didn't have to look up to know another phoenix—or perhaps the same one—barreled toward them again. Shang grabbed her arm, broke into a run, and yanked her after him into a small stone building along the fortress wall.

He pulled her inside just before fire hit the pavement.

Meiling blinked against the sudden darkness of the enclosed space, her nostrils filling with the scent of oil, soot, and iron.

Metal glinted.

She screamed.

Shang, who seemed to have lost his broadsword, shoved her aside and dodged out of the way of a falling axe. Meiling hit the ground and scooted backward, scrambling to get away as Shang threw himself bodily at the enemy in the darkness. Scuffling boots and grunts filled the small space, followed by a loud crash. She groped for something, *anything*, and her hands closed around what seemed like an iron poker. She shoved up to her feet, holding the poker in front of her as a *crack* split the air.

Something caught the sparse light—*ice*—before it plunged into soft flesh.

A body hit the ground.

Silence.

"Shang?" It was half-whisper, half-whimper.

"I'm here," came a low voice from behind her.

She whirled, dropping the poker with a clang. She couldn't control herself, couldn't stop her legs from running, her arms from opening. And then she'd flung herself straight into his chest, her cheek pressed against his breastplate as she shuddered in this small, terrifying space that was almost a refuge from the storm outside.

"Shang, Shang, Shang," she gasped, choking on tears, clinging desperately to him.

Slowly, one of his strong arms came around her, pressing her closer. "We can't stay here. We have to get *out*."

"But are you hurt? You've been fighting so much—"

"Don't worry about me. Slow down your breaths; you're hyperventilating."

She stared up at him, at the face she couldn't see in the darkness. And then she burst into tears, crumpling. "I can't! I can't go with you, Shang! Feiyan is still here—we have to help her! I can't leave her behind! He'll kill her if we don't. He'll kill them all!"

Two firm hands gripped her shoulders, giving her a gentle shake. "Meiling. Stop it. *Stop it.* You need to hold it together just a little bit longer. Be strong for me. *Please.*" Did his voice just break? "I know this is the most terrifying thing you've endured, but you *must* stay strong until I get you out of here. Then you can cry all you want. Understood? Meiling, can you promise me this?"

A sob wracked her entire frame, and she shook her head. "You're not listening! *I. Can't. Leave. Feiyan.*"

His grip on her tightened, turning to ice. "We *can't* save Feiyan. But we must save you before it's too late. Your powers in Zedong's hands mean the destruction of our entire empire. I have to get you out, even if it means leaving others behind."

A terrible cold washed down Meiling's spine.

Was *this* why Shang had come to save her? Why Pa had sent an army to rescue her? Because her magic was too great a threat? Not because they cared for her? Would they have left her behind with Feiyan and the rest if her magic had been different—or if she hadn't had magic at all?

You came for me.

Of course I did—

—because I'm one of the only people who knows the danger you are to Zheninghai.

She didn't want to believe it. She didn't *want* to. But she couldn't convince herself it wasn't true. Since she'd been dragged through that portcullis, everything she'd believed was questioned, thrown into doubt. Maybe she'd been slammed into that tower wall harder than she realized, because she couldn't make any sense of the thoughts careening through her head.

What if those words spoken in her mind while she'd wielded black magic were truer than she'd been willing to admit at the time? Was her naivete and hopefulness not allowing her to see the obvious reality around her?

She was a stupid girl who'd dreamed of the moment Shang would come and save her because he *cared* for her. She'd just made a fool of herself, throwing herself into his arms, as if he wanted her there. And maybe, just *maybe*, he did. But had he given her any reason to believe that?

Not truly.

She couldn't be the weeping princess during a battle, hiding away in a little hole, begging for comfort from one of her father's warriors.

Feiyan needed her.

Meiling stepped back from Shang, drawing in a deep breath, and wiped away her tears with the back of her filthy sleeve. She probably only succeeded in smearing blood across her face. Nevertheless, she lifted her chin in the darkness, ignoring her own traitorous sniffle and the way her voice quivered.

"Tan Shangdi, as your princess, I order you to help me find and free Feiyan."

Two heavy, booted footsteps, and then Shang's breath ghosted across her face, making her hands spasm. "I don't take orders from you—not ones that go directly against His Imperial Majesty's. Don't you realize that this entire rescue mission is about *you*? And the longer you don't cooperate, the more lives are being lost? *For you?*"

Those stupid tears threatened once more, her heart twisting in a bitter knot. "But it *shouldn't* be just about me! There are so many others—"

"If you cared about others, you'd come with me. Right now."

"Help me, Shang! Help me find her, and I'll come! Please don't ask me to abandon—"

He caught her chin in an iron grip, forcing her face up toward his. Another warm breath washed over her skin, and she thought she might break in two. "Don't make me tie you up and throw you over my shoulder like a sack of rice. Because Meiling, I *will* do it. We don't have time to argue about this! We need—"

The door swung open.

Meiling whirled, a scream dying on her lips.

There, framed in the light of the dying sun and fire, was Shuren.

Shang had already unholstered his *jiaun* and taken aim.

"No!" Meiling shrieked, throwing herself bodily into Shang's arm, knocking his shot wide as arrows careened through the open doorway.

"Mei-*ling*!" Shang shouted furiously, betrayal staining his tone.

But she was *not* about to let him kill the only ally they had inside this fortress. She wrestled with his arm, struggling to keep her hold as he fought to pry her off without hurting her.

"Come with me, Highness, and he won't die," said Shuren, his tone roughened.

"She's not going *anywhere* with you," Shang snarled. With that, he twisted her wrist, forcing her to break her hold, and shoved her behind him.

"Where is Feiyan?" Meiling cried, scrambling back up and throwing herself at Shang when he lifted his *jiaun* again, ignoring his curses.

"The battle is over."

Those words were spoken with the finality of a deathblow. Meiling staggered, and it was enough for Shang to grab her, twist her wrists behind her, and yank her face-first into his side. His hand gripped her wrists like shackles, his arm pinning her to him. Restraining her—so she couldn't stop him when he lifted the *jiaun* and aimed straight for Shuren's face.

"Don't kill him!" Meiling screamed as he fired.

The arrows whizzed straight through the illusionist's face into the world beyond. The image went fuzzy around the edges and then sharpened once more. Shang's body slackened with realization. He turned horrified eyes down to Meiling, and it was like she relived that moment in the valley before Liafugen all over again.

Because she saw the very moment he realized Shuren hadn't lied.

The battle was over.

And they'd lost.

A loud *bang* echoed through the small space. Shang's eyes shuttered. His grip on her laxed.

He crumpled to the ground.

Meiling screamed, bending over him, searching for signs of wounds, for signs of life—his name echoing against the stone all around her, over and over again. Strong hands grabbed her arms, hauling her to her feet, ignoring her screams, and she barely registered it was the real Shuren, or that he'd set the flat of his blade on the ground.

Her vision was too full of Shang's collapsed form. His closed eyes.

She twisted, tears streaming down her face, trying to break Shuren's hold on her as he dragged her out into the courtyard. "Did you kill him? Is he dead? Don't let him die! Please, *please* Shuren, I beg you. He can't be dead. I can't—I can't lose him! *Shang!*"

I did this.

I did this.

I did this.

He's dead.

I killed him.

She'd tried to save one—and killed the other in the process. Killed and doomed them both.

In that moment, Meiling hated herself more than she'd ever hated anything in her entire life. More than being a societal outcast because of a lie. More than Fang Zedong.

She was never getting out of this fortress. No one would stop Zedong. Her loved ones would never be safe. She would be the death of them all.

"Allow me this mercy," Shuren whispered to her between her screams.

Before she processed what was happening, he pressed a cloth over her mouth and nose. Sweetness exploded across her senses. Her head went light as a cloud.

Then everything went black.

CHAPTER 17

MEILING HAD COME to the vault—a small room, presumably underground, with not a scrap of furniture to soften the hard stone edges—with her head in Feiyan's lap, their hands clasped, and guards standing over them like pillars of stone. Her mind was foggy, her cheeks tight from dried tears, her eyelashes crusty. Her body, however, had never felt better, despite the many, *many* hours that had passed since she'd last eaten. When she tentatively reached up to her face and touched her nose, there was no pain. Not a single bruise marred her skin.

Her heart was another matter.

He's dead. It's better that you reconciled yourself to that terrible fact and moved on, part of her said. The other part screamed, wept, wailed. *He can't be dead. He isn't dead. I won't accept it. He's alive. I'll do anything to make him be alive.*

This was a nightmare she would never wake up from.

Feiyan's free hand stroked Meiling's hair, working through tangles. Gentle and soothing. It only served to make her number. Eventually, Meiling forced herself to sit up. When she stole a glance at her friend's face, the healer didn't return the look, keeping her profile turned. On that profile, teeth nibbled a quivering lower lip.

When Meiling squeezed her hand, Feiyan finally turned. Her eyes were full of gleaming, unshed tears. Nevertheless, she offered a shaky smile and a shrug. Then she turned away, biting her lip harder.

The sight cut Meiling like a blade. She scooted closer, wrapping her arm around Feiyan and leaning her head on the healer's shoulder. Feiyan responded at once, laying her head on Meiling's, her face crumpling as a few tears slipped free.

Shuren, who watched from the opposite side of the room, didn't stop them.

Did you kill him?

She was too terrified to ask. As long as she didn't confirm Shang was dead, there was always the hope he was alive. She didn't think she could face a world that didn't have him in it.

"We should get some sleep," said Feiyan in a brisk tone that seemed a cover for her covert tears. "We might be in here all night."

They settled on the floor. No blankets, no head cushions. They rested their heads on hard stone, facing each other with clasped hands between them. Meiling closed her eyes; a shuddering breath escaped her lungs. It would be a miracle if she fell asleep in such an uncomfortable position, and yet, there was no denying the deep exhaustion creeping like a phantom behind the influences of Feiyan's healing magic.

Much faster than she thought possible, she lost herself to tormented dreams of Shang's bloody face, his horror-struck eyes, and the ghosting memory of his breath across her lips.

The silence after battle was thicker than the blood that pooled on flagstone.

When they were finally let out of the vault, it was after dawn, and not a single body remained. The phoenixes perched on their towers, their flames flickering lazily, their bellies protruding. She wanted to vomit.

The long night had passed. Daybreak shone red and bloody. The fortress stood. Zedong's defenses held. And Shang was most likely dead. Dead because of her.

She had to push away that thought. Otherwise, grief and guilt would shatter her into a thousand pieces.

She was exhausted. Exhausted, and very, very hungry. When Zedong came to retrieve them, he looked, in some ways, even worse than she felt. But that mad light shone in his eyes, and there was a determined swing to his step that scared her.

She and Feiyan were given bread to scarf down before Zedong ordered her to that dreadful chamber he reserved for her magic. There wasn't an ounce of warmth in him this morning, no veneer of kindness. Meiling didn't resist when one of the brigands escorted her up the flight of stairs, didn't resist when he kept prodding her to move faster.

Had Zedong taken prisoners?

The door opened in front of her. Her eyes roved in the dimness, trying to catch any sign of Shuren. Any sign of whether the threats she was about to face were real or painted by magic. But there was no looming shadow. Only Zedong standing with a strange look on his face, arms crossed and legs braced wide. At his feet, a man in armor knelt in chains.

Not Shang.

Zedong must have taken some of the Zheninghai warriors captive specifically for this purpose—for her to hunt through their minds and divulge their secrets.

Zedong spoke without greeting or preamble. His voice cracked slightly, as if he had been yelling all night. But his words were no less authoritative. "Confirm the purpose of last night's attack. Find any other information about where and how the emperor will strike next."

No threats. No knives held against quivering flesh. No tears or blood.

He expected her to obey.

He need not threaten her anymore. Not verbally. She knew as well as he by now that he could make her do anything. All his threats hovered in the air, compelling her feet forward toward the bed. Making her sit down on its hard surface.

At least this time, she did not think she would need help falling asleep. She was so exhausted after a night of restless dozing. Even so, before she could prepare herself, Zedong stepped forward and plunged his blade into her finger. She cried out—a thin, hollow sort of cry. Blood flowed.

Meiling rose out of her body, numbly taking stock of the room.

The prisoner knelt with his head down, but the rest of his posture indicated no submission whatsoever. His strong hands were balled into fists around the chains connecting his shackles, his young, broad shoulders set with stubbornness. What sort of mind did he possess? Would he even have the information that Zedong sought? He didn't bear the insignia of a high-ranking officer.

Her gaze strayed to Zedong, whose gaze hadn't shifted from her limp body. The gray in his hair seemed more prominent now, as did the lines forming on his face. He could only be in his forties, but he suddenly seemed so much older now. Black magic reached out like groping tentacles from his chest, overpowering whatever his natural soul-glow was.

She was tired of being his puppet. Tired of letting him win. Tired of letting him steal and take from her while clothing her in finery. Tired of listening to his lies and manipulations.

She was tired of losing those she loved to his evil machinations. She was sick that his vengeance was why someone as good, noble, and brilliant as Shang had been another body lying on the ground last night.

Feiyan fought despite knowing she would lose. She never gave up. She was no one's puppet. Feiyan was her own self. Only a fool would fight like her. A fool, or someone who refused to give up hope. Someone who believed that someday she would win. If she bided her time and fought faithfully every chance she could scrape together, someday she was bound to win.

And then no one would ever bind her again.

Pa had come to save her. Shang had come—even if it *was* just because of her magic. She was not forgotten. How many lives had been lost to recover her? How many more would be during this war?

Because they were in a war now. No more vague mentions of barbarians amassing on the northern borders. Zheninghai was at war.

They had tried to save her, and they had failed.

There was no knowing when a second attempt could be made. At least weeks, as the troops reassembled, recovered themselves, and planned a better strategy. One that probably involved taking out those deadly phoenixes sooner rather than later.

And she did not want to stay here for weeks longer.

Which meant . . .

Which meant she needed to save herself. And Feiyan.

Meiling glanced at the kneeling, rebellious, yellow-glowing wielder. She followed his angry gaze to the towering, black-clad form who held his hands behind his back. A stance of power and dominance.

Escaping was not enough.

Fang Zedong would burn the world if he could. He would tear through cities, razing as he went, all in the name of his new society that would remove shame from magicless people. A society that would be built solely around loyalty to his power. An empire forged on manipulations and deceptions and false hope.

She needed to defeat Fang Zedong. More than she needed to escape, more than she needed to be free, more than she needed anything else in the world. No one knew him like she did now. No one could have seen the destruction he was capable of, the blood he was willing to shed.

“Meiling,” Zedong growled. “Enter his mind.”

How did he know she hesitated?

She floated to the man. Someone she very much did not want to see slow-sliced to death before her. She had no choice, did she?

With a burst of speed, Meiling flung herself into his mind.

Not the young wielder’s mind.

But Fang Zedong’s mind.

CHAPTER 18

FOG CLUNG TO her awareness.

It was like walking through a dream. Meiling moved as though a syrupy marshland bogged down her limbs. Empty, darkened hallways stretched before her vision, clouded by dense, obscuring fog. It was mostly silver, but the edges were laced with blackness.

This place was familiar. Meiling recognized it from when she visited Yun and Hou while they trained. This was the Academy.

It was colorless.

She struggled to penetrate deeper into Zedong's mind. If the threshold was so difficult, what about those hidden passages where he hid his deepest secrets and fears? The things that she needed to find?

Undaunted, she slogged forward. And gradually became aware that she was not alone.

A shadow whispered on the edge of her awareness. Was that a wisp of hair that flicked away, just at the end of the hallway? She plunged after it. Having a tangible goal made the fog stop clinging so heavily and she was able to move a little faster.

Not fast enough.

As soon as she burst around the corner, she barely caught sight of a ghostly hand disappear into one of the many partitions that made up the Academy dormitories. Growling with frustration, Meiling hurried faster. She dared not speak, not in this mind. He would hear her and know she was here.

She slid open the flimsy, paper-like door and glimpsed a red robe embroidered with blue lotuses. Then the shadow was gone. There was nowhere for it to go in this tiny room, so she backed out of it and stared down the colorless hall. The fog grew thicker, shrouding her view.

There was a flash of glossy black hair.

Meiling chased it.

She chased it because she knew it. There was no one else it could be. There was no one else in this mind. Except . . .

Except voices. Voices much like the ones that had haunted her when she'd touched the purple, sharp-edged, poisonous leaf. Voices . . . No, there was only one voice. But it was muddling and speaking over itself again and again, incessantly. She could hardly make out the words.

Then, as though the sun broke through clouds, she heard them clear as day just as she almost caught up to the vanishing shadow.

I pity you. I pity you. I pity you.

A woman's voice. A gentle, brave woman's voice. A voice edged in heartfelt emotion, in honesty.

Pity, pity, pity, pity, pity.

That one word rung out above the rest. Meiling reached out and her fist closed around vanishing lotus-embroidered robes.

At long last, she cried out, *Ma! Come back to me! Stop running!*

The figure kept running. She laughed sweetly, and Zedong's mind reacted to that sound. Beneath the choking fog was the pulse of a beating heart. This voice, this *memory* of her mother, was much younger than when she had ever heard it. Tinges of raw emotion, of hopefulness and belief.

Of naivete.

A roar sounded above. The dormitory walls shredded and crashed in a rustle to the smooth, cold floor. Plaster fell straight through Meiling's formless spirit.

Blackness descended.

Something lowered from the ceiling. It crawled with the stealth of a spider, chittering almost silently as it came. It wasn't a soul, wasn't part of Zedong's mind, and yet it was *almost* sentient. Its aliveness burned her nostrils.

Then, its intention wafted over her with the force of a tsunami.

It was going to eat her. It was going to swallow her—devour her soul.

There was nowhere to run and nowhere to hide as it bore down on her with dizzying speed.

Meiling's physical eyes flew open as her body was smashed into the stone wall of Zedong's fortress.

No sound could escape from her throat as she lay stunned on the ground. Not even a low, guttural groan. The pain had not set in yet. Her body still thought she was asleep, still thought she was about to be eaten by whatever terrifying thing lived and breathed in Zedong's mind. Her mind still thought she watched snatches of her mother flitting through Academy dormitories, still felt the very distinct lack of memory threads lacing through those colorless halls.

So when Zedong dragged her up again and hurled her into the wall with unnatural strength, Meiling didn't try to brace her fall with her hands. She hit hard, slumped again.

Belatedly, pain burst across her mind.

A scream broke through her shock. Self-preservation kicked in, and she tried to scramble away from Zedong's booted foot. He kicked her in the ribs—something cracked—and she screamed again.

He was yelling. The words slowly coalesced in her brain.

"I would have made you my own princess! I would have made you my own daughter, my own heir! And instead, you fight me! You throw my kindness in my face! Wicked girl!"

With her last strength, Meiling lifted her bruised face heavily from the floor, iron burning her tongue, warmth dribbling down her chin. She could not raise herself high enough to look him in the eye, but she could lift her eyes to see his knees.

"I never wanted to be anyone's princess," she croaked.

Another blow landed, followed by another. And another.

They were falling too fast for her to process, to hardly even feel. All she knew was that she was dying.

She curled into a tight ball, the pain slowly growing more distant with every heartbeat, enough that she could spare a thought that she had been brave. That bravery cost her life, but she had stood up to Zedong for once. She had not let him continue to manipulate her and threaten her. She had fought back. Truly fought back. Not just resisted only to comply later.

She had *defied* him. This was a death worth dying. And maybe on the other side of death, in the afterlife, she'd find Shang, and he would hold her close and kiss her until she forgot the pain she'd experienced in this fortress. This life and death would be nothing but an obscure dream. It wouldn't compare to the joy she'd experience to be once more reunited with Shang.

Her awareness vanished into darkness.

The world was flowing warmth. A bath of steamed milk and honey, refusing to let her leave that warmth.

Her mind cleared slowly, bit by bit.

"You really got yourself banged up. You must have stirred up some *steep* mischief indeed. I'm impressed."

"Feiyan?" She opened her eyes, but everything was still dark. She tried again, to no avail. Was she blind? The sudden thought zapped through her brain like a flash of lightning. "I can't see!"

"You're in the dungeon, sweetheart," Feiyan said. "Some guards came and dropped you here a while ago. I've been busy trying to heal you. For a moment there, I thought you were too far gone. But we're managing. It just has taken a long time."

"Huh?"

She was lying on her back on the stone-cold floor of the dungeon. If not for Feiyan's warm, healing hands warding off the cold, she would be shivering in an instant. "Thank you," she mumbled. "I thought I was dead."

"What could you have possibly done to get beaten to a pulp like that? One minute you're the queen of this place and the next you're half dead back in the dungeon. Did you try to escape?"

"I defied him," Meiling whispered. She could not help the grin that spread across her face. "It wasn't much . . . but I went into his mind instead of the prisoner's."

Feiyan whistled under her breath.

"It was only a little, but I still stood up to him."

Like you.

Then Meiling whispered, "How are you so brave?"

Feiyan laughed and squeezed Meiling's hand. "I've told you before. I'm not brave. I'm just stupid."

Meiling scooted up into a seated position, not daring to let go of Feiyan's hands. "When the battle happened . . . I was trying to find you. And I ran into Shang."

There was a tiny little gasp on the other side of the bars, paired with a slight jolt of the muscles in Feiyan's hands. Things Meiling knew Feiyan hoped she had not noticed.

Hu Fen had said something ages ago on their journey to Liafugen. That the healer from the Academy had harbored feelings for Shang. Meiling closed her eyes, almost wishing she could have taken back the words.

"Was he one of the wielders here?" Feiyan asked, trying to make her voice sound light.

"He tried to rescue me."

"Was he killed?" she asked quickly. "Trying to save you?"

That bitter panic from yesterday swelled in her heart, the memory of her own screams rattling around her thoughts. She could barely get the words out. "I . . . I don't know. I'd been trying to convince him to stop, to help me find you, and then . . . then he was hit. Shuren drew me away before I could tell if he was alive."

"What? Are you an idiot?"

Meiling blinked, her grief forgotten in her confusion. "I beg your pardon?"

"You tried to convince him to go *back* for me, instead of getting yourself out of here? You're so *stupid*! You should have taken your opportunity, for the fathers' sakes!"

"I couldn't leave you behind! I don't think they knew all the captives were kept here. They only knew I was here." Her cheeks burned. But Feiyan had a right to know. "They were only coming for me. If I had gone with Shang, they would have left. They would have left you and the others here."

Feiyan was silent.

"If he's still alive, then he must hate me now," Meiling mumbled. It was a useless thing to say, stupid to voice, but she couldn't have swallowed back the words if she'd tried.

Feiyan didn't seem to mind. "That would make two of us that Shangdi hates. Then again, he never cared about anything except earning the next accolade and being better than everyone else. Going from indifferent to hated in Shangdi's mind is not difficult."

Those words were bitter.

"He thought I betrayed him."

"Well, he can think what he wants, can't he? What matters is that you know you didn't." She shifted in her cell and her boot scraped on stone.

Meiling licked her lips. "What do we do now?"

Feiyan shrugged. "We escape before it's too late. You know what? I think they forgot to feed us. I could be wrong . . . I don't exactly have a way to tell time in here. But I'm *pretty* sure they forgot to feed us."

Just then, a loud, distant sound of a door resounded through the stone.

"On cue." Feiyan seemed to smirk. "I'm famished. You want to know something interesting? As long as I'm touching you, you can't starve. Pretty nifty, huh?"

"Very," Meiling said. As much as she hated the darkness and coldness and stench of the dungeon, it was very good to be back with Feiyan.

Light flared painfully in her eyes when their door opened. It calmed immediately, however, with Feiyan's grip. Feiyan, on the other hand, shielded her eyes. But instead of shoving food under the door, the two figures approached Feiyan's cell. One silhouette was tall and familiar—*Shuren.* He turned a key until it shrieked.

"Don't fight me," he said in a low voice, tinged with exhaustion. "Please, Feiyan."

Feiyan recoiled at the sound of her name. She let go of Meiling and stood up. "Give me one good reason. Because I'm seeing a very good reason *to* fight. Several, now that I think of it."

"We're taking you to another cell. Separating you two," Shuren replied, glancing over at Meiling. "Orders."

All Meiling's hopes dashed to tiny pieces.

"Coward," Feiyan spat, prowling against the far wall of her cell. "Dragon-blasted *coward.*"

He stiffened. "Please. I don't want to fight you."

"Too bad."

Shuren muttered something in another language and the guard behind him stepped forward as Shuren withdrew a cloth from his pocket.

"Last chance or else I'm going to drug you," Shuren said, his voice tight.

"Feiyan!" Meiling cried, trying to reach toward her through the bars.

Feiyan's gaze snapped to hers, fiery in its intensity. Meiling wanted to tell her that she shouldn't fight, that Shuren would subdue her anyway, and he did not want to hurt her. But she held her tongue as she held Feiyan's eyes.

Feiyan shifted her focus to the two men approaching her. She barred her teeth.

The guard lunged first, took the brunt of Feiyan's quick maneuvers. Right behind him, as she almost pinned the first guard, Shuren leapt and grabbed the back of her head, smothering her face with the cloth.

She passed out almost instantly.

"Feiyan!" Meiling cried.

Shuren swept her limp body into his arms and strode out with the other guard. They took the lantern with them, and soon Meiling's world was plunged into darkness.

CHAPTER 19

D*RIP, DRIP, DRIP.*

Meiling huddled in the cold darkness, alone. Numb. This was not how she had imagined things ending up. She hadn't thought that she would find herself alone in the dungeon. She should have known—should have considered the possibility. After all, Zedong was not stupid. She was weaker alone.

That was why she had wanted to believe his lies. She had been alone.

At least now guilt over special treatment didn't gnaw at her gut. She was just another captive now. Just another wielder, far from home, a slave to a wicked man who would break her until she was no more than crumbling dust.

But she had defied him and even now, after her bones had been broken and reknit, after she sat in the darkness for hours, she smiled.

It took effort and probably did not look much like a smile, but what did that matter?

She was not a coward anymore.

Or, at least, she was less of a coward than she had feared.

She tilted her head to lean against the iron bars separating her from Feiyan's old cell. Hair fell in her face, and she made no move to wipe it away. Instead, it puffed upward with each breathy exhale, then returned to cling to her face when she inhaled.

Zedong had seemed, in many ways, to understand her better than anyone else. He understood what it was like to be forgotten, and unlike Ma, he was no longer a low magic-wielder. He was powerful. Like Meiling was powerful.

Half the time he had guessed correctly at her thoughts. He had a finger on the pulse of her hesitation. He'd sensed her weakness and brought her out of the dungeon, courting her allegiance because he knew she'd experienced the same flaws in the empire.

He understood her.

And yet . . .

Yet he hated her.

The thought made her remember the dark magic spewing out of Meiling's memory of Ma's voice.

You think you are only misunderstood.

That was how she had felt with Shang and Feiyan. And . . . everyone, if she was honest. She'd always thought that, if they knew her, if they saw the richness of her mind, if they saw how deeply she loved, if they saw who she really was—then they would love her.

Zedong had plucked on that very belief when he had enticed her with promises of a society with no shame for those without magic.

In some unnamed, hidden part of her heart, she had always thought that if Shang took the time to get to know her, he would love her too. But he had seen the depths of her devotion only last night, and he had hated her for it.

The black magic had indeed brought out her greatest flaw. She faced it now with wide, dilated eyes in the darkness. That who Meiling was—who she *truly* was—would not be enough for many people.

Many people would bear no affection for her, and she had always placed this on them. *They* did not try to understand her. *They* jumped to conclusions about who she was. *They* believed falsehoods.

When truthfully, Meiling had faults. Loves, joys, cares, fears. And some people would hate her for the very thing that made her special in someone else's eyes. Some people simply would not like her. Their personalities would not mesh.

Shang's was probably one of them.

Shang, who bristled at thwarted plans. Shang, who refused to entangle himself with "distractions" like Feiyan and Meiling unless specifically and strictly commanded.

Please don't be dead, Shang. Please, please.

Could she ever erase that memory of his eyes as realization dawned? Would she ever be able to see him like she had remembered him until last night—tall in his saddle, Fen held before him, and with a slightly crooked smile on his face? Shang, pleading for the brigands to be gentle with Meiling? Shang, holding her to his chest and comforting her in his arms? Or were those memories lost to those vivid, furious black pupils in her mind's eye that even now glared at her with venom? Or worse, his collapsed, motionless form?

She should sleep. She should . . .

Spattering blood spells!

Ma would never forgive her for that language.

But why was she still trapped in her mind? Surely she had torn enough down that she could have slipped out?

Meiling growled. She whirled, trying to catch her bearings in the glittering palace of her mind. There. That was the way to the palace entrance. There, she could inspect the bindings and see if she could escape them.

She ran through brightly lit corridors, flinging open doors and thick silk dividers. She looked over her shoulder, suddenly afraid to glimpse a horrible black shadow. But as far as she could tell, she was alone.

When she glanced behind her, there was a flash of white. Looking down, she found she wore only her silken nightdress. Her feet were bare and fuzzy around the edges, where they hovered a breath above the floor.

Irrelevant.

Meiling pushed forward through her mindscape. She was almost to the entrance. Maybe there were still tatters of the crown lying at its base; then she could tear away at the rest of Zedong's spell that held her captive here.

That was impossible. She had thrown away the leaf. If there were remaining traces of the black magic, shouldn't she be able to hear its distinctive humming? The horrifying whispers? Shouldn't she see shadows trying to catch up to her?

She rounded the corner and there was the entrance.

Meiling let out a piteous wail. *No!* She staggered back, falling into a heap on the ground, when her ankle caught on the hem of her nightdress.

Before her vision, the black barrier throbbed in full strength—stronger, even. The little peeks through to the other side had been filled in, and the black magic extended higher and wider along the wall encasing the door.

No, she whimpered.

All of that work. Pointless.

Had Zedong renewed it? Or had it regrown?

Dragons blast it! She only wanted to be free! She would be willing to obey Zedong's orders about how she could use her magic if he would only let her be free. Was there no escape from this dungeon? From herself?

She stopped. She looked up at the white ceilings trimmed with polished gold. Memory threads shimmered next to her fingertips. At least . . .

At least she found her mind to be an interesting place.

She grabbed a memory thread. Whatever was nearest. It sparked in her fingers. It thrummed with life, with a flavor of her older brother. Smiling, she followed it through familiar hallways until she reached his chambers. She glimpsed Yun chasing her straight here when they had been little. A peel of childlike laughter drifted past her.

If I catch you, I'll blow you to smithereens! Yun had threatened, tearing around the corner as Meiling screeched with delight and flung herself into his room. She slammed his door shut in his face and, with a satisfied little girl smirk, locked it with the slide of a bolt.

You don't dare burn the door, she had told him with a giggle. *Pa will kill you.*

Aww, not fair! Come back out!

And then a little burst of fire licked under the door, close enough for heat to radiate into her feet. *Yun!* she shrieked, jumping to the side.

He laughed at her. *Come out or I'll burn your toes off.*

She was laughing too. High-pitched and near squealing. She danced around Yun's flames, quite literally playing with fire.

What are you doing? An adult voice sounded with alarm on the other side of the door. *Prince Yun!*

Young Meiling slipped the bolt open in a flash and scurried under Yun's bed to hide. Outside, a sound like he scrambled to his feet and spewed out some sort of explanation to his nursemaid. *You are ten years old,* the older woman reasoned patiently aloud to him. *You should remember to be the dignified prince you are.*

Bless the fathers, he did not snitch on Meiling. As soon as he had dutifully received his scolding, he tried the door and found it gave. He closed it in a hurry and then hissed, *Where are you? I'm going to murder you!*

Her hand over her mouth was not enough to muffle her giggle. And then Yun dropped to the ground, snatched her leg, and dragged her out from under the bed as she tried to kick him in the face.

Meiling laughed at the memory, smiling as she relived the heat of Yun's touch and lively play. He had always been the more fun sibling. Hou had spent much of her younger days pouting and complaining, and when she grew older, she just liked to pick fights. Besides, since she had been so much younger than them, she could hardly be considered a playmate.

Yun was only two years older than Meiling—though he had often lorded those two years over her head when they were children.

Back then, her lack of magic wasn't a problem. Of course, there had always been the hope that she would develop it later. Everyone hoped this, except for Ma and Pa, who knew the truth about her magic. When they were young, magic and meeting their empire's expectations hadn't been a concern. They had just been three siblings. Fighting, playing, wrestling, learning.

Eventually, they learned how terrible a thing it was that the daughter of a powerful emperor had no magic. Eventually, Yun and Hou inevitably suffered because of Meiling's supposed curse. Eventually, she sensed the divide between them. Between her and Yun.

Yun had always been good to her. When he wasn't singeing her clothes, tripping her, or pulling her hair, that is. But he had never been good at hiding his feelings. So when he started being uncomfortable when she visited him while he was around his Academy friends, she noticed.

Meiling followed memory threads through her visits to the Academy. She had always loved watching him fight in the arena and how he grew better and better. At first, he had been happy to see her there. He'd received her excited congratulations afterward with a brotherly shrug and blush of pride. Slowly, it had changed, until she realized how aware he was of how his friends perceived her. His gladness never shifted, but it was overshadowed.

She started saving her visits for big battle examinations rather than his weekly arena fights. When she congratulated him, she waited until she found him alone—or mostly alone—and then she gave him her heartfelt praise.

He appreciated it. He never said so, but she knew he did. It was clear he disliked the way people thought of her, but he was so immersed in the world of the Academy. Strength, power, and prowess were everything.

As far as Yun knew, she was as devoid of those things as a fuzzy, yellow duckling.

Meiling sat sprawled in the hallway outside Yun's room, reliving so many memories. Now that she did so, she could catch glimpses of Shang in the background, in another arena fight. He had always been there, on her periphery, and she had never noticed him.

In all her memories, he looked very stern. Even when he was much younger, he had been so solemn. Focused.

Please don't be dead.

She grabbed frustrated fistfuls of her should-be scraggly hair. It was thick, glossy, like she had just brushed it for bed. Soft, unlike how her hair must feel in the waking world. Why was Shang always so close in her thoughts? She almost wished that she dared let him into her mind. Like Shuren had let Feiyan. Then maybe she could have someone to talk to, maybe it would take the edge off the constant ache of her heart.

Such considerations were foolish. She didn't deserve to think about that when she was the reason he was dead.

But the thought of his name brought a flood of memories. The time he'd kept her from falling into the lotus pond at the Graduation festival. All the days he'd helped her mount and dismount. His constant determination to keep her safe, to throw himself in harm's way to protect her. The time he'd pulled her sopping wet self out of a river and carried her to shore, commandeering Fen's cloak for her. Him holding her close in the saddle they shared when she lost her balance. His growls when she tended his wounds. And . . . and when he'd leaned down . . .

Now was not the time to be remembering how it felt when he had awkwardly cradled her in his arms and kissed her.

She should wake up.

The dungeon was not as dark as it had been when she had fallen asleep. It was also not as quiet.

There was a blinding light and a terrible ruckus of echoing banging.

Oh.

Brigands had come for her.

Every bone and muscle in her body was stiff with cold and sleep. That did not stop the brigands—no sign of Shuren—from hauling her to her feet and dragging her between them like a ragdoll.

They could only be going to one place.

At least, the way Meiling figured, Zedong had one and only one use for her outside of the dungeon. He should have no other reason to send for her.

Afternoon sun blinded her like fire-hot irons. No matter how tightly she squeezed her eyes shut, she could not make them stop burning. Not until the light dimmed and she found herself thrown to splintery floorboards at someone's feet.

"Princess Meiling," Zedong's ice-cold voice rumbled.

She blinked and was able to look up almost high enough to meet his gaze. "Fang Zedong," she returned, not caring to hide the venom in her voice.

"I gave you a chance. Many chances." His voice grew darker with each word. He readjusted his stance, stepping closer to hover menacingly over her braced body. "You refused my kindness. Alas, you leave me no choice but to threaten."

Meiling gritted her teeth. She flashed defiant eyes up at him. "When have you ever not threatened me? When have you been kind to me?"

Zedong crouched before her, one knee slamming into the floorboards and making them shudder. He snatched Meiling's chin and dragged her face upward to meet his gaze. "I said I had use of you," he seethed. Metal scraped against metal. Her blood turned to ice. Cold steel pressed sharp against her cheek and fear clambered up her throat. "But I can mar your pretty face beyond recognition. I can torture you within an inch of your life, and still make you my slave. I can make you watch this fellow—" He jerked her chin so she could see stubborn eyes flashing between hair that fell in the young wielder's face. "I can make you watch him suffer and die. And as much as I *prefer* using your magic, old fashioned torture will work in a pinch. I am not afraid to kill you, little one. The more you fight, the less useful you are." He pressed the blade harder under the curve of her cheekbone and she winced at the sting, then again as wetness dripped down her cheek.

Her breaths were shudders. Every muscle was braced with fear. She held her tongue—she had nothing to say, anyway. She breathed in and out and stared past the hand holding the knife against her face, her gaze latching on that lotus clasp holding Zedong's black cloak in place.

There was a long, exhaling sigh. The knife eased away and Zedong stepped to his feet, loosening his hold on her chin. "I believe I have made myself clear. Go into this prisoner's mind and confirm the purpose of last night's attack. Find any other information about future plans. You have one hour."

Before she could speak, could think of a way around it, could try to fight again, Zedong grabbed her hand and plunged something sharp into her now-callused fingertip. A little cry escaped her lips, and she burst free of her body.

Immediately, there was no mistaking the difference. Zedong's

Immediately, there was no mistaking the difference. Zedong's mind was hedged in black, angry magic. It swarmed around his head so tightly that she could not even make out his face. He had taken precautions. He never wanted her in his mind again.

She didn't want to go back either.

"I'll make this easier." Zedong's voice rang out in the sparse chamber above the same young wielder chained before him. "Every ten minutes, my blade will take one slice of his flesh. Here's the first."

The young wielder could not stop his cry. It burst into her floating shadow body, rattling her tether. She screamed soundlessly as blood poured from a shallow cut in the man's neck. His breaths came hard and fast.

Meiling flew into his mind without another delay.

CHAPTER 20

SHE STOOD IN darkness.

It was not complete darkness. It was not a hungry, devouring darkness like the dungeon. Neither was it the colorless gloom of Zedong's mind. Instead, this mind was dark, but edged in light that seemed to have no source.

Before her, tall walls rose until they disappeared into blackness. Forbidding stone formed the ground beneath her and the walls framing her. Meiling stepped forward and in the strange, unexplainable light in the darkness, found a jagged scrape sunken deep into that stone.

Claw marks?

Is anyone there? a man's voice, tight with strain, spoke.

I am here, Meiling whispered in response. Awareness of his name permeated the air in his mind. *You are . . . Cao Renshu?*

And you are Princess Meiling? I thought you had no magic.

Apparently, it was safer as a secret, she muttered. She took a few steps into Renshu's mind and the path split in two. More claw-like scrapes were scattered erratically on the wall, sometimes on the floor, too.

Do you have a monster in your mind?

A wave of confusion rolled through him. *Um . . . I don't think so.*

Why are there claw marks on the walls? Is this a labyrinth? Strange questions, she knew, but they needed to be asked.

Understanding seemed to flash. Was it a trick of her eyes that it suddenly seemed a little brighter?

Oh. Well, this is embarrassing. I . . . uh . . .

He was thinking it, so she knew it before he spoke it.

I sometimes lose my temper.

So you destroy your mind? Meiling raised an eyebrow. There was something about this mind that instantly put her at ease in a way she hadn't experienced . . . maybe ever? *An interesting coping method.*

I don't destroy it! I just add personality.

Meiling snorted.

What? he demanded. *You can do whatever you like with your mind.*

Fair enough. Meiling held up her hands in a placating gesture that he could not sense. *I must look through your mind. I will be as swift as I can.*

A shudder coursed through him, followed by grim determination, and the cut on his neck throbbed like it sliced her own skin.

I will be as fast as I can, she repeated. She reached out with her fingers and touched the threads shimmering around her. How different these memories were from hers! The vast majority of them involved the Academy in some form or another. She touched a thread and her heart lurched in response. *You are close friends with Shang?* she asked suddenly, almost desperately. Shang hadn't seemed the type to have friends.

Yeah, Renshu said. Her words brought his memories of Shang to the forefront of his mind, and the thread in her hand glowed brighter.

He was with you during the battle, she spewed. *Do you know if he lived? I saw him, but I wasn't sure . . .*

A question flickered through Renshu's mind but was immediately swept away as unimportant. *I do not know what happened to him. Many died.* A fierce stab of emotion followed his words. Guilt, sorrow—*deep* sorrow—and fear.

Physical pain swept those emotions away, sweeping like wildfire in his veins, flaring in his hand. A voice—

"In another ten minutes, I'll slice again."

Meiling redoubled her efforts, her mind reeling with the throbbing of his pain. She wanted to soothe him somehow, but she needed to focus. She felt along the threads. More Academy memories—history lectures, early morning training, late nights in the library studying with Shang, battles in the arena.

Renshu was apparently one who possessed unnatural strength. When she had seen him chained in the chamber, he certainly looked tall and strong, but his physical body did not look capable of the strength she found in his memories. Strength that was now bound.

That was when she noticed the subtle hums of black magic. She thought she heard them—under the floor?

Where's your soul tether? Meiling asked, hoping he could hear her over the flashes of pain he now braced against. *He's bound your strength.*

My what? Renshu's strained voice echoed in the stone labyrinth of his mind.

The very center of you. The thing that binds your soul to your body. Where is it?

There was prickling confusion. A sense of lostness. *I don't know what my mind looks like,* he said at long last. *I don't know how to guide you anywhere.*

Meiling bit her fleshless lip. The threads of his mind must lead back to his soul tether. Mazelike as his mind was, could she grab hold of a memory thread and follow it back to the center?

Her fingers closed around spider silk. She tore off down rising hallways of darkness and strange low light. *I suppose the easiest thing is to ask you what the purpose of that battle was.*

To rescue you, Renshu said simply.

Nothing else?

Nothing else that I knew. I'm not exactly a general, though.

In different circumstances, she would like to sit and talk to Renshu. His instinctive good nature, easy humor, and kindness permeated her as his heart pulsed with deep feeling.

He seemed a fitting companion for one as icy as Shang.

Did you know that the twelve captive wielders are here, too? Li Feiyan is one of them. The healer.

Surprise jolted through his body, followed by sharp concern at the mention of Feiyan's name. And . . . something else. Something . . .

Meiling blinked, almost shocked by the realization. Shuren, it turned out, was not the only one to harbor feelings for the vibrant healer. Unlike Shuren, these feelings had been here a long, long time.

No, I did not know. I do not think the others knew either. Is Li Feiyan alright?

She's lively and undaunted as ever, Meiling replied.

A curl of tension eased from his shoulders. *I'm glad to hear it.*

It was as she had suspected. Feiyan and the other wielders had not been abandoned; their whereabouts were simply unknown. Had a band of wielders tracked Meiling while the three brigands dragged her halfway across the country to this fortress?

If she did not have a tight hold on the threads of Renshu's memories, she would have lost herself in the twists and turns of his mind. Phoenixes take this disorder! If this were Shang's mind, she would be able to find everything within a snap. His memories had to be stored in the cabinets at the back of the hallway that formed his mind. They were probably meticulously labeled and organized.

Would you rather tell me everything or have me hunt for it? Meiling asked suddenly, bolting down another twist. The ground gave way to stairs, and she hurled down, floating at the last second before she smashed into the floor and lost her physical projection of her body. *If you tell me what he wants, we can finish this quickly and you won't be hurt anymore. If you don't tell me, then I might not be able to find everything he wants. In which case, we will take the full hour and you will be sliced several more times. If he's not satisfied, he'll send me in again later.*

Gritty determination formed in Renshu's chest. *You find it. Perhaps the fathers will bless us and you won't find the important things.*

Several things hovered just beneath his subconscious. Thoughts—information—he tried desperately *not* to think of. He quickly realized the folly of such a plan and, in an effort to keep those thoughts out of his mind, he made conversation.

How do you know Shang?

Once she found his soul tether, she could find where all the memory threads converged in one place, so she could inspect each one until she found the ones she was looking for. While she followed strands, she did not need to think much. So she obliged his desire for distraction.

He and Hu Fen were my guides and protectors when the palace was deemed too dangerous for me to stay. How ironic life had become.

The secret mission he was not very excited about. Renshu connected the little smidges of information he had received. *He could not tell me much, but he was frustrated. Said he was going to be gone for a month. I did not understand why he was mad. It seemed like whatever it could be was a prestigious thing.*

Shang does not seem to be motivated only by that which is most prestigious, Meiling responded, hurling down another staircase and taking a hard left. This path was particularly scraped up, but she kept her comments to herself.

Indeed. He hates showy prestige. Always has. Thinks it's stupid. There was a smile behind that voice. A smile that was immediately cut off by another burst of searing pain.

Renshu! Meiling cried.

Don't . . . He gasped aloud at the pain, and the walls of the labyrinth closed in on themselves until the space for her to run was hardly wider than her own small shoulders.

She rushed onward, refusing to despair. She was getting closer to that tether. *Closer, closer.* She had to be! Small, unused memory threads converged in the one she was holding, making it thicker and stronger. She gripped it tighter, hardly feeling anything but the skin of her own palms and fingers as she ran, ran, ran.

She broke through the winding maze and stared down into a long, straight path that stretched for dozens of li until it disappeared into blackness. In the center of that blackness, a pinprick of light blazed.

That had to be the tether. It *had* to be. Meiling abandoned her physical projection and flew as fast as she could. The light grew from the size of a pinhead to a fingertip, then to the size of a strawberry, a dinner plate.

Why must it be so far away?

Faster and faster she flew until the light was almost blinding. For a split second, she blinked out of Renshu's mindscape and found herself staring through his eyes at drops of blood spattered on the wood planks. She quickly blinked again and slowed so she did not pass straight through the soul tether.

His tether glowed, shimmering with life. Renshu's life, his very soul and essence, anchoring his spirit to his body. A horrifying thought crossed her mind. Could she . . . *break* that tether? Could she sever his life?

She didn't want to find out.

Another flash of burning pain. Another gasp from Renshu and the walls closed in tighter. A burst of blackness sputtered and flared around the soul tether. Meiling fell backward as the surge of black magic restrained his power. Preventing him from using his feral strength.

She needed to act fast. She reached out and touched his soul tether. It buzzed with Renshu's very personality, his character, the loves that shaped his life, his beliefs, his very *himness*. Despite the stress and strain of the moment, she was in awe of this ability to touch, feel, to know what made another person who he was.

Renshu was brave, good-hearted, and willing to lie down his life for a stranger in a heartbeat. He did not get caught up wandering round and round on decisions. He acted quickly, purposefully, but not rashly. He was loyal to his empire, devoted to his younger sister and his mother. His heart still ached at the loss of his loving father, but it was not a bitter ache. It was one that was tinged with joy because of the goodness of their relationship. Nothing triggered his anger like injustice, and he could hardly contain himself when faced with wrongness.

No wonder Shang loved him.

Meiling followed the tether until it began splitting into hundreds of leads. Then she closed her eyes and touched each one. Quickly, only enough to get a faint impression. There was one fat thread that led to his life at the Academy. Another fat one leading to his family memories. Finally, she landed on a sapling of a memory thread, one that was young and tenuous. His career thread.

She gripped hold of it and followed it back down the long, dark corridor. Whenever it frayed into smaller threads, she touched those and chose one to follow. With each step, she came closer and closer to the information she needed.

This had been so much easier in Wan's mind. She had not needed to find Wan's soul-tether. He stored his memories of the palace *at* the palace. His mindscape was familiar. She knew the layout of it well. But Renshu's mind was quite literally a maze.

One of his career threads faintly hummed of a classmate. Another friend. A friend who did not get the appointment she wanted. She had gotten something much lower, something that was both unsuitable for her talent and lower than her skill deserved. There were claw marks on the wall here.

Finally, she reached the part of his mind that held the information he knew about the war. She stood at the bottom of three flights of stone stairs, the walls disappearing high into the blackness on either side of her. Another slice of his flesh sent her sprawling back. This one had been deeper. He made no sound, but stone began crumbling and falling down the stairs. Walls pushed closer, so close that she had to adjust herself sideways. Eventually, she would need to abandon her physical projection altogether.

If she did not hurry, could she be crushed in this mind? Crushed by the strain and pain he bore?

Was his life the only one at stake?

She reached the end of the thread.

Where was his knowledge? In Wan's mind, it had been carefully filed away. But there was no furniture here where he could store knowledge. It was only stone, stone, and more stone. Meiling threw herself against the wall, running her palms along the cool, rough surface. Nothing gave. There did not seem to be any knowledge stored in the stone.

Renshu, where is your knowledge? I cannot find it! Meiling spewed in frustration. *I'm looking everywhere!*

I can't help you. His limbs trembled and his strength wavered. A new wave of determination pushed back the walls, easing her claustrophobia. *Even if I could, I won't. I'm not helping you give this qilin-spawn anything.* Then, *you only have ten minutes.*

Panic flared bright in her chest. She reached out and grabbed the thread again. She didn't want to do this, but it seemed the only option. Closing her eyes, she lost herself in his memory.

Renshu strapped on his armor. Beside him, Shang did the same. They were both silent. The plan seemed risky, and Shang had told him two options he had come up with that he thought would cost fewer lives. But they were to follow orders, and even when Renshu suggested Shang tell his ideas to the lieutenant, he had shaken his head wordlessly. Renshu was to be part of the force attacking the wall of the fortress, while Shang was to be one of the few who would sneak over the opposite wall to infiltrate the fortress while the majority of Fang's forces were occupied. Renshu did not dare voice his fear for Shang's life. There were so few of them that if Fang suspected such a maneuver, they could be quickly and easily eradicated.

Shang had not been surprised at this assignment. Renshu had been, partially because they were often paired together. It would make sense that the young, inexperienced wielders would be the ones thrown in as a distraction. Yet Shang was placed in the special force. Either because his skill was considered much beyond his years, or because his life was considered more expendable. Renshu hoped it was the first.

If they failed at recovering the princess, they'd bring a full set of troops and there had been talk of siege, but that was deemed too risky. There was always the chance of Fang using the princess as leverage. That was what limited their military action.

There was also talk of marching on Butagin in a counterattack to intimidate Fang and his forces. So many things hinged on how this attack went. If they could successfully free the princess from being a bargaining tool, that would give them many more options.

Renshu clapped Shang on the back. "Get the princess and don't die, all right?"

"Likewise." Shang smiled, tight lipped, and gripped Renshu's arm in a brotherly gesture. "Be careful."

Renshu nodded once, and they strode opposite directions, neither looking back—

Meiling hit something hard. In her physical body. She . . . she was in her physical body. She opened her eyes to find the world spinning. Tilting on its axis. She was going to slide all the way down the tilting floor until she went flying against the walls that rocked around her.

Flinging her arms wide to brace herself, she swallowed obsessively to keep from vomiting. She was gasping, falling one way, then the other.

And then she was being hauled to her feet. Meiling scrabbled with her hands, trying to find anything solid. Slowly, the world stopped shifting and tilting, and she found herself blinking up at Zedong's snarling face.

"What did you find?"

She opened her mouth, wanted to hurl an insult at his face, but a tortured cry broke through her awareness. "Renshu!" she cried, trying to shake herself free of Zedong.

"Tell me!" Zedong shook her shoulders vigorously, making her head snap back and forth on her neck painfully.

"Their goal was to rescue me," Meiling sputtered. "They were planning to have two groups, one to attack—"

"Yes, I am aware of how they attacked us. What are their next steps?"

She glanced at Renshu, bleeding from multiple wounds all over his body. She gasped for air, but her chest was too tight for a full breath. "It depended on whether they rescued me or not. He did not seem to know."

Zedong loosed his hold on her and she fell to the ground in a heap. She was scooting away from him, trying to reach the wall so she could lean against it, when he shouted, "Next!"

The door opened again.

She closed her eyes, shuddering against the cold wall. Not another one. She was too exhausted, too drained to keep fighting. Why did he wake her so violently? It took her so long to recover. A sob clogged in her throat. She bowed her head and let her tangled hair fall over her face.

"Infiltrate this prisoner's mind," Zedong growled harshly. "Find out what the empire's next plans are."

Meiling said nothing, staying crumpled against the wall, as far away from him as she could get. But in two strides, he was crouching beside her, gripping her arm painfully and hauling her up.

Too fast, he backhanded her across the face.

Stars spun in her vision, pain erupting across her face. She couldn't think, not through her dizziness, not through the searing burn on her cheek.

"Did you hear me, girl? Answer me!" Zedong shouted, grabbing her jaw and forcing her to look at him. At his wild eyes.

Meiling could only nod mutely.

Then she glanced at the prisoner, forced to kneel with his hands chained behind his back. He watched her with widened black eyes, his mouth open in horror.

It was Shang.

CHAPTER 21

MEILING'S HEART GAVE a painful, frantic, hiccupping thud. "Shang!" She wrenched free of Zedong's grip and hurled herself toward Shang. The world spun around her, and she stumbled more than ran, but it did not matter.

Alive, alive, alive, alive.

She flung her arms around his neck, despite how he jerked back, startled. And then she pressed her face into his neck, trembling like a leaf swept up in an autumn gale. "Shang, Shang, oh Shang you're alive," she gasped, tears streaming down her cheeks as she pressed against him. "I thought you were dead!"

His jaw tensed, followed by a thick swallow.

Arms still shackled behind him, he tilted his head toward hers. For a wild, heady moment, she thought he was softly nuzzling his nose into her hair, above her ear. A lightning bolt shot straight to her gut when his exhale warmed the side of her face.

Then he spoke, and she realized it was not a tender gesture at all.

"You're giving him leverage," he hissed into her ear, deep and dark. "Stop clinging to me."

Meiling froze, the tiniest of gasps escaping her mouth. For a fraction of a second, she held on longer and squeezed a hair's breadth closer to his warmth and strength. Then, the heat of a dozen fires burning her cheeks, she pulled away. She could not meet Shang's or Zedong's eyes as she scooted back. Her vision went blurry. Her heart ached too much for words.

"Interesting," Zedong muttered.

Oh, what a fool she was! When would she stop revealing her weaknesses to Zedong? When would she stop making herself an idiot in front of Shang?

"I'll make a deal with you, little one," Zedong announced, taking one step closer to her, so he could tower over where she huddled on the floor. "I will give you all the time you want in his mind. I will not hurt him either. In exchange, I want every shred of information this . . . *friend* of yours knows about the empire's plans, secrets, and weaknesses."

Meiling could say nothing. She was still reeling. The power of Shang's gaze pierced her, a berating question in the silent air between them.

Why didn't you come with me?

Zedong did not wait until Meiling was settled on the firm bed. He whipped out his knife, snatched her hand, and pierced her skin. She grimaced but kept the cry from wriggling free of her clenched teeth.

Blackness wrapped around her vision as something gave a hard, distant *thump*.

Her spirit was flung out into the room and though she turned and tried to launch herself back into her fallen body, there was a firm black wall preventing her. Meiling whimpered inaudibly and turned.

"Go into his mind. Remember, I control whether this young man lives or dies. Do as I say," Zedong growled.

Yet again, she found herself with no choice. Shang held many secrets! Had he not told her himself that he made it a point to know what threats faced the empire? To know its weaknesses as if they were his own?

If only there was something she could do!

Perhaps Shang would have an idea. Of course he would have an idea. Shang would know what to do. Had she not often wished for his presence for this very reason?

She hesitated only a moment longer and then slipped slowly into Shang's familiar mindscape. The tall windows rose on either side of the hall, red drapes still drawn tight against them. The pillars supported the ceiling, their dragons curling around them in decoration. How comforting this place was to her.

He was looking at her crumpled form in the middle of the floor, blood streaming from her finger, her cheek. Noting that she wore the same robes he had last seen her in, only now they were filthy, stained, and tattered. *Is he going to leave her lying there on the floor like that?* A sharp bolt of fury cut through the simmering rage and hatred filling him.

Shang! Shang, I'm here in your mind, Meiling called out, hardly noticing how weak, thin, and desperate her voice sounded. *I don't know what to do. I can't go back to my body and if I don't give him enough information, he will hurt you. I can't let him hurt you! I've already lost you once—I can't go through losing you again. He can make me do whatever he wants and I'm powerless against him. And now you're captured too!*

Shh, calm down, Meiling, his familiar voice rumbled. His stirring emotion was too complicated for her to name, but lined with firm conviction. *We're going to be fine, understand? You need to be strong, like you were when Fen was wounded. Remember?*

She was spiraling out of control. Seeing him again after she'd been so sure he was dead, after all she'd endured at Zedong's hand . . . It was too much. She wished they had this conversation in person, so he could hold her and she would not have to be afraid. *Ugh*—this thinking was nonsense; he had just practically shoved her away from him. And he hadn't forgiven her for last night.

That was different, she whimpered.

But if you were strong then, you can be strong now. Control yourself. The words were hard, but not unkind. *I'm going to get us out of here. Understand? I'll come up—*

Don't plan anything! Meiling practically shouted. *I don't want to know anything! I don't want to hunt in your mind. I know you hate it when I'm here, but I don't know what else to—*

Meiling! Calm down! Shang said sharply. *Hunt in my mind, like he said. Find whatever you need.*

Forgive me. She drew in a gasping breath, trying to compose her frayed nerves. *Please forgive me, Shang. I think I am going mad in this place with him.*

A question flashed in his mind before he could erase it—*then why didn't you come with me?* A question not exactly intended for her, but aimed at her nevertheless. Beneath it was a deep ache in his soul.

She was the source of that ache. She hated causing him pain.

Is Fen still alive? she asked instead of answering his unspoken question. *What happened after I was taken?*

A faint memory seemed to appear before her eyes, in the rich hallway of his mind. A memory of Fen lying in a bed, bleary-eyed and bandaged.

It's not important what happened. But we're both alive and mostly well.

They did not kill you both for how things ended? She phrased it carefully, not trying to imply that Shang had failed her in any way.

He chuckled mirthlessly. *Not yet. But don't worry about that. Go hunt for what you need.*

She hesitated. A thousand thoughts and words and emotions flew to her lips, bubbling into something like a sob. *Shang? I'm . . . I'm sorry for the part I played in getting you caught. I never . . .*

Meiling, he said firmly, and a slight thread of exasperation wound through him. *You're overthinking things again.*

She ducked her head. Then, in an attempt to prove she wasn't falling apart at the seams, she said, *I need your help. I have to give Zedong information. He won't accept it if I claim there's nothing useful to him in your mind. Can you help me figure out what to tell him and what to hide?*

Part of his hard determination cracked, exposing something soft and warm. *Of course I will help you, Meiling.*

Tightness unwound from her chest.

But I won't willingly offer up any information. Shang's voice echoed around the cavernous hall. *Find what you are able to find, and then I will help you decide what to share. Perhaps the fathers will be merciful and you won't find anything crucial.*

He didn't know how good she was getting at finding secrets. Especially in a mind so organized as Shang's.

Thank you, she whispered.

Seemingly in an effort to keep his thoughts from being evident to her, Shang focused his attention on studying the floorboards before his vision. His mind seemed to war with him, fighting his instinct to survey the room for weaknesses and threats. He evidently itched to make a plan.

But he fought those tendencies, resorting to describing aloud in his mind the patterns he saw on the wood.

There's a chip in the corner of that board. The grain runs vertically.

It was dull, but it served its purpose. There was no more delaying of her work. Her work of finding the empire's secrets and betraying them all.

She approached the apse of the hall, where its panels and doors set into the wall. On her first glance, she'd missed them, but she was so confident in what they contained that she did not even reach out for memory threads, did not try to find his soul tether.

She suppressed the sudden urge to search for his tether, to open the curtains and discover what lay beyond them, to uncover what world lay just behind the door at the far end of the hall.

But no. She had to stay focused.

Meiling approached the cabinet-like drawers. She opened the first one to find parchment filed carefully under labels. Similar to Wan's, except that the categories were much narrower, so they held fewer documents. Where Wan had a file for *Academy,* Shang had one for *Academy Practices, Academy Arena Battles,* and *Academy Language Class,* to name a few.

There was an entire slough of files for his family. She had always wondered . . . She shouldn't pry . . .

Giving into impulse, she pulled the first parchment out, letting the light streaming from around the edges of the curtains wash over it. Her grip suddenly tightened, for while Wan's parchments had held detailed records, Shang's were images.

In her hands, she held a picture of stern, dark eyes under a sharp brow. A face that resembled Shang's, yet different and distinct. The picture seemed to be painted from the vantage point of someone much shorter than the man. It had the flavor of youthfulness about it, and the longer Meiling stared at it, the more immersed she became in it—

"Shangdi, my son, you are young, but I know you will be powerful. You will live up to your heritage and be a son worthy of the Tan lineage. You must work hard. Do not let anyone see you struggle. You must master all. Understand?"

I nod. He speaks the words gravely. He is so very serious. He is counting on me. I am the only child; my family's only chance at honor.

I will never let him down. He will be so proud of me some day. "*I understand, Father.*"

"*I know you do.*"

He places his hand on my shoulder and smiles. I beam. Father does not smile often.

I will make him proud. So proud that he is always smiling.

Meiling shoved the memory back, trying to keep herself from gasping. Before her mind could catch up to her actions and caution her, she retrieved another. It bore the same face as the previous memory, but this time, the face was twisted in disapproval. He already looked several years older.

"*What is this I have been hearing? That you are the laughingstock of the Academy?*"

I meet Father's hard eyes, even though I want to look anywhere else. But I will not show the weakness that he seems to think characterizes me. I stand up straighter, despite the coil of dread knotting in my stomach. "*It is nothing, Father. They only tease me.*"

"*Because you were losing a fight to the point that a master had to intervene and save your life? Shangdi, you disgrace me!*"

All the heat drains from my skin, leaving my hands clammy. I swallow a lump in my throat, but I do not shrink away from his gaze. "*They always pair new students with older students so they can learn from their failure.*"

"*You, Shangdi, will* not *learn from failure! You will learn through success, understand? To think, losing to the point of needing intervention . . . Shangdi, Shangdi . . .*" *Father shakes his head and turns away.*

I cannot bear it. Yet I must. I cannot lose any more fights. Never again. No more failure. Ever.

The next was a picture of a dark library, lit only by one candle. As Meiling stared at it, it flickered in her vision.

My eyelids are so heavy, my body sore from combat practice. Everyone else is long asleep. I wish I can sleep too, but I must keep going. Father will kill me if I do not get a perfect score on this exam. His face flashes before my mind's eye. I cannot escape that disapproving frown. He wears it so much more than his smile. I cannot earn his approval by my grades; I can only avoid his disapproval.

If it takes studying all night, dragons curse it, I'm going to get a perfect score on this exam.

I lower my head again and continue my studying.

Meiling shoved the memory back into the drawer and slammed it shut. She could not bear the shame blooming in her breast. At least he didn't know where she poked and prodded. She didn't *want* him to know.

He was still trying to focus his thoughts on boring things, so he betrayed nothing to her.

Meiling opened the next drawer. She froze.

There, under one of the labels, was her name, written perfectly in an elegant script. *Meiling.*

She shouldn't.

Something stronger than curiosity—something akin to desperation—made her yank open the drawer wider. It was fuller than she would have guessed.

Was she wrong to think some of these memories were strong, as if recently accessed?

Fear made her stop. But she had to know.

She pulled the first parchment out.

There was her face. Spread in a wide grin, with her eyes alight and sparkling, limp vines hanging from tree branches behind her. The image was startling—almost *shocking*. It was just her face, and yet, it wasn't the face she saw in the mirror each morning. It was *far* more beautiful than what she'd found in a reflection.

This is how he saw me.

She blinked, momentarily stunned. Then she grabbed several more images, only to find all of them were of her in different places, different orientations. Sometimes it was her profile as she stared out at a vast landscape, her hair whipping into her face. Others were of her crouched on the ground, laughing as she played with the panda cub they'd rescued. As she flipped through image after image, her heart beating faster, she could almost make out the low timbres of his voice, speaking aloud the thoughts he'd had during those moments.

She's so beautiful. What a lovely smile.

She's a puzzle I cannot figure out.

She moves with the elegant grace of a dancer.

Now, wait a minute—he'd berated her for the way she moved, saying it gave her away as royalty! But he actually . . . *liked* how she moved?

She shouldn't be surprised. This was probably the most *Shang* thing ever. And yet, it didn't calm her racing heart or make it any easier to breathe. They were captive in an enemy fortress, being forced to betray their homeland, and yet all Meiling could think in this moment was: *He thinks I'm beautiful. He thinks I'm beautiful.*

He liked her smile.

She was going to *die*, but in the most glorious way possible.

How long is this going to take? Shang's question rang out overhead, not aimed at her, but at himself. It startled her so much she dropped half the memories she was holding. Cursing in her mind, she fell to her knees, scooped them back up, and shoved them back in their drawer. Hopefully, the order didn't matter? She cursed her stupidity once more and went to slam the drawer shut.

Something stopped her.

She could find out if . . . if . . . he *cared* about her.

That would be a horrible breach of privacy. She wasn't here for games or to fan the flames of her vanity. But dragons blast it, if Shang *did* care about her, he'd never tell her, and if he didn't, then it would help her not make a fool out of herself.

Her people were on the line, and she was wasting time over nonsense.

She would move on. Close the drawer. Shut away Shang's thoughts and feelings and memories of her.

Phoenixes burn this place down—she couldn't resist pulling just one more page out of that drawer. It was an image of the horse they'd shared and the back of her head. A light breeze ruffled her hair, her robes, moving the image until it filled her vision, and she was no longer herself.

Giving in at last, I slip my arm around Meiling's waist and tug her back against me. A little gasp escapes her lips. She wants this. She softens against me, leaning into my chest, laying her head on my shoulder.

My heart thunders wildly.

Fen isn't here. Father isn't here. No one is here except me and her. There's nothing to stop me from brushing aside her hair and pressing my lips to the soft skin of her neck.

I shouldn't be imagining this.

Meiling jolted out of the scene with the suddenness of a lightning bolt, her face on fire. That . . . *that* was not a memory. That hadn't ever happened. She would certainly have remembered. He'd been nothing but distant, professional, and cold when they'd shared a saddle.

The image on the next page sent her stumbling back a step, pressing the side of her fist against her parted lips as a wave of dizziness flooded her.

It was a picture of Shang holding her close in that cave and . . . *kissing* her. His hand in her hair, the other wrapped around her waist, as he leaned into her and pressed his mouth to hers.

That was it. She would never breathe again. She slammed the drawer shut and turned away, pressing a hand to her heart as though to make it calm its erratic rhythm.

But a thought lingered behind the fantasy she'd just locked back up. One of Shang's thoughts.

This mission is turning me desperate and foolish. These ridiculous impulses will leave me alone once we arrive. I'll master myself again, and that will be the end of this stupidity.

The faint echoes of those words left Meiling rooted to the spot. Where she'd been hot mere seconds ago, she was now cold.

At least she had her answer.

What Shang felt for her was an inconvenience to him. Something he intended to get rid of just as soon as he could.

She needed to stop dallying and get to work.

CHAPTER 22

NUMBLY, MEILING OPENED the next drawer, and the next, until she finally found a label that read *Zheninghui Security Threats.*

Her hands hesitated. *Shang?* she called.

Yes, Meiling?

One of these days, her stomach would stop flipping whenever he said her name. She shoved the sensation aside, drawing a deep breath to focus. *I found all the threats you've cataloged. I have not opened them yet.*

There was a flicker of emotion. Fear? Dread? She was not sure.

Yes?

I don't want to betray the empire. I don't want to betray Pa—the Glorious Emperor, I mean.

What choice have you? If you resist, he'll punish you.

I'm more afraid of what he will do to you, she whispered. *He'll kill you. I know he will. He knows it will be more effective than beating me.*

Another flash of emotion. More anger, a tinge of real fear, and a strong protective urge. *The empire is more important than my life,* Shang said. Behind it was a tiny, whispering thought: *Her father will protect her if I cannot.*

I want an option that involves keeping your life and not betraying the empire.

That would be a nice option indeed, he muttered. *But you must be realistic. Any chance we have to escape cannot come until Fang leaves us. Which he does not seem inclined to do. This means that you need to give him the information, or I need to die.*

You're supposed to have a better idea, she said dryly. *Military strategist and all.*

His body suddenly warmed. There was a trace of amusement in his emotions. And . . . was that a feeling of—no, surely not—*missing* her? Behind it, was there really a flash of longing, of wanting to . . . to *hold* her in his arms?

He shoved those feelings away, almost frantically.

She tried to ignore the stab of hurt.

He exhaled. *You must make your decision. I'm not going to make it for you.* Because he knew what decision he *should* do, and that decision did not align with the fact that he didn't want to die. Fear pulsed through him, followed by mounting determination and the will to face whatever came to him.

Pa's voice echoed in her mind, tainted by black magic: *Will you trade all you love because you do not understand the meaning of sacrifice?*

She did not merely need to escape Zedong. She needed to defeat him. Which meant she should refuse to give him the information he wanted. She should let Shang die, should have the spine that would make her Pa proud.

I'm not going to let him kill you, Meiling growled fiercely.

Relief and warmth flowed through Shang, followed by guilt and his conscience telling him he should argue with her. He said nothing, but when Meiling blinked to his vision, he stared at her unoccupied body lying in a crumpled heap on the floor. His eyes ran the length of her, noting each uncomfortably twisted limb, each bruise, each drop of blood.

His anger was too strong for him to hide.

Well, she said, *I suppose I should get to betraying everyone then.*

A stab of guilt went through him.

This isn't your fault, she said quickly. *And it's not your choice. It's my choice.*

If you had just come with me—

I couldn't, Shang! she said sharply, almost angrily. *I know you think I've betrayed us all. I know you're angry with me. But I couldn't leave Feiyan. You must understand!*

I don't have to understand anything, he returned coldly.

Meiling tried to fight the hurt creeping into her soul. This was his decision to remain angry, not hers. And her decision was that she was not going to let the man who was furious with her die.

So she opened the file with secrets. One by one, she pulled every secret out of Shang's mind. Uneducated as she was in this type of thing, she did not understand half of it. Most of the things that did not sound serious, like one vague *"Shi Family,"* he had labeled as a serious threat. And most of the things that sounded serious—like one of the courtiers presumed to be a spy for Zedong—he had labeled as a mild concern.

Several times, she almost asked for clarification or explanations. But she held her tongue. The less she understood, the better.

The more Meiling looked into the documents, the more amazed she grew. She had never known this side of him. He had often snuck around at the Academy, listening to conversations between masters and high-ranking officials that came in to scope out the students for appointments. These last few weeks, he had done the same at Liafugen, becoming little more than a shadow himself. These were his less preferred methods, however. He had several key relationships with masters at the Academy, relationships that he would maneuver for information.

"Knowledge is power, my son," his father had told him.

He had taken that to heart.

The next secret in his folder surprised her.

Princess Lu Meiling's magic. Risk: High.

He'd gathered information about her mother, about the nature of her friendship with Zedong back at the Academy.

Once she had delved into the secrets that Shang knew, she pulled out the folder labeled *Butagin War Strategy.* Naturally, he knew much more than Renshu. Even while he had been recovering from his wounds, he had been doing everything he could to learn and understand both his enemies and the ways Zheninghai prepared to confront them.

Was this why her parents had kept so much of this information from her? To keep her from being any more valuable to their enemy than she already was with her magic?

Shang, on the other hand, was a vault of secrets. Zedong would learn everything he'd carefully harvested all these years.

Meiling groaned when she discovered plans for an ambush on Zedong. They had planned to let him march across the border, and when he reached the Silk Highway—the only road he could take to reach the capital city through the mountains—they would ambush him.

It might have worked.

More and more information she found. Each new shred of information was a new betrayal. Each piece sent her more and more into a panic, until she cried, *Dragons take you, Shang! Did you have to know so much? Was it really necessary?*

I believed it was, he said hoarsely, defeat and guilt lining every word. His shoulders stooped—just a tiny bit. *You found it all, then?*

This is . . . this will ruin everything! There are so many things he can use. I don't know what to tell him. Can I hide any of it? Oh, but I'm afraid that he will hurt you, as I'm telling him, making sure that I'm saying it all. I could not bear it, Shang! He will make me tell him everything and I cannot do anything to stop him.

Tell him what he asks. It's as simple as that, Shang growled. He attempted to quell his own agitation for her sake.

But I need to know what to hide! What to share? You must help me! I should hide the ambush, right? What about the security threats? Which ones can I safely share? What can I—

Meiling, shh. It doesn't matter anymore. I had hoped you wouldn't find as much as you did, but you did. We don't have time to go over everything. Right now, it's most important that you placate him, Meiling. Don't make him angry and don't let him believe you are keeping anything from him. Answer his questions. Give him what he asks.

I cannot! Shang—Shang! I'm so afraid! I do not want to leave your mind. I'm so afraid—

A surge of emotion followed her words and Shang could not stuff it back soon enough. He was alarmed, and a stray thought broke through his walls of defense: *She is never like this.* When he spoke in his mind-voice, however, his tones were even and controlled. Firm and strict. *He can't hurt you. You're too valuable. You don't have to be afraid.*

If you think that, you do not understand Fang Zedong at all, Meiling returned, trembling so much that she became more shadow with every passing minute.

His soul's strength faltered for the barest of instants.

She continued ruthlessly. *He can make me do terrible things. He can't hurt me, but he can make me hurt others. He's . . . he's breaking me. I can feel it. He's making me hurt so many people and do things I'd never do, so other wielders aren't tortured in front of me.*

There was another crashing wave of emotion. Anger. Vicious, burning anger. Followed by the almost overwhelmingly violent urge to rip Zedong to pieces. He quickly controlled himself, however. *It's time to wake up,* he said firmly.

But I have so many more questions! How is my family? Why did you come? Is Fen going to be okay?

Meiling, he chided, *everything will be all right. Wake up.*

Her fight, her desperation, her determination all fled away like birds at the faintest trace of winter. Without even answering, she rose out of his mind, looking down for only a split second at his kneeling, shackled form. Then she glanced toward Zedong, standing against the wall, gazing with fiery light in his eyes at Shang. The hunger in his gaze frightened her.

She slipped to her body—and immediately ran into a block. Panic hit her soul like a blow. She darted back into Shang's head.

There's something wrong about his gaze. Shang's thoughts rang out overhead when she hurtled into the dimmed, grand hallway.

I cannot wake up! He's blocked me!

Shang glanced at her body again and very suddenly, very briefly, an image flashed in his mind of Meiling's face cradled in his arms, a blue and purple bruise on her forehead, her lips slightly parted.

Then it was gone. He spoke aloud to Zedong. "She cannot wake up."

She watched out of Shang's eyes as Zedong smiled a slow, cruel smile. He pushed off the wall and took a few steps toward Shang.

Shang thought to himself, *I am not intimidated by you standing over me.*

"That will not be necessary." Zedong strode past Shang and beckoned to the guards, who grabbed Shang's arms and dragged him upward even as he scrambled to get to his feet on his own. Dread fell sick and heavy on him, and the luxurious hall went dimmer than before. His mind was whirling with thoughts so fast she couldn't keep up.

What? Why? Why won't that be necessary? Meiling cried out in Shang's mind.

It's his magic.

His magic?

Then she remembered. He could hear the nonverbal transmission of information between people. Which usually wasn't beneficial, but in this case . . .

The weight of Shang's words fell like a millstone around her neck. *He knows everything.*

What? No! she cried. *Wait, where are they taking—*

The door slammed shut, and she was sent flying out of Shang's mind. *Shang! Shang!* she screamed into nothingness. *Shang, don't leave me! Please, please!*

But he was gone.

Doors had never been a hinderance to Meiling's magic. But as soon as the door had shut, black magic flared to life, discordant and ugly, blocking escape from the room. Nothing else remained in the room except the one bed and her fallen, twisted body on the ground.

She was trapped.

CHAPTER 23

OF COURSE, ZEDONG had heard every conversation, every mental exchange of information.

It was so obvious, she should have guessed it from the start.

Wildly, Meiling ran through the things she'd discovered in Shang's mind. Things about the empire, about the war they were drawn into against their will, things about Shang's thoughts of her.

Even if Shang didn't love her, even if she was just his duty, he still had a weakness for her. A weakness that Zedong could exploit. She'd betrayed enough of her own thoughts and feelings to expose her to even worse manipulation than before. All Zedong had to do was threaten Shang's death—he could threaten her with much less, so long as it hurt Shang—and she would do what he asked.

Renshu.

She hadn't told Shang that Renshu was captured here! A thousand more things she should have told him flooded her mind as she drifted uselessly around the confines of her stone and wood prison. A thousand things far more useful than whimpering about being frightened. Things like the layout of the fortress—he probably knew that already, though—the garden she had found, the things she had learned about Zedong.

Was there any hope of escaping this room? If she could escape it, she could find Shang and tell him everything. She could find Renshu and Feiyan. She could be a messenger for the three of them, and together, they could plot an escape. She could go into anyone's mind and find exactly when the guards would be where, the location of the prison keys, anything they needed to know. It might take a while, but if Zedong thought she was trapped here, she might have quite a bit of time.

Besides, she didn't trust Zedong one minute not to hurt Shang now that he knew what he meant to her.

Meiling approached the door. When she first blinked, it was like her vision cleared, and it was only a room with no enchantments. The longer she fixed her gaze on the door or the walls or the window, the black magic would slowly emerge from the woodwork, the masonry. It started as tiny, translucent threads, before it thickened into cords big enough to clench in her fists.

She tried the walls, the door, the window, the floor, the ceiling. She even slid under the bed and scraped her fingernails along every inch, looking for the slightest hint that he had overlooked something.

Zedong was apparently a master of the dark arts. He left no rock unturned, no exit unsealed. She could not even return to her body, which grew paler by the moment. At least her soul tether hummed with life when she grasped it. Faint, certainly, but still there.

Meiling plopped in a puddle of soul shadow on the ground. Gone seemed the days of flying to the highest heights of whispering stars, of reaching tendril-like hands of smoke into a midnight sky, bathed in moonlight and singing in starlight.

Freedom.

That was her one dream. It had always been her dream. Freedom to be what she wanted to be, to do what she wanted to do, and not be bound by the pressures of society to fit into an identity that was not hers.

Meiling was not a magicless princess. She was not even a low-magic wielder.

By all rights of the word and all society-accepted definitions, she was a powerful wielder. She was honing her skills, learning how to penetrate minds and hunt for information. Here, in Zedong's fortress, she was getting the practice she had always wanted.

Before she had traveled across the countryside, she'd sometimes considered her palace home a prison. As she had traveled with Shang and Fen, she'd considered herself a fugitive.

Meiling had never known captivity. She'd had more freedom than she realized . . . and she'd *squandered* it. She had not been grateful for it like she ought.

Even with Shang now here, escape seemed even less possible than before.

But she would not despair. No matter how exhausted she was of this place, of this game, of this prison, she would escape. She would fight. She would be brave. Her hair might be gray and her bones rattling in their sockets when she left. But by all the fathers, they would make it out.

She had to.

It was near dusk when the door opened again. Meiling's heart soared at the prospect of *anything* besides sitting here, trapped. Maybe Shang was back? Maybe she could tell him all the things that she needed to.

She shouldn't be so optimistic, but she couldn't help herself.

It was not Shang who Zedong dragged in for Meiling to infiltrate. No, and when she caught sight of the form that was hauled in, spitting and fighting and spewing insults, her heart dropped.

No, not Feiyan.

Feiyan was shouting at Zedong's turned back. Shuren held one arm, his other hand planted firmly on her back as he pressed her to her knees. A brigand gripped her other arm. Together, they restrained her.

Zedong turned mildly to regard her. "Li Feiyan—"

She spit in his face. It was a well-aimed, well-timed shot. She should not have been able to spit so far. But it hit Zedong right in the nose and dribbled down into his beard. "What have you done to her?" Feiyan shrieked, her eyes darting from Meiling's body to Zedong.

He retaliated immediately.

His backhand would have sent her sprawling except for Shuren's grip on her. Their hold made her take the blow even harder, momentarily stunning her. Blood welled from her lip and dripped down the corner of her mouth. Shuren's face was a stern mask, betraying nothing.

"I would understand such rash behavior if you had the ability to heal yourself," Zedong said. "But I admit, I'm baffled by your insistence upon injury."

Feiyan met his gaze as blood smeared on her face, stained her teeth. "Maybe I'm a fool who's not afraid of pain," she answered defiantly.

Zedong smiled down at her, and Meiling trembled with deep dread. "A fool you are indeed, my little healer. A fool you are indeed."

Feiyan grinned. It was a strange sight: blood dripping from her split lip, down her chin, and into her mouth. Yet, it did not seem false in any way. She smiled like she knew something Zedong didn't. Or like she enjoyed some private joke.

Zedong did not know what to do with that smile.

Perhaps Meiling should have tried to smile more often.

"Daughter of Liena," Zedong barked, "enter her mind. Extract her secrets." Then, as if sensing Meiling's immediate resistance, he whipped out his knife and bent next to Feiyan. He held the blade harshly against the soft, exposed flesh of her neck. She flinched, but the look in her eyes hardened.

Meiling glanced quickly at Shuren, but other than a tight swallow, he was still expressionless as he restrained Feiyan.

"I know what she means to you, Daughter of Liena," Zedong said loudly, threatening.

Of course he did. Because Meiling and Shang had discussed her refusal to leave because of Feiyan. He'd overheard.

"Do it quickly. You may think I will not kill the healer, but you can be certain that I will make her suffer." He pressed the blade hard enough that Feiyan flinched again. Hard enough to draw a thin line of crimson blood. "And there's always your handsome Shang I can kill."

Without hesitation, Meiling flew into Feiyan's mind. She could not fight, not when Feiyan and Shang were on the line. She couldn't stand by and let their blood be spilled.

Instead, she would spill the blood of her family and the entire empire.

With an ache like death in her gut, she stepped into Feiyan's mindscape.

Barefoot, clad in rough wool trousers and a wrapped tunic, standing in tall grass, Meiling breathed deeply the smell of pine. She stood in the middle of a forest of unnaturally tall evergreen. She stared up at them, letting her gaze follow up higher and higher until they disappeared into a cloudy sky.

It was both sunny and misty at once. The sunlight caught on the mist, making it sparkle like the light of a thousand diamonds. It was beautiful, serene. Nothing like the mind she would have guessed for one like Feiyan.

A broad, rather short figure stood outlined by mist. He was only a few feet away, yet remained obscured. She knew him. She called out to him, not in her mind voice, but in a heart voice that did not belong to her.

Papa!

She was running toward that figure, no longer Meiling anymore. In only a few strides, the mist cleared, offering a full view of the man before her.

He looked almost nothing like Feiyan. While she was average height and slender as a reed, with chiseled, beautiful features and striking eyes, he was much plainer. He was stocky, with a build that clearly had once been very muscular. His face held no sharp angles like hers; his cheeks were a little round, and he bore a little tuft of moustache above his upper lip. His eyes were soft, gentle, and full of affection—nothing like Feiyan's.

Meiling ran straight into his open arms as his arms tightened around her in a warm embrace. He chuckled, sighing softly. *My little Feiyan.*

This seemed like the sort of intimate thing Feiyan would not want Meiling intruding upon. She jerked away from Feiyan's father—the only person she could sense in this mind—and she turned, closing her eyes against the beauty of the pine forest.

I'm in your mind, Meiling said. *I'm so sorry. I want to fight it, but I cannot.*

Feiyan snorted back. *What do I care? I have no secrets. Pillage what you want.*

Meiling wanted to say more. But Zedong was listening, catching every word between the two of them. Now that she knew he had access to whatever she found, she would need to tread carefully.

Feiyan was thinking about all the ways she could kill Zedong. It was a little morbid, glancing the flashing images of her shoving him out a window, slipping him poison, stabbing him with a knife she had previously pilfered off a guard and now was tucked in her boot, knocking him unconscious and then decapitating him and slicing off each of his fingers and toes.

A little morbid? Meiling asked about the last option.

Feiyan laughed. Out loud, in her physical body. She fixed her eyes on Zedong and spoke aloud. "Never too morbid." She grinned. Her thought strayed—*he's unnerved by me.*

Meiling wished she had ever thought that in her life. Unfortunately, Zedong had been the one doing all the unnerving in their relationship.

"Take the knife out of her boot," Zedong said.

Anger burst through Feiyan's mind, making the trees sway under her wrath. "Excuse *me?* I worked very hard to snatch that knife." Her thoughts flashed, and Meiling caught that battle instinct that she had seen in Shang and Fen. She took advantage of Shuren's shifting movements as he stuck his hand into her boot. She jerked free, elbowed him in the gut, and tried to spin on the guard.

"Drug her," Zedong snarled.

It happened in such a flash. For one second, Meiling was seeing double—the pine forest, and the world outside Feiyan's eyes—and then a cloth swiftly approached Feiyan's face. Blackness, and so much avalanching frustration in Feiyan's soul.

Cowards! she spat in her mind.

A strange stillness fell over the forest, leaving Meiling inside.

She closed her eyes, reaching out for Feiyan's memory threads. Her father's awareness burned into her as she worked. Did Feiyan always feel this way? He seemed to always be hiding just behind the clearing of her mind—obscured, waiting, and watchful.

The first memory thread hummed faintly. A memory not recently accessed, not treasured. A pluck of pain. A vision flashed before her eyes. Two women, one beloved by Feiyan and the other despised by her, stood arguing with each other. Foggy silhouettes of siblings hovered in the background. Not true siblings, not except one little brother. There was Feiyan's father, approaching the fighting women and saying something harsh to the beloved woman. The woman startled and slipped away into another room. The father embraced the other woman.

Two wives. Feiyan's mother was one of two wives.

It was an uncommon practice, but not extraordinarily unusual. Some men did it to increase their likelihood of having a magic-wielding child.

Meiling touched the next memory. It was an argument between Feiyan and a stepsister similar in age, during one of the times that Feiyan had come home from training at the Academy and she was furious with her stepsister for derogatory comments she'd made about Feiyan's mother. Her father intervened and had taken her on a walk to this very clearing. He had told her there that he loved her mother more, that he treasured her and was prouder of her than he was of any of his other children.

She'd felt guilty about the favoritism, especially how it affected her younger, magicless brother. She'd struggled with feeling like the reason she was her father's favorite was because she was his only magic-wielding child, and a healer at that. The first healer they had seen in decades.

She'd brought more honor to the Li family than they could have asked for, could have ever dreamt.

But Feiyan craved her father's love, her father's special attention and favoritism in a house where she was an outcast. Her half-siblings outnumbered her and her brother four to two.

And then . . . Meiling's fingers touched the next thread, following it down a little ways. She kept her eyes closed so she could see the quick flashing memories.

Then Feiyan's mother had died. That had changed things.

Meiling followed the cords of grief until her own heart ached with sorrow, with longing, with the desire to see this stranger's face just one more time. Feiyan remembered her mother's face in perfect clarity. This memory was strong, protected, treasured. But there were moments of forgetting that struck panic deep into her core.

There was a hard conversation between Feiyan and her father. It happened after Feiyan had seen the change in his relationship with her stepmother. Her stepmother was now the only woman in her father's life, and her children took every opportunity to lord it over Feiyan and her brother that their father loved their mother more than Feiyan's mother. It was a bitter rivalry for love and attention.

Nothing in Feiyan's mind came close to the bond between her and her father. Nothing except a fierce protectiveness for her younger brother that was present in every memory of him. The only other things that came close to the strength of emotion was the hatred she harbored for her stepmother and stepsiblings.

And—Shang? Was that Shang?

Meiling hurried after that memory thread, squeezing her eyes tighter as her heartbeat increased. The throbbing in Feiyan's memories of Shang echoed in Meiling's breast. There was a flash of a younger Shang, stern and so focused on his work that nothing could turn his eye. Feiyan's frustration that he would not notice her rippled through her, coupled with her deep admiration. *This is someone Papa would be proud for me to marry.*

As Meiling followed the threads linking Feiyan's memories of Shang, she caught more glimpses of his life at the Academy. His close friendship with Renshu, his determination to be the best, his tenacity to rise above every obstacle. She felt Feiyan's admiration like it was her own.

Then one memory thread burned brightly, throbbed painfully, and it was thick and strong. Accessed often. The memory was more vivid, so vivid Meiling barely kept herself from being pulled into it. Instead, she watched as Feiyan sat next to Shang in the darkened library. The two of them studied by candlelight, saying nothing to each other. Shang studied because he always studied late. Feiyan studied because she was busy healing each day and this was the only time she had for her schooling.

Apparently, they had often studied together at this late hour. They rarely spoke. Only sat side by side, not even sharing a candle. More than half the time, Renshu studied with them.

This night, however, Feiyan was especially tired. Especially frustrated with her studies. Especially worn from a letter she had received from her little brother that made her heart ache. And especially emotional.

Renshu wasn't there.

While they were studying, Feiyan turned to Shang. Sensing her gaze, he looked up. A flood of wild impulsiveness rushed like heady wine through Feiyan's body.

And she lunged in for a kiss.

Shang jerked back, slammed his textbook shut, and stood in a rage. "Don't be a fool," he hissed as he started packing up his studying materials.

Feiyan stared at him, jarred with pain, but undaunted. She met his eye, refusing to flinch under his furious gaze. "We're all fools, Shangdi."

He glared at her and picked up his candle. He turned away, but his low voice carried. "I'm not."

That was when Feiyan's heart broke. That was where her dreams had shattered of bringing home a boy like Shang to meet her papa. That was when she'd resolved that she was tired of being hurt by people she loved.

"What was I thinking?" Feiyan said into the dark library. Her candle flickered a small circle of yellow on her work. "I cannot marry. I'm too busy for marriage."

That was very true. Meiling followed more spider silk, through years upon years and days upon days of healing the masses. Exhaustion tainted every memory. Fighting with her masters, telling them that she could not do everything they wanted. She literally did not have enough time to heal every day while still completing the full coursework at the Academy and not work herself to death.

Feiyan had apparently wrestled often with her gift. Meiling found many strands splitting off that one lead. Some more often traveled than others. Feiyan wished she were not a healer, but she was glad she could help so many people. She wished helping others did not come at such a high cost to herself.

She wished she could fade into the background. Be a decently powerful wielder, enough to bring her family honor, but not enough that it became obligation that outweighed everything else.

Feiyan wanted freedom like Meiling did, but she needed it far more than Meiling.

Her leisure was someone else's death.

Meiling touched the next thread and immediately jerked away from it. *Shuren.* If she went down this road, it could endanger his life. She did not know what Feiyan knew about his loyalties and feelings, but she could not find out. If Feiyan even suspected his disloyalty, Zedong would have a phoenix murder him.

Meiling hesitated. She opened her eyes and found she'd wandered farther into the pine forest, away from that clearing. She turned, her eye catching on green boughs wrapped in golden mist and that stocky figure watching her.

With that, she flew upward and out of Feiyan's mind. She poured out of the space above Feiyan's head, into the air of the ether. Shuren and the guard had stepped backward and watched nothing happen between the two crumpled bodies on the floor.

Meiling caught her soul tether in her smokey hands. It had strengthened since last time. Should she try it? With something like a deep breath, she slid one leg into her own mind—and discovered no resistance.

A cry of relief escaped her lips when she opened her physical eyes to floorboards. And Zedong's booted foot. She quickly tried to sit up and scoot away from him. Oh, how everything ached! Her wrist, her back, her hip, her neck, her entire body ached with the rudeness of the position in which she had been left.

Zedong's hand caught Meiling's jaw and wrenched her gaze upward to meet his.

"I found nothing, I swear!" she cried, sputtered, as he arched her neck painfully.

He waved one hand dismissively back toward Feiyan. Immediately, Shuren and the guard grabbed her and hauled her out of the room, her head swinging limply. "I know you are resisting me in every way you can. You didn't look hard enough. I confess, little princess, that I am growing desperately weary of your games and stubbornness."

The door opened again, and two brigands strode into the small chamber. Meiling's jaw was still gripped in one of Zedong's clenching fists, but her eyes darted to them, away from his terrifyingly blue gaze.

He let go abruptly and flung her back to the ground.

"How long should we make her sleep?" one of the brigands asked, a middle-aged woman with cropped hair, coming to crouch beside Meiling on the floor.

Sleep? Was this different from whatever magic Zedong had placed on her that prevented her return to her body? Fear darted through her mind, down her spine, into her heart. She pressed both her hands into the floor and shoved herself upward. She tried to scramble to her feet, but the other brigand—an old, old man with a hood covering most of his face except a long, white beard—placed a heavy hand on her back, forcing her back to the ground. Unnatural strength radiated through that one touch. He could smash her into the floor without hardly exerting himself.

Zedong stared down at Meiling from his towering height. His eyes had grown so much colder, his face so much harder. His voice was mostly indifferent but edged in bitterness. "A hundred years. She can wither and die in this room for all I care. Perhaps as the years go by, she'll grow more malleable." His teeth flashed when he spoke.

Those words almost made her faint dead away, but she pressed her hands harder into the floor, trying to shove herself upward despite the brigand's restraint. But the brigand was far, far stronger than her. Worlds stronger. He pressed more heavily into her, forcing her elbows to bend.

A hundred years.

Was this . . . was this the last time her soul would reside in her body? Was this the last time she would feel the prickling cold of autumn seeping through the open window? The warmth of the sun on her face? The cold of stone, hear the creaking of floorboards in her own ears? Would she ever see Shang, Feiyan, or her family ever again?

"No!" Meiling cried, throwing herself forward and trying to grapple free of the old man's hold. He restrained her easily and pressed her painfully into the floor, belly down. She tried to fight, tried to wrestle, to free herself. She desperately clawed at anything, but she was no match for the strength of the brigand.

Zedong was staring at her with an unknowable emotion on his face. Then, he crouched beside the woman, who was mixing something in a vial. He placed one long finger under Meiling's chin and jerked her gaze upward to face him. She winced, gasped hard to breathe.

"I had so many plans for you. So many hopes. A pity to close those beautiful eyes forever. Goodnight, daughter of Liena."

The woman pried open her mouth and poured scalding liquid down her throat. Meiling choked. She gasped for air around the burning that caught and blocked her breath. Her stomach heaved, and for once, she would have gladly vomited. But the old man brigand clamped her jaw shut and held her firm, despite how much she coughed and tried to gasp. She took quick, sputtering breaths through her nose as she tried to swallow.

The world went black.

CHAPTER 24

MEILING'S SPIRIT HURLED out of her body. Zedong and his brigands rose and left, leaving her sprawled on the floor just two short feet away from the bed. This was how they were planning to leave her for a hundred years?

No! Let me out! What have you done? she cried into the emptiness of the chamber. Now, blocking her vision of the stone walls and the wooden floorboards, the door, and the window, was nothing but raging black.

Blackness. Everywhere she turned. But this was not just the absence of light. It flared with life, tinged with colors invisible to the human eye. Colors that Meiling could not begin to describe. This blackness was alive and breathing in a way that was entirely inexplicable to her, and it imprisoned her from everything else alive and beautiful in this world.

How could she escape an enchantment this strong? Her soul tether thinned to less than a thread of silk, barely holding on, barely keeping her alive.

Then a shocking and frightening thought occurred to her.

If her tether snapped, would she die like everyone else? Or would she live onward, a formless, wraith-like spirit with no home in the world? With no means to interact with other humans except by invading their mind?

Could Meiling even die? Could her soul be dragged like the *mó guǐ* she had seen, upward into the sky, for whatever afterlife awaited her? Would her soul be forever lost to wander the world?

Or would she remain an eternal prisoner here in this fortress, a weapon for anyone with power to wield? Would she be lost to blackness until this world was burned away with a purging fire? Would she *then* go on to the afterlife? Or would she be snuffed out into oblivion?

Was there any hope now? For her, for her empire, for the people she loved?

Day by day, Meiling hunted through minds.

Her body lay sprawled amid black magic, waiting for it to finally devour her. One after another, Zedong brought in prisoners for her to infiltrate. Sometimes he even brought his own guards and brigands, and she never knew what happened to any of them once they left her prison.

He never brought back Shang or Feiyan or Renshu. He did, however, threaten her with Shang's torture and death. For all she knew, Shang could already be dead. So long as the possibility remained that he still lived, she couldn't let him be hurt.

Meiling was Zedong's slave.

But while her body still breathed, laying face down in seeping black magic, she fought wherever she could.

Mind after mind, she searched and hunted. She grew faster at navigating minds, better at blocking out their distracting thoughts. She worked quickly and efficiently, learning how to avoid being drawn away by fascinating parts of their life. Soon, she was even bypassing the most important people in their lives, to avoid learning who they were and what they meant to the person. That was information that Zedong could use, but it was not the information he asked for. Meiling was determined to keep personal secrets hidden so that the person whose mind she invaded could not become a slave like her. The fewer things that Zedong knew about his prisoners, the better. She even tried to notice less about their mindscapes, for those too revealed much about a person.

Memories, my darling, are treacherous. Never trust them.

So Meiling learned how to not pry, how to go straight for their soul tether, how to not tarry and experience their humanness and uniqueness beneath her fingertips, how to block out memories she had no business knowing. She learned how to quickly find exactly what Zedong asked. She learned more about the empire, the problems her Pa faced, the beginning devastation of this war.

When Meiling floated in her prison, hovering near Zedong's mind locked behind bars of black magic, she hurled defiant words toward him. It was the only time he couldn't hear what she said, and it was the only thing she could do to feel less like a slave, to pretend her will was not completely subservient to his.

Day by day, mind by mind, the time slipped away.

Meiling could only tell when night fell because the stream of minds would stop and Zedong would leave her for a long stretch of time. It was impossible to tell time, surrounded as she was by so much blackness, but this helped her keep count of the days and helped her feel a little less insane.

Today, she had entered six minds. All of them had been the minds of the original twelve captive wielders. She'd discovered from Xian Hanying that Zuan Wan had died in his cell recently. She'd entered Cai Fu's mind, another high seer, hunting for visions that he had not revealed to Zedong. Because Zedong wanted to understand how siren lures worked, she'd entered Kang Lei's mind. He could only want to know such a thing if he was planning to duplicate it himself with his black magic.

Her own mind throbbed. When she grabbed hold of her fading soul tether, she sensed her body's shallow breathing, her soft and steady heartbeat.

She was exhausted. Not in the normal sense of the word, as she could never be physically tired when she was spirit. No, her essence, her soul, was weakened. She wanted to collapse to the ground, to be reunited with her body and simply lay in oblivion. She wanted to feel the stiffness, the pain of a physical body.

How much longer could she hold on to herself before she was lost to the madness of this captivity and her slavery?

Zedong was right. She was becoming more malleable. It hadn't taken years to do so. She still struggled with every inch given her, but the one thing that kept her sane was her memory.

In these long hours of blackness and night, Meiling kept a ritual.

She did not think about the minds she had entered. She did not even try to find a plan of escape. Those things had driven her mad the first few days she'd been put to sleep.

Instead, she remembered her life back at home. Her life at the palace before this all started. She thought about her mother, the nights that she had tucked her safely into her bed. She remembered the sunspots she found in the library, the books she would read. If she lost herself deeper to memories, she could make out the starry sky in winter against her closed eyelids and pick out the constellations, hear their whispers in the emptiness of the room.

She would think about her childhood with Yun and Hou. She would think about Academy visits, about the festivals they had grown up attending, the different sets of robes she had in her wardrobe. Her favorite one had been white with a pink embroidered sash. She could still remember the embroidery on the sleeves, like sand and foamy ocean.

In her mind, she would visit her favorite cliff overlooking the waves and the wharf. She would remember the ways she had wished to smell the salt and crunch the grit of sand in her teeth, how she wanted to let the wind twist and tangle with her hair.

She remembered watching the sun rise from that perch, seeing the soft purple fade to brilliant orange, until the entire mountainside was burning with gold.

There was her Pa, tall and strong and powerful, sitting on his throne. He'd tried so hard to save her. She wanted to think about whether he would come to save her again, how he might even break the spell she was under. But she could not think about the future without going mad. So she only remembered.

It made sense now why her parents had concealed her magic.

This was what they'd been protecting her from.

As strenuous, as difficult, as painful as the journey with Fen and Shang had been, she looked upon those weeks with as much fondness as she did her life back at the palace. She replayed every interaction over in her mind until she could see Fen's snarl and Shang's enigmatic black eyes. Those black eyes that said so much yet told so little. No matter how long she laid here, she would never, ever forget that slightly crooked, beautiful smile on Shang's face, directed at her. Neither would she ever forget what she'd found in his mind about wanting to kiss her.

She treasured every one of her memories that she could find. She held them close, like diamonds to her chest, and each night, when darkness fell deeper than the night before, she would recount each one.

This was how Meiling fought for her sanity. This was the only anchor for her soul, herself, in the madness that surrounded her.

She sat in the corner this night, rolling memory after memory through her mind, smiling. Even at the painful memories. She did not hope, for hope involved the future. Instead, she merely relived the past.

Her life had been a beautiful one.

Memories might be treacherous, but Zedong could never take them from her. He could take everything else, but he could not take away what she had already lived and experienced. He could not take away the love she treasured.

As they often did, her thoughts drifted to Shang. She refused to let herself imagine him chained in a dungeon far below, slowly starving. Or already dead. She did not want to think of him as anything other than the tall, strong, smart, ambitious young man who'd come to rescue her.

Yet her imagination betrayed her. She imagined the door opening, and a tall figure quickly stepping inside and shutting the door, his cloak fluttering silently around him. The blackness of the magic imprisoning her made him blurry on the edges, but nevertheless, in a few strides, he reached her. He knelt beside her form, which lay sprawled face down in black magic, one arm flung out above her head.

Gently, her imagined projection of Shang grabbed one of her shoulders and pushed it backward. He moved swiftly, as Shang would, and with another gentle push on her waist and hip, completely rolled her over so she lay limp on her back. Her arm was still stretched above her, the other one flopping to her side. Her hair was everywhere, and he used his thumb to brush the dark strands out of her face.

She should not be imagining this. It would make her go insane; it would make her hope. But her imagination kept going, kept plowing forward like a wild stallion broken free of its rider and every restraint.

The cloaked figure paused for a second, kneeling in blackness. Then, swiftly, he planted a hand on either side of Meiling's face and leaned down.

She felt the moment Shang's lips touched hers like a bolt of lightning. Were imaginations supposed to be this real? She was getting carried away; she should bring herself back to reality. After all, was that not the very essence of madness? Being disillusioned about what was actually real?

Meiling felt that kiss, though.

It burned like fire through her soul tether, which suddenly glowed much stronger. Like a blaze billowed to life in a cold kitchen hearth hours before dawn, her blood started pumping again, her lungs began drawing deeper breaths, and her muscles twitched.

That inescapable pull tightened on her tether as he kissed her harder, as he moved one of his hands to cradle the back of her head, drawing her closer. She was being reeled in like a fish on a line. It was not real, of course, but suddenly she did not care. She stopped fighting.

Her eyes opened.

There was no blackness. It was dark, but it was only the dark of night, something entirely different from Zedong's enchantments. She could see the wood of the ceiling, the stone of the walls, felt the coolness of more wood beneath her. A pleasantly cool hand cupped the back of her head. The warmth of a kiss still pressed against her lips.

Her eyes focused on the face in front of hers. If this was her imagination, she was impressed at the clarity with which she recollected Shang's face, with the hard angles of his nose and jaw and brow, the dark stubble lining his jaw. His hair was messy, and plenty had escaped his queue and fallen around his face. His eyes fluttered open a second after hers, and he pulled back just far enough that their lips parted.

Their gazes locked, and Meiling wished with all her heart that she could believe this was real. That the flash in his black eyes, which bespoke so much emotion she dared not name, was not her imagination.

Then his arms went around her, crushing her against him as his mouth found hers again and again. At first, carefully, gently—and then desperately. Like he was as broken and hopeless as she was. She leaned into him, returning his kisses like there was nothing in this world but him, her arms around his neck, and the softness of his lips.

Shang, Shang, Shang, every fragmented part of her cried.

Meiling, Meiling, Meiling, his kisses replied.

A low groan escaped him as he tugged her closer, kissing her deeper than before.

Maybe she *was* insane, because she never, ever wanted to leave this moment.

And then—he pulled back.

She stared up at him as he hovered close, still pressing one hand to the floor beside her and holding her with his other. A soft exhale escaped him, and it was warm on her face. He swallowed, his jaw tensing with the movement.

"This is a good dream," Meiling mumbled with a sigh. "I wish it were real. I've wanted to be free."

Shang drew back too quickly, his handsome face half hidden in the darkness. "It is real," he said, and it was his familiar low voice that filled her ears.

"That's what dreams always say." Meiling laughed quietly up into his not-real face. "It's only when you believe that they're real that you wake up and see that they're not." She smiled at him, studying everything before she was jerked back to Zedong's binding enchantments and the hopeless future she refused to think about.

"Meiling," he growled, his hand gripping her head tighter before his hand slid down to her back to heave her up into a sitting position. "We don't have time to waste on nonsense. Come."

The light of a full moon streamed into the darkness. Was she imagining how beautiful it was? All the nights she had floated under it, gripping her tether, flying free among stars?

Meiling blinked. She frowned, and she closed her eyes, reaching out with her hands. "Where's my tether?" she cried suddenly. "Am I dead?"

He grabbed her face in both of his and hissed, "Hush! You're awake! I woke you up. I broke the enchantments he had you under. *Spitfire*, he left you lying in the middle of the floor this whole time."

Meiling blinked again, still staring stupidly up at him. He seemed so . . . *real.* She lifted one hand and touched the back of his hand with the tips of her fingers. His entire arm jolted in response. This wasn't . . . But if it wasn't, where was her tether? No matter where she was lost in a dream or the world, she could always find her tether. Unless she was dead, or she was awake. She was fairly certain this was not the afterlife, not one of the seven layers of *diyu*.

Which meant . . .

This was real. This was actually Shang kneeling over her, touching her. The stiffness of her limbs, the pounding of her heart, the ache in her back—it was real.

A whimper escaped Meiling's lips and with something like a laugh, something like a sob, she flung her arms around his neck, breaking the hold he had on her face. "Shang!" she cried. "This is real . . . You're real . . ."

One of his arms wrapped hesitantly around her as she clung to him with all the certainty in the world, drawing in a lungful of his smell. He smelled like safety. Like home. Like everything that was good and right in the world.

He patted her back like she was a child, but she felt his heartbeat increase. Then, for a split second, he wrapped both his arms around her and held her tightly, pressing his face into her hair. For that bare instant, nightmares and curses evaporated into dust, and she thought that perhaps . . . perhaps she wasn't just his duty. Perhaps she wasn't an inconvenience to him. Perhaps what he felt for her was, indeed, much warmer.

He pulled away too quickly for her to know for sure.

"Come, now is not the time for celebration." His voice was low, husky. "I'm getting you out of here."

CHAPTER 25

SHANG PULLED MEILING to her feet and turned toward the door. "Follow me," he whispered. She hurried to his side and started reaching for his arm, but stopped herself. Slowly, she regained sense of her mind, herself. She didn't want to cling to him too closely.

His side glance told her he had caught her movement, however.

"Shang," she whispered quickly, swallowing. "Are you alright? Are you wounded in any way?"

"I am fine," he said immediately, turning back toward the door.

This time, she did reach out and catch his arm. He flinched. "I'm serious, it's important to know if—"

Shang disentangled himself without another look her way. The floorboards creaked under his careful footsteps. He stood as a looming shadow of darkness, and he looked hale and whole, but she knew

Shang. "Stop worrying," he muttered. "If you're trying to ask if I have the strength to do this, I most definitely do."

She hadn't meant to insult or doubt him. He should know that was not her intention. Instead of apologizing, she said, "I am glad to hear it." She did not tell him how often his harm was the knife brandished at her throat.

They were at the door. Shang pressed his ear to it, then silently crouched and peered underneath for any sign of guards or brigands. Meiling was near giddy with the prospect of leaving this wretched chamber, her mind addled with the thrill of escape. Nevertheless, she tried to calm her breathing.

Fathers, she was *starving.*

Somehow, the enchantments had sustained her body, but now they gave way to overwhelming hunger. Her body trembled, and she went a little lightheaded, but she took several deep, steadying breaths. She would think about eating when they escaped. Until then she would survive the aftereffects of Zedong's magic.

How was it possible that one kiss could make so much strong magic dissolve into nothing? She'd spent a full night hacking into the bindings on her mind with her crown of fears and nightmares, and still had never fully broken through. Yet one kiss, and it was gone. As though it never existed.

Shang eased open the door. "Stay close to me." He moved slowly, slipping silently out of the room, and then beckoned for her to follow. Just as quietly, he shut the door.

Wordlessly, he took a left and tucked himself into the shadows of the rising columns. Meiling followed in his shadow, the sound of her own breathing loud in her own ears. At least, of everything she was unequipped in when it came to being a magic-wielder, she was quiet. She had mastered that art long ago. Thus, Shang offered no rebuke or warning glare as she followed him.

A patch of moonlight stood in the middle of the hallway, bright and betraying. Shang hesitated for one moment. When he was about to take a step, he froze. Even his wafting cloak seemed to suddenly hold stone still.

Meiling froze too.

He reached behind him with his left hand for her. His fingers, cold as ice, closed around her forearm. Her breath caught.

Someone was standing just beyond the moonlight, hidden in the shadows like them.

Shang's hand on her wrist went so cold it almost burned. His right hand, which was partway concealed by his cloak, sparkled a little. He held a palmful of deadly ice shards.

For one very long moment, the three of them stood rigid. No movements, no words, no breathing. When Meiling finally sucked in air as silently as she could, that tiny sound broke the moment.

Shang dropped his hold on her forearm and drew back his arm to fling the ice.

"I will let you escape," a familiar, almost-musical voice rumbled in the darkness ahead.

She grabbed Shang's arm with both of hers. "It's Shuren!" she whispered in his ear as she jerked him back. "Don't kill him. He's a friend."

"Friend?" Shang spat, turning angry eyes back on her.

Distrust simmered there, just below the surface. A quiet question hummed between them—*Has Zedong broken her more than I realized?*

Of course he would doubt Shuren. The illusionist had been the one to knock him out and ensure his capture.

"Shang," Meiling hissed, wrapping her arms tighter around his as he tried to pull free. "Listen to me, please. I know these people, these minds. Believe me."

He stopped jerking his arm. The tension in his body didn't relax one moment as he glanced from her to the shadows beyond the moonlight. He was listening.

"You will not betray us?" Meiling whispered around Shang's shoulder as she poked her head into the illusionist's view.

Shang was so very, very tense. Like a wildcat ready to pounce.

"Only if you take the healer," Shuren said. Even his big frame was hard to see in the shadows. She might not have seen him if Shang hadn't sensed his presence and stopped.

Shang cursed under his breath.

"Of course," Meiling answered. "We were just going to get her."

Shang immediately ripped his arm free of her grip and turned a withering glare upon her. She glared her fiercest back at him. Did he truly think she would leave without Feiyan after refusing the first time?

"You will help us?" Shang asked the illusionist, his low voice dark with skepticism.

Shuren nodded once, but said nothing more. Then he seemed to simply . . . *vanish*. Shang cursed again. Whipping his gaze back down to Meiling, he hunched down so his face was close to hers and hissed into her ear, "Do you understand that this may be your last chance of escape? If we attempt a rescue of the healer, we are far less likely to make it out. If we are caught, they will not take me prisoner this time. They will kill me, understand? They might kill you, too."

Meiling blinked up at him, her breathing coming fast and her words choking in her throat. Phoenixes scorch him for throwing her care for him back in her face! Typical Shang to find any weakness and lord it over her, to not care if his own life was her weakness. She squeezed her eyes shut against the tears, but two slipped free anyway. She lowered her head away from his gaze, but she nodded. "I know."

Shang sighed. He drew away and squared his shoulders. "Good thing I didn't put the keys back on the jailer."

Meiling raised her eyes, peeking at him. "What?"

"The keys. To the dungeons. I stashed them some place easily retrievable."

Of course. Naturally.

As they slipped past a moonbeam, Meiling glanced out the windows and was greeted with a flash of burning fire. Did Shang have a plan for getting past the phoenixes? Surely, he did. He likely had this entire escape mapped out flawlessly in his mind. There was no way he was planning to wing it when they got to the phoenixes.

Feiyan's words echoed in Meiling's mind. *Plans are for breaking. Rules are for breaking.*

She glanced up at the tall, cloaked figure only two steps ahead of her. So Feiyan had tried to kiss him years ago. He had pushed her away. She simultaneously stood in Feiyan's heartbreak and her own relief and warmth that he had never kissed anyone but her. Not that it mattered.

They neared the end of the hallway, reaching the door to the stairwell. Meiling waited as Shang started to place his hand on the door. But then he stopped and turned back to her. "Do not make a sound. No screaming, you hear me? Whatever you do, no screaming. And close your eyes."

She nodded mutely, and he looked at her a second longer, as if he did not believe her. Then he whirled and opened the door.

He acted so fast she didn't have time to close her eyes, and she hardly realized what was happening until he was beckoning her to enter the stairwell as he dragged a heavy body out of the way. She stood frozen out in the hallway until he hissed, "Meiling!"

She scampered through the doorway, starting to glance at the poor guard, who bled from a dozen little cuts on his chest. But Shang caught her chin, drew her attention to him. *"Don't look,"* he mouthed. *"Not a sound."* Then he was hurrying down the stairs, quiet as a mouse. Meiling hurried after him on wobbly legs, her stomach gnawing with emptiness. How was Shang so fast? She tried to be quiet and steady on her feet, but that came at the cost of speed. He was waiting for her at the bottom, his brow furrowed, when she finally reached him.

She almost asked if he knew the way to the dungeon and offered to direct him there. Just in time, she clamped her mouth shut. Of course he knew where it was.

When she hovered behind him, he cracked the door open. He poked his head through and then just as quickly pulled it back. She looked up at him, her heart quickening, and her eyes asked the question she dare not use her voice to utter. In the darkness, she could make out that Shang glanced at her, pursed his lips, and shook his head.

She took one tiny step closer to him.

Silence hung as heavy as the darkness of the stairwell. Meiling stepped closer to the door, trying to hear what was outside, but only silence greeted her. The barest flicker of torchlight slipped through the cracked door and landed on the lowest two steps.

The only thing audible was her own breathing. Not even the softest sound of his. Once or twice, he glanced back at her as if to say, *"Quiet down!"*

She glared at him in response.

After several long minutes, he stepped slightly forward again and peered out. This time, he motioned for her to follow. He slid into the light of the torch, and she could see how ragged and filthy his garments had become in the dungeons. She hated the thought of him there, half-starved and alone.

He'd apparently used his time well, however.

The thought made her smile to herself as she followed Shang into the light, and then back into the shadows as quickly as possible.

"Why are you smiling?" His voice was so quiet, it was barely a breath, yet tinged with alarm.

As though she'd be smiling while something was dreadfully wrong.

Then again, they *were* trying to escape the most traumatic experience she'd ever had in her life. *"Nothing,"* she mouthed to him, and he accepted the answer with wrinkled eyebrows and returned his focus to reaching the dungeon.

They stood on the very edge of the courtyard. Overhead, phoenixes circled and preened their beaks into flaming feathers while perched on the four towers. Shang hardly glanced at them and fixed his gaze instead on the guards nearby patrolling the battlements and wandering the courtyard.

Meiling's heart was in her throat at how close one of the guards was. She tapped Shang's elbow and pointed as they pressed into the shadowed darkness. He followed her gaze and nodded slightly.

There was the dungeon door, on the opposite side of the courtyard from them. Shang's attention was fixed on it, and then roamed every inch of the fortress in view. When she peered up at him, she could make out little more than his eyes blazing with that calculating light.

He started moving slowly along the wall and she followed. How long had it been since she was free in the night? Had her last true moment of freedom been after her dinner with Zedong when he had showed her his plans? When she wandered through the dark fortress and found his garden of black magic?

A sudden urge came over Meiling. If only she could take Shang there to the garden! He would know much more what to make of it than her. He might even know some about the plants, how to use them. If anyone did, Shang would.

But they were trying to escape. They couldn't afford any additional detours.

He suddenly halted, stiff as the stone they hugged. She froze alongside him. Her eyes darted up to him, but his were mostly trained on one guard that seemed to be coming this way. Every few seconds, his gaze would snap the opposite direction, and back to the guard. The guard's booted footfalls echoed on the flagstone.

Despite the slaughter of Zedong's Butagin guards during the battle, it seemed he'd enlisted more to his service, because everywhere she looked, the men guarding the fortress wore furs, beards, and those tight braids.

Meiling's heart pounded as the guard came closer. He did not seem to notice the two hidden forms, but he would if he came much closer. Tension radiated from Shang's body. He braced himself, and the air between them froze. He tilted his hand into the folds of his cloak so his ice would not catch any straying light.

She waited, not breathing, trying not to tremble so much as hunger stabbed her again and again.

The guard walked right by, hardly three feet away from them.

When he had passed, Meiling breathed. Shang's hand darted out and covered her mouth and nose with his big, frozen hand. It was not meant to cut off her air, but to tell her she was being too loud. Her face flamed, and she exhaled only a tiny bit against his palm. Slowly, he lowered his arm.

Few times had she ever seen his eyes so bright, so focused.

It was a small eternity before he motioned for her to follow him as they inched their way forward. Once or twice, he glanced back to ensure she remained close, and no one followed them. A third time, he looked back with a warning glare, like she was being too loud. She glared back; she hadn't made a sound.

They crept their way along the covered portico surrounding the courtyard. Eventually, they reached the corner and only had to walk down the last length to reach the door to the dungeon. The most obvious problem, aside from the wandering guards, was the torch ensconced in the wall by the door. It flamed and danced, threatening to reveal the slightest movements of the two shadows. Meiling kept eyeing Shang, wondering how he planned to get past it.

He stopped just outside the reaches of the torchlight. She paused behind him, her breath caught in suspense. He bent toward her ear and breathed, "You said you know the people here?"

Meiling glanced around at the posted guards. It was not as if she knew every single one, but she was familiar enough with Zedong's forces. If he was about to quiz her on names, especially barbarian names, she would miserably fail. She only nodded.

"Are there are any feral brigands nearby?" he asked, coming close so he could keep his voice lowered. He came so close that their faces were almost touching, his lips barely an inch from her ear.

She shivered and shook her head. "These are only the barbarian guards. I see no magic-wielders."

Shang nodded, lips tight. Was he impressed? Impossible to tell. "Good." His head swiveled back to the problem of the torch. He backed up a few steps, making Meiling scramble out of his way. He lifted his right arm, aimed straight at the torch.

She did not see any ice, but the torch started sizzling and spitting. One of the nearby guards turned, cocked his head, and stepped toward it just as it flickered out completely.

Shang snatched her wrist and darted forward quickly. She stumbled after him, trying hard not to make a sound. He glanced back at her, and she got the distinct sense of irritation, which only made her more irritated in return.

How easily they fell back into walking this tightrope of their relationship. One minute, warm; the next minute, cold. Her always managing to irritate him, and him being his too-capable confident self that always managed to be inconvenienced by her.

He let her go. Fast as lightning, he shot out and wrapped his right arm around the guard's neck and used the other to grip his head and create a hold for his right fist. The guard scrabbled at Shang's arm quickly, opened his mouth, groped for his knife, and then, with a tight flexing of Shang's arms, fell limp. A soft grunt escaped Shang's lips as he caught the man's body, and Meiling rushed to loop one of the fallen guard's arms around her neck and support his weight.

The whole thing was eerily quiet. They dragged the unconscious guard deeper into the shadows and deposited him without a sound. Shang's eyes met hers over the man's hanging head. And . . . he *grinned* at her, white teeth flashing in the darkness.

He was probably grinning because she was so shocked. She slipped to his side, and they hurried back to the now darkened dungeon door. With a last glance over their shoulders, he opened the door with a painfully loud creak and shoved her through before him. He pulled it shut behind them.

They were plunged into darkness.

CHAPTER 26

"IF WE'RE LUCKY, they will think the missing guard stepped in here," Shang whispered. His hand brushed her shoulder in the pitch blackness, and something shot through her spine. He patted her shoulder and then reached to grip her arm. "Careful. There're a lot of steps."

"I know," she whispered back with a smile. With her free arm, she braced herself against the crumbling wall and took tiny steps until she reached the drop. Immediately, she almost tripped and lost her balance, but Shang's grip tightened, steadying her. She caught her breath.

"Careful," he repeated, oddly gentle.

He moved much faster down the stairs than she was comfortable with, but he kept his grip on her, making sure she didn't fall.

"How did you do that?" Meiling whispered, finding the next step in the darkness. How many steps were there? "With the guard?" And

. . . everything? How had he escaped, gotten the key? Made it to where she was?

Shang shrugged. "It's a hold we learned at the Academy. Cuts off blood flow to the brain. Convenient for knocking someone out without injury. Done correctly, the windpipe is not blocked, so the victim can still breathe."

She did not want to ask why that guard had gotten this, while the other guard in the stairwell had gotten a handful of ice driven into his chest. Instead, she moved her arm, so she gripped his sleeve. It gave her a little more sense of control in the dark to be holding onto things with both hands.

"Last step," Shang said abruptly, seeming to turn back toward her.

"Oh good," she breathed and slowly placed her foot on the ground level. It was so much darker than the other times she'd been here. When they groped along until they rounded the corner, she whispered, "The lantern! It's burned out!"

"I snuffed it out when I escaped," he responded evenly. Then, with a hint of irritation, "Wasn't planning on returning."

A jangle of iron keys sliced through the air, right before Meiling stepped on something fleshy. Her head hit Shang's chest as his hand clamped over her mouth—preventing her from screaming.

"It's just a body. Don't worry."

Just a body. Just—just a body! Of course.

Shang held her against him for a moment longer as her chest heaved from the sudden fright. "Are you alright?"

She swallowed, forcing herself to nod.

He took a half step back, slipping his grip from her mouth down to her arm to keep them connected. There was that jangling iron again. "I have the keys."

"I know where Feiyan's cell is. I think I can still find it."

"You do?" he asked, clearly surprised.

"Yes, I visited her. And I was placed next to her while I was in the dungeon." A sudden thought made Meiling gasp. "Oh no!" she cried, pressing her free hand to her chest. Her head went light as hunger-weakness washed over her.

"What?" Shang asked quickly, his voice taking on a gruff edge. "What's the matter?"

"They moved her." Meiling smacked her forehead with her palm. Frustration raked through her from head to toe. "They separated us. She could be anywhere in this labyrinth of cells."

There was a long silence. Would he drag her back out of here, give up Feiyan for lost, and return to his original plan of escape? She couldn't allow it. But the thought of scouring hundreds of prison cells in the dark was enough to make her want to melt into a pile of flesh and bone on the floor.

"How long has it been since you were here, in the dungeon? Locked in here?" Shang asked, breaking the silence.

Meiling peeled her hand away from her face and looked up at where his voice had sounded, but she could not make out even the faintest glimmer of his eyes. "I think . . . I was trying to keep track of the days . . . I can't . . . quite . . ."

"It's fine," he said, giving her arm a little reassuring squeeze. "Sounds like it could be long enough that they put her back in her original cell."

"I do not know why they would do that," Meiling said, blinking against the blackness.

He shrugged. "It's the best place to start. Which door?"

It was better than wandering aimlessly. "Second on the right."

Shang set off toward where the doors must be. It seemed farther than it needed to be, but she kept silent. A sound of shrieking hinges met her ears. She winced as he pulled her into thicker darkness.

He paused suddenly, hesitating.

"I'm going to take your hand now," he said, perhaps a tiny bit too casually. "Easier to stay connected."

Meiling's face flushed, even before his cool fingers searched and entwined themselves in hers. She said nothing, though she should have at least grunted an acknowledgement. She was too lightheaded from hunger and this sudden rush of strong, heady emotion to respond. If she was not careful, she would collapse into his arms.

And that would be embarrassing. Not to mention, very awkward.

She was glad for the darkness to conceal everything her face surely betrayed. His hand was large and callused in hers, still holding an edge of ice. It was so strange and yet so right. She let her blushing self be led down another set of stairs, past iron bars so cold they froze the surrounding air. She welcomed the coolness against her heat.

"Which door?"

"The middle one," Meiling croaked.

There was the sound of a hand brushing across stone, then wood, then stone again, and back to wood as he located the door. Another wailing hinge, and Shang pulled her deeper after him. Instinctively, she clung to his forearm with her left hand. Just as soon as she did it, she dropped her grip and tried to calm herself. This was utterly ridiculous. The extent of the ridiculousness was seen in how cool he remained while her mind railed with questions about what this gesture could possibly mean. Even though she knew very well that it meant he did not want to lose the emperor's daughter in his enemy's pitch-black fortress. Nothing more.

She wanted to thank him for coming after her, for not giving up on her rescue, for letting them free Feiyan, too. The right words would not come, and her lips twisted with the effort of trying to speak. She was afraid that anything she said would showcase how much she still trembled.

Her hand in his went slick with sweat. This must be so unpleasant for him. She blushed deeper with mortification. Finally, she spoke. It was not what she had really wanted to say, but it was the only words her tongue would form. "Renshu is imprisoned too."

"What?" Shang whirled in the darkness, his hand tightening on hers and instantly chilling to near freezing. She barely contained herself from jerking her hand free.

"He was captured, too. I infiltrated his mind just before yours."

"And you did not tell me this before now?"

"There are many things I need to tell you."

His hand grew even colder, and he pulled her after him. "We have time," he said icily. It was definitely not a tone that made her want to spill everything she had seen, heard, and experienced here.

Nevertheless, she took a deep breath. "The twelve missing wielders were here the entire time. Ten remain, including Feiyan and me. Two have died."

"Died?" Shang repeated. "How? Were they not his tools? Rare magic he wanted access to? How could they be dead?"

"He can get . . . angry," she mumbled.

He paused for a heartbeat, his grip tightening on her hand. Then he grunted and pushed open another door. "If his temper makes him kill his prized tools, he is a greater fool than I thought."

She said nothing.

"What?" he prompted, pressing his thumb into the back of her hand.

She cocked her head, trying to organize exactly what she was trying to say. "I think he is growing more powerful. With his magic, I think he has less need for us than he did before, as he learns to replicate our magic with his." She paused before adding, "I think the only person who is truly invaluable to him is Feiyan. There is nothing that can replace her healing magic."

Shang stopped suddenly. His hand let go of hers, but she didn't have time to feel bereft. He had her by the shoulders in an instant, his grip hard, though not painful. And then she found herself against a freezing wall, shuddering and staring up into the darkness where Shang's face must be.

His voice carried low, but every edge of it was sharp as ice and far deadlier.

"What did he do to you?"

He'd read between the lines of what she'd spoken.

Her heart raced in her chest, her throat going dry as parchment. “Um . . .” She drew in a deep breath, tilting her head away from where his breath landed warm on her face. As if that could help her bear the intensity of a gaze she couldn’t see. “He tried to turn me to his side.”

“He wanted you to betray your family? Your empire?”

“Yes. He tried to get me to do it willingly, and when I wouldn't . . .”

His fingers tightened on her shoulders. He was so close, she could *almost* feel his lips hovering just above her brow. “What did he do to you?”

Suddenly, breathing was difficult, her lungs clenched and heaving. She swallowed back a sob, squeezing her eyes against the darkness. Oh *fathers.* She wrapped her arms around herself, ducking her head and shivering as the coldness of the dungeon seeped into her bones.

“Meiling.” His voice was edged with urgency. “*Meiling*, what did he do to you?”

She choked on the tears she fought, barely realizing how she'd begun trembling all over. This wasn’t what she wanted to think about, wasn’t something she wanted to relive even in memory. “He . . . he . . .”

His hands moved from her shoulders, up—up, until he cupped her face, his long fingers in her hair, on her jaw, while his thumbs pressed into her cheeks. Her breath snagged between her teeth when his forehead leaned against hers, and he was so close she could tilt her mouth up and kiss him.

“Tell me, Meiling.”

Getting the words out of her mouth was excruciating. Up until now, she’d just tried to forget that day when she’d invaded Zedong’s mind, when she’d refused to divulge Renshu's secrets. But now, the memories assaulted her, of the pain, of the belief that he was killing her. That she was dying.

“He beat me.”

The words were choked, followed by a gasping sob. There was a fierce growl in the darkness, and then Shang's arms were around her, pressing her to his chest as one of his hands slid up to the back of her head. It fisted in her hair as she began weeping.

"How . . ." Shang's swallow bobbed against her head. "How badly?"

She shivered, gasping a little. "I think . . . if not for Feiyan . . . I would have . . ." She couldn't finish the last word.

But she didn't have to. Shang knew.

He swore viciously. "I will kill him." Then his hands were running up and down her arms, her back, her waist, as though checking for injuries. Or perhaps assuring himself that she was whole. "He's a twisted, warped excuse of a man who deserves—"

"We need to find Feiyan," Meiling whispered, shuddering on the tears she tried to swallow.

Shang tightened his arms around her, so tightly she could barely breathe, and pressed his head against hers. "I won't let anyone hurt you like that again. I'll die first."

Slowly, the tension eased out of her body, and she melted against him. "I don't want you to die," she whispered.

They stood there for a long minute. She didn't want to waste their precious little time, but . . . but for the first time in ages, she felt truly safe. Even in the midst of a dark dungeon, at the heart of their enemy's fortress, so long as Shang held her, she was safe. Perhaps he was thinking something similar, because he gave no sign of letting her go.

It was just the darkness and the comfort of his warmth, the security of his strength.

Those few moments were enough for her heart, which had fragmented into so many tiny pieces, to start knitting back together. She started shaking, whether from relief or hunger or both, she wasn't sure. He held her through it all until she was still once more.

"Let's keep going," he said, his voice husky as he loosened his grip on her. She nodded, and he reached down to take her hand again before continuing deeper into the dungeon. "Where's Renshu?" he asked.

"I don't know. I never was able to visit him."

"Why were you visiting people in the dungeon?" He stopped suddenly, then said, "More stairs." Thankfully, he slowed his pace.

"I was trying to find Feiyan so we could plan our escape. I brought food to her and a couple of the other wielders I found."

As they continued groping in the darkness, the only sounds that touched her ear were their own scuffles and a faint drip. The stench was nearly overpowering, but Meiling had grown strangely accustomed to it. When Shang asked for the next door, she told him.

"This should be the last," she mumbled. She desperately hoped that Feiyan was here. If not, where could they look? Would they even have time?

He opened the last door, and it swung into darkness.

"Too busy. Come again later," a voice chirped from inside.

"Feiyan!" Meiling cried, dropping Shang's hand and rushing forward to fumble for the bars. Cold metal reached her fingers, and then that familiar healing warmth. "Oh Feiyan!" She wanted to weep with relief. Warmth filled her hollow belly at Feiyan's touch and swept away her pulsing weakness. "We're here to get you out. We're going to escape."

"Escape?" Feiyan asked in disbelief. "Who's with you?"

Shang was already sliding the key into the lock. It wailed loudly in the small chamber. "I'm with her."

A shocked silence followed.

"Shangdi?" Feiyan breathed. "What—?"

"Shang is here, yes. He managed to escape, and he's here to free us," Meiling said, tightening her hands on Feiyan's when they suddenly trembled.

"Us?" she repeated.

"The illusionist said he would help us escape if we took you," Shang muttered.

Feiyan withdrew her hands from Meiling so she could walk out of the cell. Shang closed it behind her and relocked it. "Apparently it's my lucky day," she said with a weak laugh. "The others? Are we rescuing them too?"

Meiling reached out again, brushed an elbow, and grasped Feiyan's hand.

"No time. There's also no way a dozen of us could escape without raising the alarm. That would be a full-out battle, and this place is fortified to the teeth. We do not even know who all is captive. But now that we know about the prisoners, there must be a second attack here to free the remaining wielders," Shang said quickly, striding back toward the door. His voice was clipped, and Meiling realized with a tinge of sadness that he was not even going to attempt a rescue of his best friend. "Where did you go, Meiling?" he grunted.

"I'm here."

His hand found hers again and tightly laced their fingers together. With another blush that flooded to her toes, she let herself be pulled after him, keeping her other hand firmly linked with Feiyan's.

"Well," Feiyan started to say as they began making their way back up through layers of penetrating darkness. "I'm pretty sure you're not so happy about me tagging along, Shangdi. But you've got to admit, I'm quite the asset for this little escapade. I've got you covered. You find yourself skewered, stabbed, dismembered, disemboweled, or even—dare I suggest such a horror?—sunburned, I can heal you. As long as there's breath in your lungs. I must admit death is a bit of a tall order for me to cure at the moment. Haven't quite figured that one out. Always worth a shot, though! I'd say it couldn't kill you, but it might actually, so I'd avoid taking too many chances."

Meiling hid her snickers.

"Cease your babble. We've got a mission to accomplish," Shang said.

Feiyan squeezed Meiling's hand, and when Meiling looked back, she could make out white teeth. Feiyan was grinning.

"I'm starving. Any votes to pause our daring little escape for a bite?" Feiyan asked. "When we reach the top, of course. I think I remember where the kitchen is."

Meiling's stomach folded over on itself, sending another wave of weakness passing over her. Food!

"Shut *up*."

"I like the food idea," Meiling quipped quickly, feeling far more daring and ridiculous with Feiyan here.

Shang whirled in the darkness. His strained voice dropped to a hiss, emotion threatening to break past his guards. "Is this a game to you two?"

Guilt stabbed Meiling. She hadn't considered enough how difficult this must be for him. To plan this all in the dark, to immediately have to ditch that plan to find Feiyan, to have to crawl through the fortress in the darkness and not get caught, then navigate through this labyrinth . . . All while bearing the burden of Meiling's life, which could cost him his. He risked his life for her in countless ways and could not even rescue his dearest friend. She hung her head, wished she did not have to hold his hand, and wished she were brave enough to apologize.

She did not have to respond, because Feiyan did. "Look. Shangdi, life isn't meant to be taken seriously. Life is ridiculous. We're all running around like pieces on a board game, smashing into others and trying to find our special little square to occupy." Feiyan's bright voice lowered, grew far more serious than Meiling had ever heard it. "Take life seriously and you break. That's all there is to it."

The silence that fell over the group could not conceal the anger and tension radiating from Shang's hand into Meiling. She wished there was anything she could do to alleviate the strain, anything to make him relax. But she was fairly certain that he would find even a little squeeze to his hand patronizing.

Impulse made her act before thinking. She pulled down on his hand, dragging his face a smidge closer. She quickly whispered, hoping he was near enough to hear it and Feiyan was not, "Thank you, Shang."

He jerked away and shoved open the next door. But his hand tightened on hers. Was it her imagination that his thumb just brushed the back of her hand? No, he was probably just readjusting his grip.

She wasn't sure if she could handle the fire in her gut in addition to Feiyan's gentle warmth and the painful silence. Her attempts to break the tension usually didn't end well, but she could almost taste it in the air between Shang and Feiyan. She hated that two of the people she loved most in the world were angry with each other.

So she asked a question she had long been wondering about. "Shang? Can you freeze people into a chunk of ice?"

"Is this really the best time for this question?"

"I was just curious," she said quietly.

Shang sighed. "Stairs."

Apparently, he had no interest in answering. She added it to her list of failed attempts at diffusing tension.

But he spoke, "People are hot. If I freeze them, all their heat must go somewhere. It'll make a small explosion. It's too risky, since I cannot freeze people from a distance. I'd blow myself up."

That was interesting. "Oh," she mumbled. "That makes sense."

"I must admit, Shangdi," Feiyan's bright voice emerged from the shadows behind them. Shang immediately tensed. "This is impressive. My plans never seemed to work. They always kept having to be thrown out the window. And then the improvisation had not worked yet. I knew it would work eventually, but this is a little more efficient."

"Improvisation?" The incredulity in Shang's voice was obvious.

"What?" Feiyan barked a laugh. "Do your plans never fail?"

Meiling tried to make out his face in the dark, tried to get a read on what he was thinking. It proved impossible.

"Have you never made a backup plan?" he asked, seeming genuinely alarmed. "Contingency plans?"

Feiyan laughed again. "Oh, those plans were something along the lines of, *'If this fails, look for something else to try.'*"

Shang balked. "Fathers above," he breathed. Meiling could almost imagine the regret racing through his mind, how he wished he could trade Feiyan for Renshu.

Between the two of them, Meiling grinned, glad they could not see.

"All right," he said, his deep voice ten times sterner than before. "Listen to me, healer. You follow my lead and my plan. I'm prepared, and I do not need to deal with impulsive ideas from you."

"Of course, Glorious Majesty," said Feiyan.

Shang exhaled through his teeth and pulled Meiling up behind him a tad harder than before. She tried not to trip on the slick ground and held on tightly to Feiyan's hand.

After what felt like hours of stumbling in the dark, hours of trying not to let herself be overwhelmed by the flush elicited by Shang's hand holding hers, they finally reached the top of the dungeon. He pushed open the last door, and they piled out of the labyrinth.

Shang, never losing his sense of direction, led them around the corner and up the last flight of stairs until they stood on the landing before the dungeon's exit. He released his grip on Meiling's hand and she quickly crossed her arms and tucked her sweaty hand into the folds of her grimy robes.

"This is the hard part," he whispered. "Follow me. We're going to get to the battlements without being discovered and then we're going to scale the eastern wall."

Meiling bit her lip. What did scaling a wall entail? The battlement was covered with guards and swooping phoenixes. It would be much harder than their earlier jaunt through the courtyard. She was glad Shang did not still hold her hand. Otherwise, he might have sensed the rapid increase of her heartbeat.

"This is going to be fun," Feiyan said, rubbing her hands together in anticipation.

"Shut up," he retorted and crept closer to the door, crouching and peering underneath it. "No more jokes from you until we're on the other side of that wall." He stuck a threatening finger in her face.

"Jokes? What jokes?"

Shang did not respond, so Feiyan whispered to Meiling, "Does he think I'm telling jokes?"

And Meiling genuinely had no idea if that question was a joke itself.

"Jokes aren't jokes unless people laugh. Pretty sure no one has been laughing," Feiyan quipped.

"Are you an idiot?" Shang whirled on her. "Shut your *mouth,* Li Feiyan."

The air grew colder, quieter. Meiling wanted to rebuke them both for this absurd behavior, but instead, she whispered very softly in Feiyan's ear, "I think jokes are still jokes even if no one laughs. They're just not funny."

Feiyan barely contained a snort. She reached out and squeezed Meiling's arm. A wordless thanks.

Shang opened the door. "Stay!" he whispered, and bolted out the door, leaving it cracked behind him.

"Yes, master," Feiyan muttered under her breath.

Meiling peeked through the opening of the door and tried to find the outline of Shang's tall form hugging close to the shadows. She spotted him not too far away, his right hand held up toward them, saying not to move, as his eyes roamed the area.

Then his eyes shot to hers, flashing wide with horror.

She barely jumped back from the door as it swung open, and an unfamiliar dark form stood in the doorway. The form halted, as if just as shocked as she was.

Feiyan leapt. Meiling could barely make out more than tousling shadows. There was a quiet grunt, not from Feiyan, and the man slumped.

"Catch him!" Feiyan hissed.

Meiling reached out just in time to support his forward-falling chest. Together, they dragged him against the wall and leaned him up so he would not fall down the stairs. As they finished, she turned and there was Shang standing in the doorway, a fistful of ice raised above his head.

He stared for a second at the guard, flicked his eyes to Feiyan, and then whirled in a flutter of tattered cloak back out the door.

"Tsk, tsk." Feiyan made the sound with her tongue. "Leaving the dirty work to the girls now, Shangdi?"

Without acknowledging her, Shang gestured quickly for them to follow.

CHAPTER 27

FEIYAN

FEIYAN FOLLOWED A step behind Shangdi and Meiling. She watched them and the sleeping fortress carefully, searching for signs that anyone had spotted them yet. Ahead, Shangdi picked their way carefully along the shadows to one of the tower stairwells. Heading to the battlements.

Shangdi's careful movements were beyond their level of Academy training. Feiyan had the privilege of a rather *unorthodox* experience at the Academy and while she would never come close to the sort of skill obvious in the Academy's prized graduates, she knew genius when she saw it.

She had seen it long ago. Back before he was popular among other students, before he'd distinguished himself. That was originally why she had wanted to study with him. Maybe, in a strange way, she had hoped some of his genius would rub off on her. If not, maybe his diligence would.

This plan of his revealed an uncanny knowledge of the doings and layout of the fortress. He had been well deserving of his appointment. So why was he here, instead of pursuing his lifelong dream and ambition? Why was he not reaping the reward of the years of obsessive schooling?

The answer crouched in the shadows behind him.

Meiling was oblivious to much of the workings of the empire. Surprisingly oblivious. Shangdi and Fen had failed their mission to deliver the princess safely to their destination. Which meant that Shangdi should be in one place and one place alone right now: prison, awaiting trial for his life.

Yet he was here.

This meant there was some strange monkeying going on in the bureaucracy. Feiyan was no stranger to this. Sometimes, whether convenient or inconvenient, certain people proved themselves too valuable for the limitations of justice.

Keeping Shangdi's form in her vision was not Feiyan's preferred way of operating at the moment. His words stung, but she had long given up on him. He was a fool, just like the rest of them. Sometimes geniuses could be the worst fools of all.

They clung to the shadows of the courtyard as Shangdi opened the door to the tower stairwell and dispatched the guard inside without a sound. Meiling blanched a little, no doubt still weakened from her lack of food. Feiyan had sensed her empty stomach when their hands touched and her magic immediately set to work sustaining her strength. It had been for Meiling's sake that Feiyan had spoken up earlier about finding food. Her own belly was empty enough, but she had eaten a mere half-day ago. Shangdi was smart, but she doubted he had food waiting for them on the other side of this wall.

Meiling hesitated only a second and then followed Shangdi's beckoning hand. Feiyan took up the rear as they crept up the stairs, stepping around the guard's body.

Instinct tolled alarm bells in her mind.

Shangdi was good, but this was too easy. She was not going to complain, but she wasn't about to blindly follow him. She searched every crevice, every patch of shadow.

That idiot illusionist Shuren was around here somewhere. He was here, and unlike Meiling, she did not trust him so implicitly. He probably watched their progress while hidden in their own shadows.

Meiling tripped, and the sound made Feiyan cringe despite herself. Shangdi did the glaring for her, however. Strangely, though, he reached out a hand, and it hovered behind Meiling's back for a second before falling back to his side when she steadied herself. "Careful," he rumbled. He leapt ahead, searching around the curve of the staircase for guards. Apparently there were none, for he continued taking the stairs two at a time, never making the slightest sound.

Feiyan smirked mirthlessly as his form disappeared around the curve.

So, the unbreakable Tan Shangdi had finally broken. It was the sweet and gentle princess who had dealt the blow. It seemed fitting. Even though there was a pang in Feiyan's heart—would there ever not be?—she could not have found a better, more worthy soul to make his resolve against tenderness crumble.

Tan Shangdi had a beating heart, after all.

In truth, she had always known this. Though recently, despite her intuition, her cynical side had begun to doubt. Papa had always told her never to listen to the cynic in her brain, and half the time she obeyed him. But more than half the time, her rational mind thought too hard about something.

She rounded the curve to find Shangdi and Meiling waiting for her. As soon as she appeared, he turned his attention toward the door that would let them out onto the battlements. This would be the hardest part of the escape, and Meiling seemed to realize it too. She put on a brave face, but the moonlight streaming through the window revealed how her hands trembled.

Shangdi noticed too, glancing down at her before returning to listening to whatever stood beyond this door.

It hurt; she wouldn't lie. More than she had expected. But life was meant to hurt. She glanced down at her own hands, hands that had relieved the suffering of thousands in her lifetime. In all her life of being around those sick and dying, while she was utterly incapable of healing the slightest ailment of her own, Feiyan had allowed that one big question to bud in her mind until it blossomed into a closely cherished belief.

Pain was never meant to be healed in an instant. Life and happiness were more than relief from pain.

Just then, her eyes snagged on the very shadow she had been searching for. A few stairs above the landing where they hovered around the door, Shuren crouched against the curve of the stairwell. Hidden by darkness. Darkness himself.

He'd let his invisibility drop barely so Feiyan could see him. There was no other explanation; he could stay invisible all he wanted. She met his tortured gaze evenly. Shangdi and Meiling couldn't see him, could they?

She knew he loved her. She'd known it from the first time he had punched her in the face. He was more of a fool than even Shangdi. Shuren knew Zedong was wrong, but he went along anyway. He did not fight with every breath.

That was why Feiyan couldn't trust him as much as Meiling clearly did. At least in this one thing, she and Shangdi probably agreed.

She turned away from him and let a long breath out of her nose. Shangdi shot her a glare, which only made her grin. Which, naturally, resulted in a scowl from him. Meiling glanced between them and seemed to be trying to figure out how to intervene. How to keep them from hurting each other. The thought made Feiyan shake her head imperceptibly and grin wider.

Shangdi cracked open the door and Meiling peered out with him. He drew back suddenly, grabbing both of Meiling's shoulders to pull her out of eyesight as well. He set her firmly against the wall by the door and then returned to listening and checking for an opening.

Feiyan slipped next to her and reached out to grab her trembling hand. Her magic slid through her fingertips to give Meiling another boost of strength. Did Meiling guess what she did? Or did she assume Feiyan just wanted a scrap of comfort?

It did not matter which she thought, since both were true.

Feiyan's thoughts strayed to her beloved Papa and his one great sin: his taking of another wife to improve his chances of producing a magical heir. If he had but waited three more years, it would have been obvious that his daughter was the only healer born in ages. If he had but waited! Her life might have been so different. She would never have to fear for her mother and brother. Since Ma had died, there was even more fear she harbored for her poor brother. She would not be so torn between protecting her brother and healing the people.

Love was not and never would be for Feiyan. Her job was to bind up what was broken, to never be free of her duty to heal—how could she rest when people were dying?—regardless of her own brokenness.

She had one choice: to never take life or herself too seriously.

So Feiyan smiled and leapt up a few more steps even before Shangdi heard the guard coming. Using surprise to her advantage, she dispatched that guard without a sound, and, certain that no one was near to hear except Shuren's invisible shadow, she chirped, "Are we almost there yet? The call of nature beckons. And, well, we all know such a call should *never* be ignored unless one wants disastrous aftermath."

Meiling cracked a smile. Shangdi managed to look grateful and impressed at Feiyan while still giving her a withering glare.

Feiyan gripped the guard's vest and shoved him carefully against the wall of the stairwell.

"Now," Shangdi growled.

CHAPTER 28

MEILING FOLLOWED SHANG closely. Eventually, she gave up and reached out to grip a fold of his cloak. Gently enough that he could wrench away without any impediment, but the slight touch comforted her as her fear threatened to make her crumple against the battlements. He did not give any indication of noticing, so she followed as quietly and quickly as she could.

Against all probability, this stretch of the battlement held no guards. Her eyes wandered to the phoenixes lighting the night sky, their fiery tails streaming into smoke. She cast one glance back at the phoenix sitting on the tower they had just left. It cocked its head, eyeing her, and snapped its beak. She shuddered and turned her gaze away from it, up to Shang's tall form in front of her.

"Where is everyone?" she breathed.

"Hush," he said.

Meiling bit her lip and clutched tighter at his cloak. Shang kept his pace mostly unhurried so that if they were seen from a distance, one might think he was another guard. Feiyan also, but Meiling was too short to fool anyone, so she kept close to Shang, hoping his shadow enveloped her.

Suddenly, his arm swung toward her and shoved her backward, behind him and against the wall. He half-crouched, poised for fight, but clung to the darkness. He turned and whispered frantically, "Feiyan!"

Too late.

The guard spotted her coming through the door.

He called something in another language. Feiyan shrugged, standing in the middle of the battlement, and Meiling desperately hoped the darkness was enough that the guard would not realize who she was.

The guard started toward her, spouting off another string of words that ended in a lilt, like a question. Feiyan gestured with her hands and pointed back at him, spewing a garbled collection of his strange sounds back into his face.

He paused, suddenly confused.

Then he drew his sword. The sound made Meiling's heart falter in her chest and she clutched Shang's shoulder and arm. As if guessing that she intended to intervene, he leaned back, pinning her against the wall with his body. A little gasp escaped her throat.

The guard turned toward the sound.

Feiyan leapt for him. She wrapped her arms tightly around the guard's neck, her legs braced around his middle. He swung to hack her off with his sword, but Shang flung ice shards directly at his hand, piercing his skin so that he cried out and dropped the sword with a resounding clang.

One more hit from Shang, and the man toppled. Feiyan bounced away from him, landing in a roll and leaping to her feet swiftly. Shang reached back, hauled Meiling to her feet, and said, "Run!"

Her heart galloped as a wave of lightheadedness passed over her. No, no, this was *not* the time to faint. This was not the time to be weak. She ran behind Shang and Feiyan, slower than both, until Shang growled at her to hurry.

When Feiyan looked back, alarm lit her eyes. She reached back quickly and snatched Meiling's hand, pulling her along after them. Renewed strength surged in her limbs, and Meiling ran harder.

"Get ready!" Shang called to Feiyan right before he burst through the next tower's door.

Two guards came at them. A door opened below them, a shout ringing out as Shang attacked the guards. Feiyan had picked up the fallen guard's sword and swung it with far more prowess than her thin frame suggested. The two of them flew into battle, and Meiling hung back wide-eyed, utter helplessness and uselessness returning in a crashing wave.

Too quickly, the guards lay dead on the floor between Feiyan and Shang. They hesitated a bare second before he snarled, "Get to the next tower!"

They ran out through the next door, onto the next stretch of the battlements. Meiling was the last through the door and pulled it shut behind her.

The quiet latch echoed through the suddenly still air.

She turned.

Shang and Feiyan both stood frozen, staring beyond them. Overhead, phoenixes gathered, lighted onto the two towers they stood between. Below, guards and brigands gathered, the sound of armor and boots and unsheathing swords and battle axes echoing in the night. And ahead, between Shang and Feiyan, she could make out . . .

Fang Zedong.

He stood in the middle of the battlement. The burning phoenixes illuminated the area much better than before, but even without that extra light, she could have easily recognized that silhouette with the billowing black cloak.

If she had not recognized him at first, his chilling voice would have ensured it. It made her knees lock. She braced herself against the wall of the battlement.

"You think I'm so stupid as to let you get away so easily? My little princess, this is *quite* a breach in our trust."

Zedong searched between Shang and Feiyan's braced warrior stances so he could meet Meiling's eye. He tsked and shook his head sadly. "I warned you, my pretty little one," he said, completely ignoring the two wielders standing directly in front of him. Ignoring Feiyan, who was easily his most valuable prisoner. "As much as your abilities are convenient to have, I do not need you." He swept an arm. "I do not need *any* of you."

Shang visibly tensed. His shoulders and legs were braced wide. His head moved very slightly, as though he scanned the area for an escape route.

Was this part of the plan? One of his contingency plans?

Feiyan tossed her braid. "Well, fortunately or unfortunately—you choose which—the feeling is quite mutual."

Zedong barked a short laugh. Shang used the fleeting distraction to take a step backward. Zedong spoke again, and his voice hardened. All trace of merriment, whether genuine or ironic, was gone.

"Blood is never my preferred method. You know this, daughter of Liena." He sighed, his eyes once again boring past Feiyan and Shang, straight into Meiling. "You also know that I am willing to spill it when necessary. Apparently, it is necessary."

Phoenix fire gleamed off his wriggling blue irises.

Meiling's hand found the door handle behind her, the cold metal harsh against her trembling flesh.

"This will be an awkward thing to explain to your mother," Zedong said, but instead of the strange false sadness he seemed to wear when speaking of Ma, he grinned. That grin was wicked but glittered of the truth. As if the thought of telling her mother that he had killed her darling daughter brought him a sickening sort of delight.

He raised his hand in the air. The phoenixes swirled in interest above him, chomping their beaks and burning the flames of their feathers and tails brighter than before.

Meiling pushed open the door as Shang whirled, dragging Feiyan and shoving Meiling through the opening. He slammed the door shut just as the resounding snap of Zedong's fingers filled the night.

Meiling moved to run down the stairwell, but Shang caught her. Low, in her ear, he growled, "Trust me." In a flash, he had his arm around her throat, the sides of her neck pressed tightly between his biceps and forearm. She tried to fight him, to scrabble at his hold with her nails. Her mouth opened, but a wave of drowsiness washed over her. The world started to go black.

"Trust me," Shang repeated as she lost consciousness.

Meiling flew free of her mind just in time to watch the fire of phoenixes burst under the door, licking around the edges, quickly devouring the wood. Shang caught her limp body and slung her over his shoulder. Her hair and arms hung like noodles down his back.

"Go into the phoenixes' minds!" Shang called into the air. "Do something to make them stop!"

Feiyan ran down the stairs, followed by Shang. Fire poured into the structure, through the windows. If the phoenixes burned down the doors and flew through them . . . Meiling's tether snapped tight with her terror, trying to pull her back to her body so she could wake.

Shang was right. She needed to enter their minds. But she had never tried to enter a *mó guǐ*'s mind before. There were so many, and so little time!

With a cry, she flung herself out through the stone walls of the tower. A phoenix flapped its wings, supporting itself in the air as it flamed the closed door, and without another thought, she sent her spirit hurling into its mind.

Magma. Fire.

Searing heat wrenched a gasp from her throat. It was so hot she suddenly was afraid it would burn through her soul tether. As far as she could see, lava boiled hot bursts of glowing yellow and orange. There was not a single respite of a charred, cooled chunk of lava.

She had to break the black magic tethering the *mó guǐ's* soul to the bidding of Zedong. Compulsion pulsed through the phoenix's sentience, binding its limbs, its will. Yet, when she searched, she found no memory threads. Nothing to guide her to the soul tether, where the curse must be implanted.

If it was *not* planted at the tether . . . No, she would not think about that yet.

Sentience swirled around the miasma. Much more sentience than she expected.

So she called out to it. *Phoenix! What is your name? I will break your curse!*

Who are you to fight my master? came the smokey reply.

She nearly gasped in relief. *I will free you! What is your name?*

My name is Ganzorig.

Ganzorig. That name emblazoned on her soul. She would never forget it so long as she lived.

Which might be only a few more seconds if she didn't figure this out.

Meiling desperately reached for anything that might guide her through the sweltering lava. She blinked through Ganzorig's vision, only to find the door nearly gone. *Slow down!* she screamed. *I will free you, but you must slow down!*

I cannot. The curse binds me.

She muttered a vile curse that seemed fitting for this mind and this panic. *Spitfire.* Then she tore off in any direction, searching for the tether. *Ganzorig, where is your soul?*

At the mention of the name, something blue glowed ahead. Ganzorig's soul tether. *Ganzorig, Ganzorig!* she screamed, rushing at the glow that burned brighter and brighter with each utterance of the name.

Then she was staring straight at blinding blueness. It pulsed with that feverish beat of life and personhood. Even in a *mó guǐ*. The tether thrummed with the creature's own individuality. The spectrum of personality was vastly narrowed compared to a human, but Ganzorig was still distinct from the other phoenixes attacking her and her friends.

Tangled with the blue glow was an ugly string of a black curse thread. Its discordant music blared like clanging cymbals in her ear. Wincing, she came closer. The frantic beat of her heart tried to tug her back to her body and wake her up. She resisted, focusing harder. She reached out with her formless hands and tried to grab the curse and rip it straight out of Ganzorig's mind.

But she could not grasp hold of it. It was like it was in an entirely different dimension, completely outside of her reach. Panic hit her hard and heavy, blow after blow, until she was panting despite the fact that she did not need air to breathe.

Then she remembered.

Her own tether had always reacted to one thing in this realm. One thing had always made her tether shudder, leaving her terrified in its wake that it would rend her soul from her body forever.

Sound.

Drawing every ounce of frustration and terror into her lungs, she belted out the loudest scream of her life.

Both tethers sang out in protest, wailing like a plucked string, but the black thread vibrated much harder than the other. And before Meiling could hardly process what happened, the thread broke.

Ganzorig swerved upward, tearing out of the pursuit and away from the tower.

You have my undying gratitude—

Help us, Ganzorig! she cried, and then she fled its mind. Immediately, the sweltering heat dissipated.

Where were Shang and Feiyan? She didn't have time to wonder, because another phoenix blasted down the bottom door of the tower, and she hardly breathed as she flung herself headlong into that mind.

Searing lava met her with such unwelcome ferocity that she cried out. *What is your name?*

Who are you—

Tell me your name! I will free you from this curse!

My name is Nekhii.

Nekhii! Meiling screamed. *Nekhii!* Blue flared ahead. She flew as fast as she could toward it and the black thread that throbbed next to it.

Zedong stole her from those she loved. He threatened her with their death. He used her to hurt others.

She screamed.

The curse sizzled away, dissolving into nothing. The phoenix howled, so terrifying and dark and deadly. She did not wait for a thanks or even stay to plead for help, already rushing out of this mind toward the next.

She could not hear Zedong's shrieks of rage, or Feiyan's screams and Shang's grunts as they fought to escape the fire of the curse-determined phoenixes. They never could have survived if they had not been near the tower to have some means of hiding from that all-consuming fire.

Mind after mind, name after name, Meiling screamed and broke the curse tethers. *Sukh. Timur. Taban. Ulagan. Batbayar. Gan. Arban.* With each one, she screamed away her own terror, pain, fear, and fury. The things she'd kept bottled up, the tears she'd cried and the tears she'd refused to cry. She screamed out every threat, every knife that hovered at her neck or others, every drop of blood spilled by Zedong. The long hours trapped in darkness, the bonds on her body and her soul.

Her soul shook with emotion, with . . . with . . . *rage.*

He made me bend.

He made me break.

But no more.

I will not bend. I will not break.

Meiling screamed. Another tether broke.

She flew as quickly as she could, but any minute, one well-aimed blast through a window could kill them all. She screamed out that fear.

Another tether broke.

She was still alive, so that had to mean that Shang was, too.

Then, suddenly, there were no more phoenixes.

She stopped, hovering, her vision tearing into the burning, charred remains of the tower for any sight of flame. Throbbing darkness met her gaze, washing away the melting, bubbling magma. Darkness and smoke, and the distant, trailing tails of phoenixes on the horizon.

Darkness, and an amassing army of barbarians and brigands.

Meiling grabbed her tether and used it to pull herself back to her body. She drew herself through holes in smoking stone and found Shang crouched over Feiyan and her body under the stairwell.

Oh, the bliss of nothing blocking her reentry into her own mind! Meiling slipped into it quickly and blinked awake. Her mind was suddenly assaulted by the stench of smoke. Hovering near her face were both Shang's and Feiyan's soot darkened, wide-eyed stares. She blinked again, realizing that she lay cradled in Shang's lap, and Feiyan's hand gripped hers. The aching in her stomach was temporarily relieved.

Feiyan gasped. "You did that . . ."

"No time!" Shang barked, shoving Meiling up so they could crawl out from under the stairwell.

"He's got an army out there waiting for us." Meiling coughed on the smoke. "They will charge in any second."

"One advantage of the phoenixes," Shang said, his voice raspy and clogged. "Here, we might be able to crawl out of that window. I might be able to make it bigger."

"Was this one of your contingency plans?" Feiyan asked as they ran up the stairs, away from the sound of charging guards and toward the window a phoenix had been blasting through.

Shang did not acknowledge the comment.

"Yeah, I didn't think so. Ow! This stone is burning through my shoes!"

The sounds of boots and swords clambered through the doorway below.

Shang cursed, grabbed Meiling, and pushed her toward the window. "Out! The drop is not high. We'll hold them off!"

The stone burned her hands when she grabbed the opening and she yelped. Covering her hands in the folds of her long sleeves, she stuck her foot onto the purchase. It was a small fit, blackened and still searing. It was much hotter than the stairs, and Meiling had to keep from crying out. She pulled herself through so she was crouched in the window, a band of scalding heat threatening to catch her clothes on fire.

The ground was so far away, and it sloped downward. Moonlight shone on the countryside, catching on rocks. If she stayed here any longer, she would burn herself beyond repair. And Shang and Feiyan would be killed.

So she leapt, desperately hoping she didn't die. Trying to think how she was supposed to roll like the others did, to prevent injuries.

Her arms flailed, her robes flying, and she screamed.

Someone appeared beneath her.

Meiling screamed as she fell straight into Shuren's outstretched arms. "Shuren!" she gasped. He quickly set her down.

"Run!" he cried, pointing. "That way! Go!"

"Come with us!" she begged, tugging on his arm even as he batted her away. "Come with us, Shuren!"

"I cannot," he said, and then he shoved between her shoulder blades, making her stumble in the direction he had pointed. She turned back as he angled himself again to catch Feiyan as she climbed into the window.

Meiling ran as fast as she could. Were those tears running down her face? She was too frantic to know. She tripped down the steep incline and fell headlong into the grass. Catching herself, she gripped fistfuls of brambles and leapt to her feet.

Something whizzed past her and lodged in the ground directly in front of her.

Arrow fletching.

She pumped her legs faster beneath her, running harder. More arrows landed in the brush and grass around her. Something slammed like a rock into the back of her calf. She stumbled, fell. A cry died into an agonized hiss on her lips.

Then Shang was heaving her up. As he did so, he let out a gasp of his own, and Feiyan yelled at them to run faster.

Meiling could hardly use her leg, but between Shang's strong, if trembling, grip and her good leg, they managed a speedy hobble away, running toward the concealing arms of a cluster of trees edging the dip into the green valley.

"Almost there," Shang cried. "Keep going, Meiling!" His arm was wrapped under her shoulder blades, holding her upward. He gasped again, a sharp, pained intake of breath. Meiling's head snapped to see another arrow lodged in his shoulder. The one that supported her. His grip weakened.

They stumbled into the shadow of the trees and Feiyan gestured wildly. "Over here! Behind the outcropping!"

With a shuddering gasp, Shang flung Meiling forward into Feiyan's outstretched arms. Feiyan pulled her down behind the rocky shelter. Then, with the last of his strength, Shang threw himself forward enough that Feiyan could drag him behind it as well.

For one terrible moment, they lay there, gasping as arrows whirred behind them. Blood streamed down Meiling's leg and every ounce of strength fled her as she lay with her face in the dirt. Her body quivered with radiating pain and weakness. The wider she opened her eyes, the closer the darkness pressed on the edges of her vision.

"We can't stay here," Shang groaned. "They'll catch up to us."

"They certainly will with you like this. Happy for you, I'm a healer," Feiyan retorted, and then she said grimly, "We don't have time for careful arrow extractions. This is going to hurt. *Really* hurt."

She braced one hand on his back and the other on the arrow's shaft. With all her strength, she yanked.

Shang's growling cry of pain split the night. It tore into Meiling's heart and made her burst into tears. She was vaguely aware that the brigands would be scaling the wall now, an army of powerful magic that the three of them were no match for. She dragged in a shuddering gasp and let out a sob when he cried out again as Feiyan yanked out the second arrow.

Feiyan bent over him and covered both wounds with her hands as he lay quaking on the ground. Her lips were pulled tight in a grim line. Blood soaked through her fingers, staining both of their clothes. Within a few minutes, the flow eased, and after a few more precious minutes, Shang gasped in relief and pulled himself upward. His eyes were no longer clouded with pain.

Meiling was next.

The pain was almost more than she could bear already, dirt mingling with the tears coursing down her face as she lay on the ground. She gasped as Feiyan approached, whimpering a little.

"Don't worry," Feiyan whispered tightly. "It'll be quick."

Shang crawled closer, keeping low under the shelter of the outcropping. He reached out toward her. "Here, squeeze my hand."

Meiling was hesitant, but her fingers closed around his just as Feiyan gripped the back of her knee and yanked. A scream burst from her throat as searing agony shot up her leg. She clutched Shang's hand as though her life depended on it. She moaned, shaking, as Feiyan pressed her already-bloody hand to her calf. Warmth spread under her touch.

Meiling wept.

Shang tightened his hold on her hand and reached out his other hand to grip the back of her head as she pressed her face into the dirt. "Almost over," he whispered, his voice still trembling, his thumb stroking behind her ear. "Almost over."

"There," Feiyan said and scooted away.

She gasped in relief and weakness, trembling. But when Shang's grip on her hand suddenly tensed, she lifted her head.

Swords glistened in the starlight, poised directly at them.

CHAPTER 29

LOWER THOSE DRAGON-blasted things out of our faces," Shang growled, swatting one away.

Meiling blinked, glancing quickly at Shang, Feiyan, and the darkened figures in front of them. Dread knotted in her stomach, but confusion kept her fear at bay. She struggled to sit up and pulled her hand out of Shang's.

"Tan Shangdi?" one of the figures asked incredulously.

"Yes. And the princess, and the healer." Shang gestured to both in turn. "We have no time to waste. An army of brigands will descend upon us at any moment." At this, he craned his head and peered back over the outcropping. "They're scaling down the wall." He gritted his teeth. "Horses, you have horses for us?"

"Princess Meiling? Then we can retreat the entire attack," the second voice chimed.

“Who are you?” Feiyan blurted.

Shang glared at her as if to say, *“Do you really not know?”* but he kept his voice quiet as the first figure spoke.

“I am Lieutenant Jadaala. Sent to rescue the princess.”

“Lieutenant,” Feiyan breathed and executed a very swift bow. “Can we go . . . *now*?”

“Yes. Come, hurry.” The swords were sheathed, and the figures turned away, breaking into jogs.

Shang gathered himself to his feet and then, with a quick glance back at the wall, held out his hand to Meiling. “Up, hurry!”

She grasped his hand, and he pulled her to her feet.

The three of them ran after the lieutenant and the others. Down the steep incline, shielded by the line of trees. She tugged at Shang’s sleeve to get his attention. He kept his pace, but tilted his head toward her. “They need to rescue the others!” she gasped between pants for air. “They still don’t know the other prisoners are there. They could rescue Renshu!”

Shang tightened his lips and gave a nod. “I’ll speak to the lieutenant when we reach the camp.”

Feiyan called, “You think they have food at this camp? I’m stupid hungry.”

Finally, they reached another patch of trees where the cloaked figures untethered horses. Shang approached Lieutenant Jadaala and lowered his head, bowing swiftly.

“Take two of the horses and follow me south. Our camp is just beyond the river. My wielders will come shortly,” the lieutenant said to Shang, who rose and nodded. “I will expect a full report.”

A wielder came forward with the leads of two horses. He held them out toward them. Shang took one. He nodded toward Feiyan, who grabbed the other. She quipped something under her breath, too quiet for Meiling to hear. Instead, she looked up just as Shang motioned for her to come with him.

He did not complain, made no comment about the discomfort of riding with another person, and did not suggest she ride with

Feiyan since they would have an easier time sharing a saddle. Instead, his black eyes fixed on her, and he laced his fingers together to boost her into the saddle.

Meiling didn't have time to hesitate. She hurried forward and slipped her foot into Shang's hands. He lifted her first and swung himself up behind her. He reached out and grabbed the reins, and she found herself a fistful of horse mane. How familiar and yet no less unsettling it was to feel her back bumping into his chest as he kicked the horse into motion.

"We'll follow you, Lieutenant Jadaala," Shang said.

Meiling looked around his arm to see Feiyan settled onto the horse next to them. She smiled and cocked an eyebrow at Meiling. Instantly, Meiling's face flamed, and she barely had the presence of mind to smile back before facing forward again. Did that look . . .? Oh lights above, Feiyan knew! She knew what went through Meiling's mind in that moment.

Meiling had little enough time to think about that as the lieutenant kicked his horse into a gallop and led them away from the horrible fortress, from the countryside that would by now be crawling with brigands.

Her leg, bumping against Shang's, still throbbed with the memory of the arrow, the pain of Feiyan extracting it. She shuddered at the memory.

"Don't worry," Shang mumbled above her ear. "You will be safe soon enough. I've got you."

Her throat closed and her breathing hitched, but she kept herself from doing anything stupid. Like sagging back against him. Tears struggled against her swift, determined swallows. Tears of relief, of gratitude, of so many emotions.

She should thank him. She should tell him how brave he'd been, how well he had planned things, compliment him on his quick thinking. She never could have escaped without him. If he hadn't broken out of the dungeon—*how* had he done that, exactly?—and come to rescue her, she would still be lying in a snarl of spelled sleep, face down on the floorboards of her chamber prison. Surrounded by raging, devouring black magic that blocked all traces of the moonlight that now washed over them.

No words came.

There simply were no words. Maybe later, she would try to thank him. For now, she let herself experience his warmth behind her, the biting wind blasting their faces, and profound relief.

"Your hair," Shang started to say and shook his head. "It's all in my face," he added with something that sounded like a smile. "It keeps getting in my mouth."

"Oh!" Meiling quickly reached up and tried to gather as much of it as she could in her hands and hold it at her shoulder, away from his face. "Sorry." She blushed.

"It's fine. That's better, thank you." He chuckled, a sound she had not heard in a long time. "Look, we get to cross another river."

Was that a . . . *joke*? About the time Fen had gotten her dunked in a river?

Was he *teasing* her?

"Good thing Fen is not here," she mumbled, face burning hot.

He chuckled and said with his low voice, "And good thing I won't let you fall."

The sound reverberated into her back and . . . her strength of will gave out. She melted against him, tilting her head so it rested against the crook of his neck and shoulder. To her utter shock, one of his hands let go of the reins, sliding around her waist and pulling her tighter against him.

"Almost there," he murmured in her ear.

She couldn't think about how much easier it was to cross a river when it had a bridge. Couldn't think about how much better it was to not be sopping wet and shivering.

All she could think about was Shang's arm around her waist and his warmth at her back.

She peeked a glance at Feiyan and found her beautiful midnight gaze set forward, a slight quirk to her lips. Feiyan was another person that she needed to thank.

Finally, they rode into a camp in the middle of a small forest. Tents were pitched on the ground, scattered around the clearing and deeper into the forest. More horses were hobbled to one side, in view of the small fires lit throughout the camp.

The sight of crackling, happy flames made her sigh.

Shang dismounted from behind her, then stood beside the horse, looking up at her. For a long moment, she lost herself in his dark eyes.

Then she realized he was waiting for her to toss her leg over the side so he could help her down. She had escaped a fortress, broken a dozen curse tethers implanted in minds full of lava, taken an arrow in the leg, survived said arrow being ripped out, and yet she could not find the strength to get her leg over the neck of the horse. She went lightheaded again, but this time the adrenaline vanished and left her in a quavering pile of bones.

A little embarrassed laugh escaped her as another hot flush spread across her neck. "I'm sorry, I think I'm stuck. I don't know—I can't . . . I feel—"

"You haven't eaten in over a week, Meiling," Feiyan said, stepping next to Shang. She folded her arms. "Of course, you're having trouble."

"What?" Shang's brow furrowed as he shot a look at Feiyan, then back at Meiling.

She gripped the horse's mane as a wave of heat washed over her. One that was not due to embarrassment. "I'm . . . I think I'm . . . about to . . ."

Shang reached up, caught her around the waist, and lifted her out of the saddle. She wrapped her arms around his neck just as darkness began clouding her vision. Carefully, he set her on her feet as Feiyan grabbed both of her hands. The darkness cleared at the healer's touch, and Meiling felt instantly better.

"I'll check the saddlebags for food," Shang said, drawing his arms away slowly, as if afraid she would fall. He turned and began rummaging through the bags. He pulled out a few rice cakes and a couple of strips of rabbit jerky. "Here. The owner won't mind."

Meiling eagerly scarfed the food, not caring how unladylike it looked.

"Slow down," Feiyan said with a laugh. "You'll be a little overenthusiastic for your stomach."

"Not if you're still touching me," Meiling said around a mouthful. "Thank you. So much." She met Feiyan's kind gaze and then dragged her eyes upward to meet Shang's. They shone with an earnest concern she had seen only once or twice before.

"Princess Meiling." The lieutenant's gruff voice yanked Meiling's focus away from her food and her friends. She shoved the rest of one cake in her mouth at the last second, earning a snicker from Feiyan, and turned to meet the lieutenant with full cheeks. She pressed the back of her hand against her mouth. The light of the campfire revealed his hard brow and heavy armor. "I see you have found sustenance. We are relieved at your recovery, Highness, and will do everything to ensure you arrive back at the palace safely in a timely manner."

"The palace?" she blurted and immediately covered her full mouth.

"Yes, as soon as the emperor heard of your capture, he ordered that you be rescued and returned to the palace at once."

Meiling nodded and lowered her head to hide the smile that spread across her face. Home! She was going home. Back to her Ma, her Pa, Yun, and Hou. Back to her library, her window, and her life as the cursed princess. The last thought made her pause slightly, but after what felt like a thousand years in that horrible fortress, she would take her previous life a hundred times before going back.

Even if it *had* been nice for her powers to be known, to be viewed as who she was. An increasingly powerful magic-wielder with unique and unprecedented abilities.

"Li Feiyan." The lieutenant turned to her. "It is a relief that you are rescued as well. Your absence has been keenly felt."

Feiyan merely nodded and bowed.

Meiling suddenly remembered the other wielders. "Lieutenant!" she spewed. "The other captive wielders are all in the fortress. Except two who have died. But the rest, including several wielders who were captured during the attack, are imprisoned there."

Shang gave her a sidelong glance. One that made her wonder suddenly if she had broken some military protocol. She stopped and shut her mouth.

"Do not trouble yourself with them, Your Highness," Lieutenant Jadaala said patiently. "We will recover them. I have already sent for reinforcements, and they should be here soon for another attack."

Meiling breathed a sigh of relief and lowered her head.

"Tan Shangdi," the lieutenant continued. "Your valiance is to be commended. This will be brought forth during the trial."

"Trial?" Her head snapped up, glancing quickly between Shang and the lieutenant.

The lieutenant glanced at Shang, clearly asking him to explain. Shang's face was hard when he spoke and he seemed to struggle to meet her eyes, but his voice did not waver. "I failed to deliver you to the fortress. Fen and I are both to be tried. There is an investigation happening as we speak into the entire journey. To determine if we deserve the death penalty."

Meiling might have passed out if Feiyan had not reached out and grabbed her arm. Her breathing came heavy and fast as realization sunk deep into her soul. She had known this was a possibility, but when she had run into Shang in the tower, she had thought . . . She had assumed he was vindicated then.

"We are currently in a state of war," the lieutenant continued. "The barbarians have struck, have razed several towns in the north. Zheninghai is retaliating. I will send more wielders back with you to the palace to ensure *this* journey does not fail." He cast one look at Shang.

Feiyan rolled her eyes. "Great. As if there weren't enough people needing healing already."

Meiling reeled in shock, barely keeping herself from stumbling back a step.

The lieutenant didn't seem to notice her distress. "Rest until dawn. You will be on your way at first light. I will send someone to find you a place to sleep, Highness. Tan Shangdi, I will summon you in half an hour for a full report." The lieutenant bowed to Meiling, and then Shang and Feiyan both bowed to the lieutenant. He turned and strode away.

As soon as he was gone, Shang leaned over and whispered, "You saw none of the trial in my mind?"

Meiling shook her head, wringing her hands. "If your mind was not—"

"Sorry?" he asked, leaning closer to hear.

She spoke up, conscious of Feiyan standing next to her and how obvious her flush must be. "If your mind was not so organized, I might have stumbled upon it. As it was, I could find everything he wanted very quickly. I tried not to pry into the other things." *Mostly.* Except for a few memories of his childhood and her . . .

"If you will excuse me, I have been *dying* to relieve myself for the past several hours," Feiyan chirped and then spun on her heel and marched away from them. Meiling was strangely relieved to have her too-perceptive gaze gone for the moment.

Shang gave her a look that seemed to say, *Can't you be a little more professional?* He sighed. "I . . . I am optimistic they will rule in our favor." His tone indicated the opposite, sending her stomach dropping even further. "With this successful mission, I stand more of a chance."

"Oh." A *chance*? She couldn't hope for just a *chance*! Shang had almost died for her more times than she could count. Under *no* circumstances would she allow him to be executed. She'd do anything.

When she looked up, his eyes searched hers, a strangely vulnerable expression on his face.

Meiling gritted her teeth. "I will speak to my father. He'll stop this. I'll testify in the trial! I'll explain everything. They'll understand."

He shook his head, a sad smile on his face. "You know his Imperial Majesty cannot gainsay the courts. But please, put this worry out of your mind. Trust me to keep myself safe." He stepped a little closer, and when she opened her mouth to protest, he lifted one finger, barely touching her lips in a silencing gesture. "Trust me, Meiling."

She glared at him. As if she was about to just stand aside and let him be killed!

A line appeared between his eyebrows as he ducked his head toward hers, lowering his voice to a deep rumble. "Now that we are going back, you must remember to keep your magic a secret. You do not want to find yourself at the mercy of the courts as a brigand."

It was a kindly meant warning, and a necessary one. But it made Meiling's heart falter even more than it already was. She'd just escaped a nightmare of imprisonment, and already her beloved empire was in a full-blown war, Shang was talking about being sentenced to death, and now she had to protect the secret of her magic again else she found herself sentenced to death too.

She wrapped her arms around her still-hungry middle. "The world is a different place than when I . . ." She shook her head and trailed off, but he nodded in understanding.

They stood in silence for a moment longer. In the firelight, his dungeon filthiness was finally visible, matching her own wretched state. He still managed to be handsome, even as blood stained his shoulder and splattered a few other places. His hair had almost entirely fallen out of his queue, and it wafted in long, dark strands in the wind.

After the silence lingered, he made to leave. "I will go find out about your tent."

"Wait!" Meiling said quickly, reaching out one hand toward him.

He stopped, turned, and she expected him to cock an eyebrow. Instead, he only stared back at her with his black-as-night eyes, waiting. He held very still, but the wind caught the edges of his cloak, his tunic, his sleeve, and his hair. Tugging softly.

"I must thank you. I fear I cannot thank you enough or as you deserve, but that must not stop me from trying." Meiling looked everywhere but his eyes and finally settled on staring at her toes. "It was . . . I don't . . . I don't think anyone else could have done that." Phoenixes blast it. Why was she suddenly tearing up? She was exhausted and had too many emotions waiting to be processed. "I just wanted to—I mean, you see . . . Ugh, I'm—this is nonsense!" She flung up her hands in frustration and had to swallow hard, giving a shaky chuckle to keep from crying. "I just . . . I think, well, you . . . Thank you. I guess that's all."

Well, if he had ever wondered, that certainly confirmed it. She was an idiot.

He was silent.

Quickly, her mind full of dread, she darted a glance up at him.

His gaze was intent on her. Serious, not at all mocking. His brow was slightly puckered, his jaw a little more tense than before. What was he thinking? She should know, having been in his mind so many times, but his face was inscrutable.

He finally said, at long last, "I appreciate your words." He took one more step and stopped again. "I likewise owe you my thanks. The phoenixes—*Meiling*, do you have any idea how significant that feat of magic was?" He turned back toward her, palms outstretched. "It was, well, a level of skill and power I've never seen before. I hate to say that I doubted you, but I was not sure you could accomplish it. I had no idea how such a thing *could* be accomplished. Yet you did it, and very quickly. You saved our lives."

Those words rendered her speechless for a moment.

Did he have any idea what that meant to her?

She ducked her head and mumbled, "It was a good idea. I wouldn't have thought of it." She peeked up at him, a mischievous smile on her face. "When you told me about that special hold, I didn't expect you to use it on me."

He smiled and shook his head, glancing toward the campfire and the line of tents. "I had hoped to not resort to that."

"Was it one of your contingency plans?" she asked, raising an eyebrow and smirking. "Not improvisation?"

He smiled again, tilting his head to one side. He stared at her for a long moment, long enough to make her start fidgeting with the once fine embroidery on her sleeves. His smile went lopsided, and he said with too much cockiness, "I never improvise, Princess."

Something like a giggle spilled out of Meiling's lips. She covered her mouth and glanced around for anyone watching, still grinning stupidly.

He grinned back at her, firelight dancing in his black pupils, and she went lightheaded again, but not at all because of hunger. Oh, she wanted this moment to last! But he turned and said over his shoulder, "I'll go see about your tent, Highness. You need rest."

Meiling wanted to spew some nonsense about not being tired since she had been asleep for over a week, but she genuinely was exhausted. As soon as Shang stepped away, the cold autumn wind bit fiercer, and she couldn't hide from the shambles of her mind. A sudden thought made her brighten, however.

She could freely use her magic again! *Finally*, she could explore the world after dark, no longer chained by Zedong's enchantments. Her heart ached with longing.

Feiyan appeared out of nowhere and sighed. "Ahh. So much better. How does it feel to be free?"

"You've been imprisoned longer than me, so it must feel even better to you," she said, wrapping her arms around herself again.

Feiyan shrugged, smiling a little. Her smile was genuine, but it was not as happy as Meiling had expected. She shrugged again. "I am glad to be free, but the thought of returning to life before this . . ." She sighed, her smile drifting away into a frown, her voice serious.

"It makes me exhausted, Meiling. Sometimes I think my abilities are more a prison than anything else. It makes me seem like a terrible person." She chuckled, shaking her head. "But I simply do not want to heal all day. Dungeons are not ideal, exactly, but imprisonment was a little . . . restful." She cocked another grin Meiling's way. "And I'm telling you, whatever that phoenix-blasted illusionist put on that cloth left me dizzy with happiness whenever I woke up. It was great."

"Princess Meiling? Li Feiyan?" A broad-shouldered, middle-aged wielder marched up to them in the darkness. "We have tents for you. This way."

When the man showed her a tent very similar to the one she'd used while traveling with Fen and Shang, she smiled. She bid goodnight to Feiyan and thanked the wielder.

Something made her stop and glance over her shoulder.

There was a girl staring at her from across the campsite. She was obviously a magic-wielder, with knives strapped to her belt and travel-worn clothes. Her brow was furrowed at first, then her eyes widened as though in recognition. She was quite pretty, and though she was likely even shorter than Meiling, her frame was muscular and well-built. Something about the glint in her eye suggested a natural wildness—a wildness that reminded her of Hu Fen. Was she a shapeshifter, too? Two men flanked her, one older and stockier, while the other was tall and handsome.

Did they fear Meiling's supposed curse?

There was no knowing.

She opened the tent flap and slipped inside. It was like stepping into a dream. How strange it was to go through mundane motions after adventures she could hardly describe. Soon, she would be home. That would be even stranger. Did Yun and Hou know about her capture? Had they missed her? Meiling's heart constricted at the memory of their broken selves in Shuren's illusion, and she whispered quietly to herself, "That wasn't real. They are safe."

Soon, she would be home again, in the arms of her Ma and Pa. Shang would be tried for his life, and the empire would head into battle.

Would she simply go back to reading books about stars and topography in the library, sitting in sunspots and overlooking Academy training? Wishing she was with them? Useful like them? Would she go back to being the empire's closest guarded secret, an unused weapon?

How much would things be the same as before? How much would things change? Meiling would have no idea until they made the trek all the way back to the palace. Until she crossed the threshold and donned her own garments and slept in her own room, she could not even begin to guess what might be awaiting her when she arrived.

She unwrapped her robes and settled down onto the bedroll, pulling the thick wool blanket up to completely cover her head.

CHAPTER 30

MEILING'S SOUL CREPT out of her body, her nervousness making her move slower than normal. Would anyone guess? Surely the lieutenant knew . . . *something* of her magic. Right? Or were Feiyan and Shang the only ones?

She stayed huddled in the safety of her tent for a long minute, stretching and savoring the flavor of freedom. Then, prowling like a cat in the night, she slipped out of the tent. Only a few people—presumably the night watch, and anyone tying up loose ends after tonight—were still milling about. Soul-glows broke through canvas tents and shone like dots of rainbow in the darkness of the forested night.

It made her smile.

It only took her a few minutes to find Shang's ice-blue aura entering the lieutenant's tent. The lieutenant glowed a darker blue.

Perhaps it was wrong of her. Perhaps she should let their conversation be theirs.

But this was Shang's life on the line, and she intended to do everything she could to save him. That started with knowing what he faced.

Shang bowed as he entered the larger tent, his hands outstretched and palms downward. "Lieutenant Jadaala."

The space was rather severe for a high-ranking military officer, with no furniture except a bedroll behind a screen, and a low table in the center of the room. Cushions were arranged on either side of the table, but only the lieutenant sat.

"Tan Shangdi. Report," came the crisp response.

Shang took a deep breath, laced his fingers behind his back, braced his feet wide, and began. He spared no detail about his involvement from the moment the attack was launched on the fortress. He told of finding Meiling in the tower and fighting off the guards trying to drag her away. When the lieutenant asked for clarification about why the princess was in the tower, Shang said, "From what I have inferred, she was something of a pet to Fang Zedong and, at times, was granted liberties that she attempted to take advantage of. I believe she was trying to locate the healer when she was caught by the guards I then killed. Beyond that, I do not know why she was in the tower at the time of the attack."

"Go on."

Shang told of encountering the illusionist and did not hide his attempt to recover Meiling by force, against her will. She glanced at the lieutenant, but his sharp-lined face was unreadable.

Shang detailed his capture, captivity, planning the escape, and being questioned. He explained that on his way back from that ordeal, he had snuck a key off a guard. His magic had been limited while he was imprisoned, but the binding was lifted when he had used the Yanzhao technique to break the princess's enchantments.

The kiss.

He hesitated at one part—when Zedong had ordered Meiling to enter his mind. She watched as thoughts seemed to war in his mind. Perhaps the lieutenant did not know about her magic after all? He resorted to saying, "He brought me into a room where the princess was and tried to use her to extract information from me."

"Did he succeed?"

"I do not know what information was extracted. There seemed to be magic involved. I believe Fang was working some sort of enchantment, though I could not see it."

At this, the lieutenant lowered one eyebrow. "How did the princess fit into this? How was she used?"

Again, Shang hesitated. "The entirety of her role was unclear to me. He handled her . . . roughly." His teeth gritted at this part. "I assumed in an effort to intimidate me and make me pity her."

"And did you?"

"Did I what?"

"Pity her. Did you pity her and thus reveal classified information to our enemy?" the lieutenant pressed.

Shang breathed through his nostrils, but otherwise did not flinch. "I did pity her, but I did not reveal any information of my own accord."

"Yet you did reveal information?"

"I believe it was taken directly from my mind. I spoke nothing. As I previously stated, I do not know what was taken. I do not know what Fang Zedong knows," he said coolly. Meiling thought she detected the faintest trace of worry lining his brow. She wanted to slip into his mind and tell him he did not need to cover for her, but she didn't want to break his focus and reveal that she was eavesdropping.

Maybe she did not fully understand the threat Shang protected her from. She should be grateful. She *was* grateful.

"Continue," the lieutenant said.

So he did. He explained their flight, how the illusionist had let them escape in exchange for Feiyan's freedom. The lieutenant pressed about this, and Shang added that Meiling had found something trustworthy about the illusionist and that she had again been unwilling to leave without Feiyan. He had decided under the circumstances that rescuing Feiyan also would be the best course of action.

When Shang reached the part about the phoenixes, he gave the briefest account possible, offering little explanation. “Fang Zedong ordered his phoenixes to dispose of us, but we ran back into the tower and were able to escape through a window.” He paused, as if waiting for a clarifying question, but there was none. He continued all the way up until the lieutenant and his wielders had found them. Then, he closed his mouth and held stone still.

The lieutenant studied his face closely, then let out a large sigh and sat back in his chair. “This was quite the rescue, young man. You are aware, I’m sure, of the glaring places you broke protocol, but you did singlehandedly recover the healer and princess. I suppose I shouldn’t be too surprised after your feat at Liafugen, yet here I am. I commend you.”

Shang bowed his head slightly. “Thank you.”

“I will send this report and my commendation along with you tomorrow to the capital. I wish it could guarantee your pardon.” He shook his head. “It truly is a shame. I could have used someone of your talent in my ranks as an officer. I know your aspirations were otherwise inclined, but it is a shame indeed that one such costly mistake should bring down one with so much potential.”

Shang swallowed. He looked down, and from where Meiling hung against the doorway of the tent, she thought she saw the slightest sagging of his shoulders. She wanted to insist that none of this was his fault. It had been her choice to give herself up to Zedong. If it was her choice, why did Shang have to pay his life for that?

It was stupid and grossly unfair.

Indignation boiled in her soul, resulting in her losing more of her shape to shadow, but she kept herself composed.

“You are dismissed, Tan Shangdi.”

Shang bowed again and strode out of the tent into the night. She followed, fluttering just behind him as he did not slow his pace toward the edge of the campsite. When he was alone, he sat on the ground, just outside the perimeter of the firelight, and buried his head in his hands. His fingers snarled in his dirty hair, and he tightened his hands into fists. Ice-blue pulsed from the center of his chest.

Meiling ached. She settled herself next to him, staring up at his silent, covered face. When she tried to place a hand on his arm, it floated straight through him.

She could offer him no comfort. Not unless she entered his mind and admitted what she had overheard, or unless she woke herself up and came out here.

He seemed to want privacy.

She rose with a long last, lingering glance. As she drew away, his grip loosened, and his hair fell into his face. He let his hands dangle from where his elbows propped on his knees. He stared directly into the fire, an unreadable expression on his face.

She left him and flew free into the night.

CHAPTER 31

THE SUN HAD already set, yet they rode onward. Meiling rode next to Feiyan and kept glancing over at her to keep from staring at Shang's back ahead of her. Her friend wore an unusually tired expression, but when she met Meiling's gaze, she tossed her a lazy smile.

"Almost there," Meiling whispered.

Feiyan sighed. "About time. My backside is going to be so callused that I won't be able to feel cushions when I sit in them."

Meiling laughed. She could think of no response, so she said nothing. There was nothing but trees ahead of her and stars above her, glistening and dancing around a sliver of a white, glowing moon. Their guides insisted they were close, so they kept going.

Shang slowed his horse until he rode alongside them. He'd kept his distance during this journey, which had felt strange after all they'd been through together. It was probably for the best, however. Things would change when they reached the city, anyway. She would slide back into the role of cursed princess. And Shang would go on trial with Fen.

Feiyan would return to healing from dawn to dusk and studying in the fringes, trying to find moments to eat and sleep and breathe. She dreaded it, and Meiling didn't blame her. She only wished there was something she could do to help. Something to repay her friendship.

"Are you ready to be home?" Shang asked Meiling with a sidelong glance.

"Nope," Feiyan interjected.

Shang spared her the briefest of glares. Meiling smiled and said, "Yes. But I'm afraid it won't be the home I left."

He nodded, his gaze settled ahead on the backs of the other wielders in their company. "It won't be the same, but it will hopefully still be home."

She smiled at him, but he did not glance at her. He seemed determined to keep a professional distance between them. Her smile faded into a thin line on her face.

"I am *very* skeptical of our being *almost there*," Feiyan said, peering intently into the dark forest surrounding them. "I think they just wanted to make us ride longer. Make our rumps a little number."

Meiling grinned and suggested, "Maybe they were only teasing us."

"We are almost there," Shang insisted with one quick tilting of his head. "Watch. We'll round the bend in only a few minutes."

"Now you're just doing the same exact thing they are." Feiyan threw up her hands, leather reins hanging between her fingers. "Your ploys cannot escape me."

He ignored her. Meiling shared a glance with Feiyan as she mouthed, *"See? Told you."* Meiling suppressed a giggle. Somehow, everything was funnier when she was exhausted and with a friend.

Life was just better with friends.

"And . . . now," Shang said.

They rounded the bend, and below them, caught in the folds of sleep and the shadow of the mountain, lay Suguan, the palace, and Meiling's home. Dots of light illuminated the city enough that she first gasped with recognition and then sighed. Beyond the city, stars and moon reflected on white ocean caps and even from here, the fragrance of salt tinted the air.

Her heart clenched with a sudden, stifled, and forgotten longing and aching. Tears threatened, but she was smiling as she clasped her hands to her chest, dropping the reins of the horse entirely.

"You're home, Meiling," Shang whispered, making her tear her gaze away from the beauty before her to find his gaze settled softly on her. The lips of his hard mouth twisted up slightly, and starlight caught in his black eyes.

She held his gaze for a long moment, too afraid to lose whatever this was, as she whispered back, "Thank you." She wanted to reiterate her promise to do everything she could to help him, or at least say something else. But no words came. Nothing besides that one paltry expression of gratitude. But she thought that perhaps, just perhaps, he saw what she wanted to say in her gaze.

He turned back and kicked his horse faster to join the other wielders in front of them. Meiling returned her attention to Feiyan.

"Whatever happens," she said under her breath, reaching through the space between them and clasping Feiyan's hand. Warmth buzzed through their touch. "We're home. And I don't want to lose . . . this."

Feiyan smiled and squeezed her hand back. "Girl, it is going to take a lot more than whatever is waiting for us to break a friendship forged in a rat-infested dungeon between bouts of unconsciousness."

Meiling laughed. She faced forward, eagerly drinking in every familiar sight and the beautiful towering heights of the regal, colorful palace. Ma, Pa, Yun, Hou. *Home.* At long last.

For that beautiful moment, long after the sun had died behind the mountain, she did not worry about being branded as a brigand, never having a chance to see Feiyan again, dealing with the repercussions of the war, stepping back into life as the cursed princess, or watching helplessly as Shang and Fen were sentenced to death.

She had escaped Fang Zedong's clutches. She was home. Safe and sound.

For this one moment, that was all that mattered.

EPILOGUE

ZEDONG CURLED HIS fist around the siren stone on his desk, wishing it had sharper edges to slice into his palm. He wanted that physical pain, the sight of his own blood. But no matter how hard he squeezed, the blood didn't come.

He'd lost the princess.

No matter.

He had what he needed for now. Liena's daughter could enjoy a respite. She could tell of the horrors of him and his men to her ugly mother. Then maybe Liena would finally see. She'd finally understand. And Nianzu—he'd at last realize it was Zedong, *Zedong*, the boy he'd scoffed at and dismissed, who'd enslaved and broken his empire's most prized wielders.

The world would at last see him. They'd see they had never understood him. They'd been wrong about him. *All* of them were wrong about him.

Then he'd tell Liena he hadn't just stolen twelve wielders, but thirteen.

The thirteenth wielder he hadn't even bothered capturing. He'd killed her with his bare hands, ignoring the screaming of her baby in the other room. A woman named Mao Shu. She'd made his and Liena's life at the Academy miserable. Last he'd heard, Shu's death had been labeled a mystery. No one had figured out who killed her or why.

Liena thought Nianzu was the only one who could save her from those that meant her harm. She was wrong.

Zedong hadn't forgotten the name of a single person who'd mistreated her and him. He'd hunt each one down, drag them to her feet, and slaughter them before her.

Last of all, he'd break Liena.

And he knew exactly who to use to do it.

Meiling.

He slammed the siren stone back on his desk with such force, one of his parchments fluttered to the ground. He planted his hands on his desk, shoved up to his feet, and barked, "Send for Shi Yong!"

A pair of footsteps outside his door broke into a run, hunting down that dragon-blasted evanescer. As Zedong waited, his mind shifted to the young warrior who'd *somehow* managed to break his two prized captives out of his fortress.

Tan Shangdi.

Zedong drew a long, slow breath between his teeth. "You want to make an enemy of me?" he whispered in the quiet of his office. "Then I'll be your enemy, Tan Shangdi."

Zedong didn't forgive. Forgiveness was injustice.

He'd gladly destroy that young man. He was everything Zedong hated most in the world. And thanks to Meiling, Zedong knew exactly how to destroy him.

He'd do it slowly, so slowly. After all, Zedong was patient. *So dragon-blasted patient.* He'd waited twenty-five years for his revenge. He wasn't about to spoil the fun by rushing.

Footsteps sounded outside the door. A knock.

"Come in!" Zedong said brightly, straightening and smiling.

Shi Yong opened the door, sweeping into the space with the warmth of Shangdi's ice. He answered Zedong's smile with one of his own, but there was no mistaking its uneasiness. "Ah, Fang. How may I be of service?"

Zedong picked up the siren stone and gave it a little toss, catching it in his palm. "Ready your brigands. I'm thinking of paying a little visit to Suguan."

Experience the heartpounding climax of the Zheninghai Chronicles *in* Daughter of Darkness and Dreams!

MORE FROM ANASTASIS BLYTHE

THE ZHENINGHAI CHRONICLES

Maiden of Candlelight and Lotuses

Guardian of Talons and Snares

Warrior of Blade and Dusk

Princess of Shadows and Starlight

Captive of Twilight and Treachery

Daughter of Darkness and Dreams

ABOUT THE AUTHOR

Anastasis Blythe makes her home in central Texas with her husband and their two adorable but rather whiny cats. When she's not writing, she is reading an unhealthy amount of fantasy novels, daydreaming about future books, and trying to keep up with the laundry.

If you would like free novels, regular behind-the-scenes updates on her writing, and an early peek at new book covers, join her community at Patreon.com/AnastasisBlythe.

CONNECT WITH ANASTASIS ONLINE AT:

Website - AnastasisBlythe.com

Instagram - @AnastasisBlythe

Facebook - Anastasis Blythe

Goodreads - Anastasis Blythe

www.ingramcontent.com/pod-product-compliance
Lightning Source LLC
Chambersburg PA
CBHW020337310726
48979CB00015B/2405/J

* 9 7 8 1 9 6 0 6 0 6 0 4 4 *